This book belongs to Eve Moore
61 Ladywell Avenue
Dundee
Scotland.
Tel: 21015

SPOOKY
TALES

SPOOKY TALES

Spine-Chilling Stories of Ghosts and Ghouls

This edition first published in
Great Britain in 1984 by

Octopus Books Limited
59 Grosvenor Street
London W1

Arrangement and illustrations © 1984 Hennerwood Publications Limited
Illustrated by Gavin Rowe

ISBN 0 86273 169 0

Printed and bound in Great Britain
by Collins Glasgow

CONTENTS

Jimmy Takes Vanishing Lessons

Walter R. Brooks

The school bus picked up Jimmy Crandall every morning at the side road that led up to his aunt's house, and every afternoon it dropped him there again. And so twice a day, on the bus, he passed the entrance to the mysterious road.

It wasn't much of a road any more. It was choked with weeds and blackberry bushes, and the woods on both sides pressed in so closely that the branches met overhead, and it was dark and gloomy even on bright days. The bus driver once pointed it out.

'Folks that go in there after dark,' he said, 'well, they usually don't ever come out again. There's a haunted house about a quarter of a mile down that road.' He paused. 'But you ought to know about that, Jimmy. It was your grandfather's house.'

Jimmy knew about it, and he knew that it now belonged to his Aunt Mary. But Jimmy's aunt would never talk to him about the house. She said the stories about it were silly nonsense and there were no such things as ghosts. If all the villagers weren't a lot of superstitious idiots, she would be able to let the house, and then she would have enough money to buy Jimmy some decent clothes and take him to the cinema.

Jimmy thought it was all very well to say that there were no such things as ghosts, but how about the people who had tried to live there? Aunt Mary had let the house three times, but every family had moved out within a week. They said the things that went on there were just too queer. So nobody would live in it any more.

Jimmy thought about the house a lot. If he could only prove that there wasn't a ghost ... And one Saturday when his aunt was in the village, Jimmy took the key to the haunted house from its hook on the kitchen door, and started out.

It had seemed like a fine idea when he had first thought of it – to find out for himself. Even in the silence and damp gloom of the old road it still seemed pretty good. Nothing to be scared of, he told himself. Ghosts aren't around in the daytime. But when he came out in the clearing and looked at those blank, dusty windows, he wasn't so sure.

'Oh, come on!' he told himself. And he squared his shoulders and waded through the long grass to the porch.

Then he stopped again. His feet did not seem to want to go up the steps. It took him nearly five minutes to persuade them to move. But when at last they did, they marched right up and across the porch to the front door, and Jimmy set his teeth hard and put the key in the keyhole. It turned with a squeak. He pushed the door open and went in.

That was probably the bravest thing that Jimmy had ever done. He was in a long dark hall with closed doors on both sides, and on the right there were stairs going up. He had left the door open behind him, and the light from it showed him that, except for the hat-rack and table and chairs, the hall was empty. And then as he stood there, listening to the bumping of his heart, gradually the light faded, the hall grew darker and darker – as if something huge had come up on the porch behind him and stood there, blocking the doorway. He swung round quickly, but there was nothing there.

He drew a deep breath. It must have been just a cloud passing across the sun. But then the door, all by itself, began to swing shut. And before he could stop it, it closed with a bang. And it was then, as he was pulling frantically at the handle to get out, that Jimmy saw the ghost.

It behaved just as you would expect a ghost to behave. It was a tall, dim, white figure, and it came gliding slowly down the stairs towards him. Jimmy gave a yell, yanked the door open, and tore down the steps.

He didn't stop until he was well down the road. Then he had to get his breath. He sat down on a log. 'Boy!' he said. 'I've seen a ghost! Golly, was that awful!' Then after a minute he thought, 'What was so awful about it? He was trying to scare me, like that smart aleck who was always jumping out from behind things. Pretty silly business for a grown-up ghost to be doing.'

It always makes you cross when someone deliberately tries to scare you. And as Jimmy got over his fright, he began to get angry. And pretty soon he got up and started back. 'I must get that key, anyway,' he thought, for he had left it in the door.

This time he approached very quietly. He thought he'd just lock the door and go home. But as he tiptoed up the steps he saw it was still open; and as he reached out cautiously for the key, he heard a faint sound. He drew back and peeped round the door-jamb, and there was the ghost.

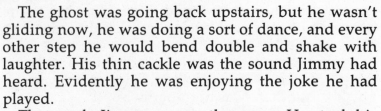

The ghost was going back upstairs, but he wasn't gliding now, he was doing a sort of dance, and every other step he would bend double and shake with laughter. His thin cackle was the sound Jimmy had heard. Evidently he was enjoying the joke he had played.

That made Jimmy crosser than ever. He stuck his head further around the door-jamb and yelled 'Boo!' at the top of his lungs. The ghost gave a thin shriek and leaped two feet in the air, then collapsed on the stairs.

As soon as Jimmy saw he could scare the ghost even worse than the ghost could scare him, he wasn't afraid any more and he came right into the hall. The ghost was hanging on the banister and panting. 'Oh, my goodness!' he gasped. 'Oh, my gracious! Boy, you can't do that to me!'

'I did it, didn't I?' said Jimmy. 'Now we're even.'

'Nothing of the kind,' said the ghost crossly. 'You seem pretty stupid, even for a boy. Ghosts are supposed to scare people. People aren't supposed to scare ghosts.' He got up slowly and glided down and sat on the bottom step. 'But look here, boy; this could be pretty serious for me if people got to know about it.'

'You mean you don't want me to tell anybody about it?' Jimmy asked.

'Suppose we make a deal,' the ghost said. 'You keep quiet about this, and in return I'll – well, let's see; how would you like to know how to vanish?'

'Oh, that would be swell!' Jimmy exclaimed. 'But – can you vanish?'

'Sure,' said the ghost, and he did. All at once he just wasn't there. Jimmy was alone in the hall.

But his voice went right on. 'It would be pretty handy, wouldn't it?' he said persuasively. 'You could

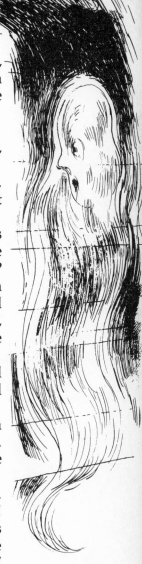

get into the cinema free whenever you wanted to, and if your aunt called you to do something – when you were in the garden, say – well, she wouldn't be able to find you.'

'I don't mind helping Aunt Mary,' Jimmy said.

'H'm. High-minded, eh?' said the ghost. 'Well, then . . .'

'I wish you'd please reappear,' Jimmy interrupted. 'It makes me feel funny to talk to somebody who isn't there.'

'Sorry. I forgot,' said the ghost, and there he was again, sitting on the bottom step. Jimmy could see the step, dimly, right through him. 'Good trick, eh? Well, if you don't like vanishing, maybe I could teach you to seep through keyholes. Like this.' He floated over to the door and went right through the keyhole, the way water goes down the drain. Then he came back the same way.

'That's useful, too,' he said. 'Getting into locked rooms and so on. You can go anywhere the wind can.'

'No,' said Jimmy. 'There's only one thing you can do to get me to promise not to tell about scaring you. Go and live somewhere else. There's Miller's up the road. Nobody lives there any more.'

'That old shack!' said the ghost, with a nasty laugh. 'Doors and windows half off, roof leaky – no thanks! What do you think it's like in a storm, windows banging, rain dripping on you – I guess not! Peace and quiet, that's really what a ghost wants out of life.'

'Well, I don't think it's very fair,' Jimmy said, 'for you to live in a house that doesn't belong to you and keep my aunt from letting it.'

'Pooh!' said the ghost. 'I'm not stopping her from letting it. I don't take up any room, and it's not my fault if people get scared and leave.'

'It certainly is!' Jimmy said angrily. 'You don't play fair and I'm not going to make any bargain with you. I'm going to tell everybody how I scared you.'

'Oh, you mustn't do that!' The ghost seemed quite disturbed and he vanished and reappeared rapidly several times. 'If that got out, every ghost in the country would be in terrible trouble.'

So they argued about it. The ghost said if Jimmy wanted money he could learn to vanish; then he could join a circus and get a big salary. Jimmy said he didn't want to be in a circus; he wanted to go to college to learn to be a doctor. He was very firm. And the ghost began to cry. 'But this is my home, boy,' he said. 'Thirty years I've lived here and no trouble to anybody, and now you want to throw me out into the cold world! And for what? A little money! That's pretty heartless.' And he sobbed, trying to make Jimmy feel cruel.

Jimmy didn't feel cruel at all, for the ghost had certainly driven plenty of other people out into the cold world. But he didn't really think it would do much good for him to tell anybody that he had scared the ghost. Nobody would believe him, and how could he prove it? So after a minute he said, 'Well, all right. You teach me to vanish and I won't tell.' They settled it that way.

Jimmy didn't say anything to his aunt about what he'd done. But every Saturday he went to the haunted house for his vanishing lesson. It was really quite easy when you know how, and in a couple of weeks he could flicker, and in six weeks the ghost gave him an examination and he got a B plus, which is very good for a human. So he thanked the ghost and shook hands with him and said, 'Well, goodbye now. You'll hear from me.'

'What do you mean by that?' said the ghost

suspiciously. But Jimmy just laughed and ran off home.

That night at supper Jimmy's aunt said, 'Well what have you been doing today?'

'I've been learning to vanish.'

His aunt smiled and said, 'That must be fun.'

'Honestly,' said Jimmy. 'The ghost up at Grand-father's house taught me.'

'I don't think that's very funny,' said his aunt. 'And will you please not – why, where are you?' she demanded, for he had vanished.

'Here, Aunt Mary,' he said as he reappeared.

'Merciful heavens!' she exclaimed, and she pushed back her chair and rubbed her eyes hard. Then she looked at him again.

Well, it took a lot of explaining and he had to do it twice more before he could persuade her that he really could vanish. She was pretty upset. But at last she calmed down and they had a long talk. Jimmy kept his word and didn't tell her that he had scared the ghost, but he said he had a plan and at last, though very reluctantly, she agreed to help him.

So the next day she went up to the old house and started to work. She opened the windows and swept and dusted and aired the bedding and made as much noise as possible. This disturbed the ghost, and pretty soon he came floating into the room where she was sweeping. She was scared all right. She gave a yell and threw a broom at him. As the broom went right through him and he came nearer, waving his arms and groaning, she shrank back.

And Jimmy, who had been standing there invisi-ble all the time, suddenly appeared and jumped at the ghost with a 'Boo!' and the ghost fell over in a dead faint.

As soon as Jimmy's aunt saw that, she wasn't

frightened any more. She found some smelling salts and held them under the ghost's nose, and when he came to she tried to help him into a chair. Of course, she couldn't help him. But at last he sat up and said reproachfully to Jimmy, 'You broke your word!'

'I promised not to tell about scaring you!' said the boy, 'but I didn't promise not to scare you again.'

And his aunt said, 'You really are a ghost, aren't you? I thought you were just stories people made up. Well, excuse me, but I must get on with my work.' And she began sweeping and banging around with her broom harder than ever.

The ghost put his hands to his head. 'All this noise,' he said. 'Couldn't you work more quietly, ma'am?'

'Whose house is this, anyway?' she demanded. 'If you don't like it, why don't you move out?'

The ghost sneezed violently several times. 'Excuse me,' he said. 'You're raising so much dust. Where's that boy?' he asked suddenly. For Jimmy had vanished again.

'I'm sure I don't know,' she replied. 'Probably getting ready to scare you again.'

'You ought to have better control of him,' said the ghost severely. 'If he was my boy, I'd take a hairbrush to him.'

'You have my permission,' she said, and she reached right through the ghost and pulled the chair cushion out from under him and began banging the dust out of it. 'What's more,' she went on, as he got up and glided wearily to another chair. 'Jimmy and I are going to sleep here at night from now on, and I don't think it would be very clever of you to try any tricks.'

'Ha, ha,' said the ghost nastily. 'He who laughs last . . .'

'Ha, ha, yourself,' said Jimmy's voice from close behind him. 'And that's me, laughing last.'

The ghost muttered and vanished.

Jimmy's aunt put cottonwool in her ears and slept that night in the best bedroom with the light lit. The ghost screamed for a while down in the cellar, but nothing happened, so he came upstairs. He thought he would appear to her as two glaring, fiery eyes, which was one of his best tricks, but first he wanted to be sure where Jimmy was. But he couldn't find him. He hunted all over the house and, though he was invisible himself, he got more and more nervous. He kept imagining that at any moment Jimmy might jump out at him from some dark corner and scare him into fits. Finally he got so jittery that he went back to the cellar and hid in the coal bin all night.

The following days were just as bad for the ghost.

Several times he tried to scare Jimmy's aunt while she was working, but she didn't take any notice, and twice Jimmy managed to sneak up on him and appear suddenly with a loud yell, frightening him dreadfully. He was, I suppose, rather timid even for a ghost. He began to look quite haggard. He had several long arguments with Jimmy's aunt, in which he wept and appealed to her sympathy, but she was firm. If he wanted to live there he would have to pay rent, just like anybody else. There was the abandoned Miller farm two miles up the road. Why didn't he move there?

When the house was all in apple-pie order, Jimmy's aunt went down to the village to see a Mr and Mrs Whistler, who were living at the hotel because they couldn't find a house to move into. She told them about the old house, but they said, 'No, thank you. We've heard about that house. It's haunted. I'll bet,' they said, 'you wouldn't dare spend a night there.'

She told them that she had spent the last week there, but they evidently didn't believe her. So she said, 'You know my nephew, Jimmy. He's twelve years old. I am so sure that the house is not haunted that, if you want to rent it, I will let Jimmy stay there with you every night until you are sure everything is all right.'

'Ha!' said Mr Whistler. 'The boy won't do it. He's got more sense.'

So they sent for Jimmy. 'Why, I've spent the last week there,' he said. 'Of course I will.'

But the Whistlers still refused.

So Jimmy's aunt went round and told a lot of the village people about their talk, and everybody made so much fun of the Whistlers for being afraid, when a twelve-year-old boy wasn't, that they were ashamed, and said they would rent it. So they moved in.

Jimmy stayed there for a week, but he saw nothing of the ghost. And then one day one of the boys in his class told him that somebody had seen a ghost up at the Miller farm. So Jimmy knew the ghost had taken his aunt's advice.

A day or two later he walked up to the Miller's farm. There was no front door and he walked right in. There was some groaning and thumping upstairs, and then after a minute the ghost came floating down.

'Oh, it's you!' he said. 'Goodness sakes, boy, can't you leave me in peace?'

Jimmy said he'd just come up to see how he was getting along.

'Getting along fine,' said the ghost. 'From my point of view it's a very desirable property. Peaceful. Quiet. Nobody playing silly tricks.'

'Well,' said Jimmy, 'I won't bother you if you don't bother the Whistlers. But if you come back there . . .'

'Don't worry,' said the ghost.

So with the rent money, Jimmy and his aunt had a much easier life. They went to the cinema sometimes twice a week, and Jimmy had all new clothes, and on Thanksgiving, for the first time in his life, Jimmy had a turkey.

Once a week he would go up the Miller farm to see the ghost and they got to be very good friends. The ghost even came down to the Thanksgiving dinner, though of course he couldn't eat much. He seemed to enjoy the warmth of the house and he was in very good humour. He taught Jimmy several more tricks. The best one was how to glare with fiery eyes, which was useful later on when Jimmy became a doctor and had to look down people's throats to see if their tonsils ought to come out. He was really a pretty good fellow as ghosts go, and Jimmy's aunt got quite fond of him herself.

When the real winter weather began, she even used to worry about him a lot, because, of course, there was no heat in the Miller place and the doors and windows didn't amount to much and there was hardly any roof. The ghost tried to explain to her that the heat and cold didn't bother ghosts at all.

'Maybe not,' she said, 'but just the same, it can't be very pleasant.' And when he accepted their invitation for Christmas dinner she knitted some red woollen slippers, and he was so pleased that he broke down and cried. And that made Jimmy's aunt so happy, she broke down and cried.

Jimmy didn't cry, but he said, 'Aunt Mary, don't you think it would be nice if the ghost came down and lived with us this winter?'

'I would feel very much better about him if he did,' she said.

So he stayed with them that winter, and then he just stayed on, and it must have been a peaceful place for the last I heard he was still there.

THE SHADOW-CAGE

Philippa Pearce

The little green stoppered bottle had been waiting in the earth for a long time for someone to find it. Ned Challis found it. High on his tractor as he ploughed the field, he'd been keeping a look-out, as usual, for whatever might turn up. Several times there had been worked flints; once, one of an enormous size.

Now sunlight glimmering on glass caught his eye. He stopped the tractor, climbed down, picked the bottle from the earth. He could tell at once that it wasn't all that old. Not as old as the flints that he'd taken to the museum in Castleford. Not as old as a coin he had once found, with the head of a Roman emperor on it. Not very old; but old.

Perhaps just useless old . . .

He held the bottle in the palm of his hand and thought of throwing it away. The lip of it was chipped badly, and the stopper of cork or wood had sunk into the neck. With his fingernail he tried to move it. The stopper had hardened into stone, and stuck there. Probably no one would ever get it out now without breaking the bottle. But then, why should anyone want to unstopper the bottle? It was empty, or as good as empty. The bottom of the inside of the bottle was dirtied with something blackish and scaly that also clung a little to the sides.

He wanted to throw the bottle away, but he didn't. He held it in one hand while the fingers of the other cleaned the remaining earth from the outside. When he had cleaned it, he didn't fancy the bottle any more than before; but he dropped it into his pocket. Then he climbed the tractor and started off again.

At that time the sun was high in the sky, and the tractor was working on Whistlers' Hill, which is part of Belper's Farm, fifty yards below Burnt House. As the tractor moved on again, the gulls followed again, rising and falling in their flights, wheeling over the disturbed earth, looking for live things, for food; for good things.

That evening, at tea, Ned Challis brought the bottle out and set it on the table by the loaf of bread. His wife looked at it suspiciously: 'Another of your dirty old things for that museum?'

Ned said: 'It's not museum-stuff. Lisa can have it to take to school. I don't want it.'

Mrs Challis pursed her lips, moved the loaf further away from the bottle, and went to refill the tea-pot.

Lisa took the bottle in her hand. 'Where'd you get it, Dad?'

'Whistlers' Hill. Just below Burnt House.' He frowned suddenly as he spoke, as if he had remembered something.

'What's it got inside?'

'Nothing. And if you try getting the stopper out, that'll break.'

So Lisa didn't try. Next morning she took it to school; but she didn't show it to anyone. Only her cousin Kevin saw it, and that was before school and by accident. He always called for Lisa on his way to school – there was no other company on that country road – and saw her pick up the bottle from the table, where her mother had left it the night before, and put it into her anorak pocket.

'What was that?' asked Kevin.

'You saw. A little old bottle.'

'Let's see it again – properly.' Kevin was younger than Lisa, and she sometimes indulged him; so she took the bottle out and let him hold it.

At once he tried the stopper.

'Don't,' said Lisa. 'You'll only break it.'

'What's inside?'

'Nothing. Dad found it on Whistlers'.'

'It's not very nice, is it?'

'What do you mean, "Not very nice"?'

'I don't know. But let me keep it for a bit. Please, Lisa.'

On principle Lisa now decided not to give in. 'Certainly not. Give it back.'

He did, reluctantly. 'Let me have it just for today, at school. Please.'

'No.'

'I'll give you something if you'll let me have it. I'll not let anyone else touch it; I'll not let them see it. I'll keep it safe. Just for today.'

'You'd only break it. No. What could you give me, anyway?'

'My week's pocket-money.'

'No. I've said no and I mean no, young Kev.'

'I'd give you that little china dog you like.'

'The one with the china kennel?'

'Yes.'

'The china dog with the china kennel – you'd give me both?'

'Yes.'

'Only for half the day, then,' said Lisa. 'I'll let you have it after school-dinner – look out for me in the playground. Give it back at the end of school. Without fail. And you be careful with it.'

So the bottle travelled to school in Lisa's anorak pocket, where it bided its time all morning. After school-dinner Lisa met Kevin in the playground and they withdrew together to a corner which was well away from the crowded climbing-frame and the infants' sandpit and the rest. Lisa handed the bottle over. 'At the end of school, mind, without fail. And if we miss each other then,' – for Lisa, being in a higher class, came out of school slightly later than Kevin – 'then you must drop it in at ours as you pass. Promise.'

'Promise.'

They parted. Kevin put the bottle into his pocket. He didn't know why he'd wanted the bottle, but he had. Lots of things were like that. You needed them for a bit; and then you didn't need them any longer.

He had needed this little bottle very much.

He left Lisa and went over to the climbing-frame, where his friends already were. He had set his foot on a rung when he thought suddenly how easy it would be for the glass bottle in his trouser pocket to be smashed against the metal framework. He stepped down again and went over to the fence that separated the playground from the farmland beyond. Tall tussocks of grass grew along it, coming through from the open fields and fringing the very edge of the asphalt. He looked round: Lisa had already gone in, and no one else was watching. He put his hand into his pocket and took it out again with the bottle concealed in the fist. He stooped as if to examine an insect on a tussock, and slipped his hand into the middle of it and left the bottle there, well hidden.

He straightened up and glanced around. Since no one was looking in his direction, his action had been

unobserved; the bottle would be safe. He ran back to the climbing-frame and began to climb, jostling and shouting and laughing, as he and his friends always did. He forgot the bottle.

He forgot the bottle completely.

It was very odd, considering what a fuss he had made about the bottle, that he should have forgotten it; but he did. When the bell rang for the end of playtime, he ran straight in. He did not think of the bottle then, or later. At the end of the afternoon school, he did not remember it; and he happened not to see Lisa, who would surely have reminded him.

Only when he was nearly home, and passing the Challises' house, he remembered. He had faithfully promised – and had really meant to keep his promise. But he'd broken it, and left the bottle behind. If he turned and went back to school now, he would meet Lisa, and she would have to be told . . . By the time he got back to the school playground, all his friends would have gone home: the caretaker would be there, and perhaps a late teacher or two, and they'd all want to know what he was up to. And when he'd got the bottle and dropped it in at the Challises', Lisa would scold him all over again. And when he got home at last, he would be very late for his tea, and his mother would be angry.

As he stood by the Challises' gate, thinking, it seemed best, since he had messed things up anyway, to go straight home and leave the bottle to the next day. So he went home.

He worried about the bottle for the rest of the day, without having the time or the quiet to think about it very clearly. He knew that Lisa would assume he had just forgotten to leave it at her house on the way home. He half expected her to turn up after tea, to claim it; but she didn't. She would have been angry enough about his having forgotten to leave it; but what about her anger tomorrow on the way to school, when she found that he had forgotten it altogether – abandoned it in the open playground? He thought of hurrying straight past her house in the morning; but he would never manage it. She would be on the look-out.

He saw that he had made the wrong decision earlier. He ought, at all costs, to have gone back to the playground to get the bottle.

He went to bed, still worrying. He fell asleep, and his worry went on, making his dreaming unpleasant in a nagging way. He must be quick, his dreams seemed to nag. *Be quick . . .*

Suddenly he was wide awake. It was very late. The sound of the television being switched off must have woken him. Quietness. He listened to the rest of his family going to bed. They went to bed and to sleep. Silence. They were all asleep now, except for him. He couldn't sleep.

Then, as abruptly as if someone had lifted the top of his head like a lid and popped the idea in, he saw that this time – almost the middle of the night – was the perfect time for him to fetch the bottle. He knew by heart the roads between home and school; he would not be afraid. He would have plenty of time. When he reached the school, the gate to the playground would be shut, but it was not high: in the past, by daylight, he and his friends had often climbed it. He would go into the playground, find the correct tussock of grass, get the bottle, bring it back, and have it ready to give to Lisa on the way to school in the morning. She would be angry, but only moderately angry. She would never know the whole truth.

He got up and dressed quickly and quietly. He

began to look for a pocket-torch, but gave up when he realized that would mean opening and shutting drawers and cupboards. Anyway, there was a moon tonight, and he knew his way, and he knew the school playground. He couldn't go wrong.

He let himself out of the house, leaving the door on the latch for his return. He looked at his watch: between a quarter and half past eleven – not as late as he had thought. All the same, he set off almost at a run, but had to settle down to a steady trot. His trotting footsteps on the road sounded clearly in the night quiet. But who was there to hear?

He neared the Challises' house. He drew level with it.

Ned Challis heard. Usually nothing woke him before the alarm-clock in the morning; but tonight footsteps woke him. Who, at this hour – he lifted the back of his wrist towards his face, so that the time glimmered at him – who, at nearly twenty-five to twelve, could be hurrying along that road on foot? When the footsteps had almost gone – when it was already perhaps too late he sprang out of bed and over to the window.

His wife woke. 'What's up, then, Ned?'

'Just somebody. I wondered who.'

'Oh, come back to bed!'

Ned Challis went back to bed; but almost at once got out again.

'Ned! What is it now?'

'I just thought I'd have a look at Lisa.'

At once Mrs Challis was wide awake. 'What's wrong with Lisa?'

'Nothing.' He went to listen at Lisa's door – listen to the regular, healthy breathing of her sleep. He came back. 'Nothing. Lisa's all right.'

'For heavens' sake! Why shouldn't she be?'

'Well, who was it walking out there? Hurrying.'
'Oh, go to sleep!'
'Yes.' He lay down again, drew the bedclothes round him, lay still. But his eyes remained open.

Out in the night, Kevin left the road on which the Challises lived and came into the more important one that would take him into the village. He heard the rumble of a lorry coming up behind him. For safety he drew right into a gateway and waited. The lorry came past at a steady pace, headlights on. For a few seconds he saw the driver and his mate sitting up in the cab, intent on the road ahead. He had not wanted to be noticed by them, but, when they had gone, he felt lonely.

He went on into the village, its houses lightless, its streets deserted. By the entrance to the school driveway, he stopped to make sure he was un-observed. Nobody. Nothing – not even a cat. There was no sound of any vehicle now; but in the distance he heard a dog barking, and then another answered it. A little owl cried and cried for company or for sport. Then that, too, stopped.

He turned into the driveway to the school, and there was the gate to the playground. He looked over it, into the playground. Moonlight showed him everything: the expanse of asphalt, the sandpit, the big climbing-frame, and – at the far end – the fence with the tussocks of grass growing blackly along it. It was all familiar, and yet strange because of the emptiness and the whitening of moonlight and the shadows cast like solid things. The climbing-frame reared high into the air, and on the ground stretched the black criss-cross of its shadows like the bars of a cage.

But he had not come all this way to be halted by moonshine and insubstantial shadows. In a businesslike way he climbed the gate and crossed the playground to the fence. He wondered whether he would find the right tussock easily, but he did. His fingers closed on the bottle: it was waiting for him.

At that moment, in the Challises' house, as they lay side by side in bed, Mrs Challis said to her husband: 'You're still awake, aren't you?'

'Yes.'

'What is it?'

'Nothing.'

Mrs Challis sighed.

'All right, then,' said Ned Challis. 'It's this. That bottle I gave Lisa – that little old bottle that I gave Lisa yesterday –'

'What about it?'

'I found it by Burnt House.'

Mrs Challis drew in her breath sharply. Then she said, 'That may mean nothing.' Then, 'How near was it?'

'Near enough.' After a pause: 'I ought never to have given it to Lisa. I never thought. But Lisa's all right, anyway.'

'But, Ned, don't you know what Lisa did with that bottle?'

'What?'

'Lent it to Kevin to have at school. And, according to her, he didn't return it when he should have done, on the way home. Didn't you hear her going on and on about it?'

'Kevin . . .' For the third time that night Ned Challis was getting out of bed, this time putting on his trousers, fumbling for his shoes. 'Somebody went up the road in a hurry. You know – I looked out. I couldn't see properly, but it was somebody small. It could have been a child. It could have been Lisa, but it wasn't. It could well have been Kevin . . .'

'Shouldn't you go to their house first, Ned – find out whether Kevin is there or not? Make sure. You're not sure.'

'I'm not sure. But, if I wait to make sure, I may be too late.'

Mrs Challis did not say, 'Too late for what?' She did not argue.

Ned Challis dressed and went down. As he let himself out of the house to get his bicycle from the shed, the church clock began to strike the hour, the sound reaching him distantly across the intervening fields. He checked with his watch: midnight.

In the village, in the school playground, the striking of midnight sounded clangorously close. Kevin stood with the bottle held in the palm of his hand, waiting for the clock to stop striking – waiting as if for something to follow.

After the last stroke of midnight, there was silence,

but Kevin still stood waiting and listening. A car or lorry passed the entrance of the school drive: he heard it distinctly; yet it was oddly faint, too. He couldn't place the oddness of it. It had sounded much further away than it should have done – less really there.

He gripped the bottle and went on listening, as if for some particular sound. The minutes passed. The same dog barked at the same dog, bark and reply – far, unreally far away. The little owl called; from another world, it might have been.

He was gripping the bottle so tightly now that his hand was sweating. He felt his skin begin to prickle with sweat at the back of his neck and under his arms.

Then there was a whistle from across the fields, distantly. It should have been an unexpected sound, just after midnight; but it did not startle him. It did set him off across the playground, however. Too late he wanted to get away. He had to go past the climbing-frame, whose cagework of shadows now stretched more largely than the frame itself. He saw the bars of shadows as he approached; he actually hesitated; and then, like a fool, he stepped inside the cage of shadows.

Ned Challis, on his bicycle, had reached the junction of the by-road with the road that – in one direction – led to the village. In the other it led deeper into the country. Which way? He dismounted. He had to choose the right way – to follow Kevin.

Thinking of Whistlers' Hill, he turned the front wheel of his bicycle away from the village and set off again. But now, with his back to the village, going away from the village, he felt a kind of weariness and despair. A memory of childhood came into his mind: a game he had played in childhood: something hidden for him to find, and if he turned in the wrong direction to search, all the voices whispered to him, 'Cold – cold!' Now, with the village receding behind him, he recognized what he felt: cold . . . cold . . .

Without getting off his bicycle, he wheeled round and began to pedal hard in the direction of the village.

In the playground, there was no pressing hurry for Kevin any more. He did not press against the bars of his cage to get out. Even when clouds cut off the moonlight and the shadows melted into general darkness – even when the shadow-cage was no longer visible to the eye, he stood there; then crouched there, in a corner of the cage, as befitted a prisoner.

The church clock struck the quarter.

The whistlers were in no hurry. The first whistle had come from right across the fields. Then there was a long pause. Then the sound was repeated, equally distantly, from the direction of the river bridges. Later still, another whistle from the direction of the railway line, or somewhere near it.

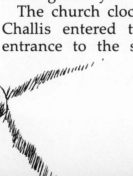

He lay in his cage, cramped by the bars, listening. He did not know he was thinking, but suddenly it came to him: Whistlers' Hill. He and Lisa and the others had always supposed that the hill had belonged to a family called Whistler, as Challises' house belonged to the Challis family. But that was not how the hill had got its name – he saw that now. No, indeed not.

Whistler answered whistler at long intervals, like the sentries of a besieging army. There was no moving in as yet.

The church clock had struck the quarter as Ned Challis entered the village and cycled past the entrance to the school. He cycled as far as the

Recreation Ground, perhaps because that was where Kevin would have gone in the daytime. He cycled bumpily round the Ground: no Kevin.

He began to cycle back the way he had come, as though he had given up altogether and were going home. He cycled slowly. He passed the entrance to the school again.

In this direction, he was leaving the village. He was cycling so slowly that the front wheel of his bicycle wobbled desperately; the light from his dynamo was dim. He put a foot down and stopped. Motionless, he listened. There was nothing to hear, unless – yes, the faintest ghost of a sound, high pitched, prolonged for seconds, remote as from another world. Like a coward – and Ned Challis was no coward – he tried to persuade himself that he had imagined the sound; yet he knew he had not. It came from another direction now: very faint, yet penetrating, so that his skin crinkled to hear it. Again it came, from yet another quarter.

He wheeled his bicycle back to the entrance to the school and left it there. He knew he must be very close. He walked up to the playground gate and peered over it. But the moon was obscured by cloud: he could see nothing. He listened, waited for the moon to sail free.

In the playground Kevin had managed to get up, first on his hands and knees, then upright. He was very much afraid, but he had to be standing to meet whatever it was.

For the whistlers had begun to close in slowly, surely: converging on the school, on the school playground, on the cage of shadows. On him.

For some time now cloud-masses had obscured the moon. He could see nothing; but he felt the whistlers' presence. Their signals came more often, and always closer. Closer. Very close.

Suddenly the moon sailed free.

In the sudden moonlight Ned Challis saw clear across the playground to where Kevin stood against the climbing-frame, with his hands writhing together in front of him.

In the sudden moonlight Kevin did not see his uncle. Between him and the playground gate, and all round him, air was thickening into darkness. Frantically he tried to undo his fingers, that held the little bottle, so that he could throw it from him. But he could not. He held the bottle; the bottle held him.

The darkness was closing in on him. The darkness was about to take him; had surely got him.

Kevin shrieked.

Ned Challis shouted: 'I'm here!' and was over the gate and across the playground and with his arms round the boy: *'I've got you.'*

There was a tinkle as something fell from between Kevin's opened fingers: the little bottle fell and rolled to the middle of the playground. It lay there, very insignificant-looking.

Kevin was whimpering and shaking, but he could move of his own accord. Ned Challis helped him over the gate and to the bicycle.

'Do you think you could sit on the bar, Kev? Could you manage that?'

'Yes.' He could barely speak.

Ned Challis hesitated, thinking of the bottle which had chosen to come to rest in the very centre of the playground, where the first child tomorrow would see it, pick it up.

He went back and picked the bottle up. Wherever he threw it, someone might find it. He might smash it and grind the pieces underfoot; but he was not sure he dared to do that.

Anyway, he was not going to hold it in his hand longer than he strictly must. He put it into his pocket, and then, when he got back to Kevin and the bicycle, he slipped it into the saddle-bag.

He rode Kevin home on the cross-bar of his bicycle. At the Challises' front gate Mrs Challis was waiting, with the dog for company. She just said: 'He all right then?'

'Ah?'

'I'll make a cup of tea while you take him home.'

At his own front door, Kevin said, 'I left the door on the latch. I can get in. I'm all right. I'd rather – I'd rather –'

'Less spoken of, the better,' said his uncle. 'You go to bed. Nothing to be afraid of now.'

He waited until Kevin was inside the house and he heard the latch click into place. Then he rode back to his wife, his cup of tea, and consideration of the problem that lay in his saddle-bag.

After he had told his wife everything, and they had discussed possibilities, Ned Challis said thoughtfully: 'I might take it to the museum, after all. Safest place for it would be inside a glass case there.'

'But you said they wouldn't want it.'

'Perhaps they would, if I told them where I found it and a bit – only a bit – about Burnt House . . .'

'You do that, then.'

Ned Challis stood up and yawned with a finality that said, Bed.

'But don't you go thinking you've solved all your problems by taking that bottle to Castleford, Ned. Not by a long chalk.'

'No?'

'Lisa. She reckons she owns that bottle.'

'I'll deal with Lisa tomorrow.'

'Today, by the clock.'

Ned Challis gave a groan that turned into another yawn. 'Bed first,' he said; 'then Lisa.' They went to bed not long before dawn.

The next day and for days after that, Lisa was furiously angry with her father. He had as good as stolen her bottle, she said, and now he refused to give it back, to let her see it, even to tell her what he had done with it. She was less angry with Kevin. (She did not know, of course, the circumstances of the bottle's passing from Kevin to her father.)

Kevin kept out of Lisa's way, and even more carefully kept out of his uncle's. He wanted no private conversation.

One Saturday Kevin was having tea at the Challises', because he had been particularly invited. He sat with Lisa and Mrs Challis. Ned had gone to Castleford, and came in late. He joined them at the tea-table in evident good spirits. From his pocket he brought out a small cardboard box, which he placed in the centre of the table, by the Saturday cake. His wife was staring at him: before he spoke, he gave her the slightest nod of reassurance. 'The museum didn't want to keep that little old glass bottle, after all,' he said.

Both the children gave a cry: Kevin started up with such a violent backward movement that his chair clattered to the floor behind him; Lisa leant forward, her fingers clawing towards the box.

'No!' Ned Challis said. To Lisa he added: 'There it stays, girl, till *I* say.' To Kevin: 'Calm down. Sit up at the table again and listen to me.' Kevin picked his chair up and sat down again, resting his elbows on the table, so that his hands supported his head.

'Now,' said Ned Challis, 'you two know so much that it's probably better you should know more. That little old bottle came from Whistlers' Hill, below Burnt House – well, you know that. Burnt House is only a ruin now – elder bushes growing inside as well as out; but once it was a cottage that someone lived in. Your mother's granny remembered the last one to live there.'

'No, Ned,' said Mrs Challis, 'it was my great-granny remembered.'

'Anyway,' said Ned Challis, 'it was so long ago that Victoria was the Queen, that's certain. And an old woman lived alone in that cottage. There were stories about her.'

'Was she a witch?' breathed Lisa.

'So they said. They said she went out on the hillside at night –'

'At the full of the moon,' said Mrs Challis.

'They said she dug up roots and searched out plants and toadstools and things. They said she caught rats and toads and even bats. They said she made ointments and powders and weird brews. And they said she used what she made to cast spells and call up spirits.'

'Spirits from Hell, my great-granny said. Real bad 'uns.'

'So people said, in the village. Only the parson scoffed at the whole idea. Said he'd called often and been shown over the cottage and seen nothing out of the ordinary – none of the jars and bottles of stuff that she was supposed to have for her witchcraft. He said she was just a poor cranky old woman; that was all.

'Well, she grew older and older and crankier and crankier, and one day she died. Her body lay in its coffin in the cottage, and the parson was going to bury her next day in the churchyard.

'The night before she was to have been buried, someone went up from the village –'

'Someone!' said Mrs Challis scornfully. 'Tell them the whole truth, Ned, if you're telling the story at all. Half the village went up, with lanterns – men, women, and children. Go on, Ned.'

'The cottage was thatched, and they began to pull swatches of straw away and take it into the cottage and strew it round and heap it up under the coffin. They were going to fire it all.

'They were pulling the straw on the downhill side of the cottage when suddenly a great piece of thatch came away and out came tumbling a whole lot of things that the old woman must have kept hidden there. People did hide things in thatches, in those days.'

'Her savings?' asked Lisa.

'No. A lot of jars and little bottles, all stoppered or sealed, neat and nice. With stuff inside.'

There was silence at the tea-table. Then Lisa said: 'That proved it: she was a witch.'

'Well, no, it only proved she *thought* she was a witch. That was what the parson said afterwards – and whew! was he mad when he knew about that night.'

Mrs Challis said: 'He gave it 'em red hot from the pulpit the next Sunday. He said that once upon a time poor old deluded creatures like her had been burnt alive for no reason at all, and the village ought to be ashamed of having burnt her dead.'

Lisa went back to the story of the night itself. 'What did they do with what came out of the thatch?'

'Bundled it inside the cottage among the straw, and fired it all. The cottage burnt like a beacon that night, they say. Before cockcrow, everything had been burnt to ashes. That's the end of the story.'

'Except for my little bottle,' said Lisa. 'That came out of the thatch, but it didn't get picked up. It rolled downhill, or someone kicked it.'

'That's about it,' Ned agreed.

Lisa stretched her hand again to the cardboard box, and this time he did not prevent her. But he said: 'Don't be surprised, Lisa. It's different.'

She paused. 'A different bottle?'

'The same bottle, but – well, you'll see.'

Lisa opened the box, lifted the packaging of cotton wool, took the bottle out. It was the same bottle, but the stopper had gone, and it was empty and clean – so clean that it shone greenly. Innocence shone from it.

'You said the stopper would never come out,' Lisa said slowly.

'They forced it by suction. The museum chap wanted to know what was inside, so he got the hospital lab to take a look – he has a friend there. It was easy for them.'

Mrs Challis said: 'That would make a pretty vase, Lisa. For tiny flowers.' She coaxed Lisa to go out to pick a posy from the garden; she herself took the bottle away to fill it with water.

Ned Challis and Kevin faced each other across the table. Kevin said: 'What was in it?'

Ned Challis said: 'A trace of this, a trace of that, the hospital said. One thing more than anything else.'

'Yes?'

'Blood. Human blood.'

Lisa came back with her flowers; Mrs Challis came back with the bottle filled with water. When the flowers had been put in, it looked a pretty thing.

'My witch-bottle,' said Lisa contentedly. 'What was she called – the old woman that thought she was a witch?'

Her father shook his head; her mother thought: 'Madge – or was it Maggy –?'

'Maggy Whistler's bottle, then,' said Lisa.

'Oh, no,' said Mrs Challis. 'She was Maggy – or Madge – Dawson. I remember my granny saying so. Dawson.'

'Then why's it called Whistlers' Hill?'

'I'm not sure,' said Mrs Challis uneasily. 'I mean, I don't think anyone knows for certain.'

But Ned Challis, looking at Kevin's face, knew that he knew for certain.

THE HAUNTED TRAILER

Robert Arthur

It was inevitable, of course. Bound to happen some day. But why did it have to happen to me? What did *I do* to deserve the grief? And I was going to be married, too. I sank my last thousand dollars into that trailer, almost. In it Monica and I were going on a honeymoon tour of the United States. We were going to see the country. I was going to write, and we were going to be happy as two turtledoves.

Ha!

Ha ha!

If you detect bitterness in that laughter, I'll tell you why I'm bitter.

Because it had to be me, Mel – for Melvin – Mason who became the first person in the world to own a haunted trailer!

Now, a haunted castle is one thing. Even an ordinary haunted house can be livable in. In a castle, or a house, if there's a ghost around, you can lock yourself in the bedroom and get a little sleep. A nuisance, yes. But nothing a man couldn't put up with.

In a trailer, though! What are you going to do when you're sharing a trailer, even a super-de-luxe model with four built-in bunks, a breakfast nook, a complete bathroom, a radio, electric range and easy-chair, with a ghost? Where can you go to get away from it?

Ha!

Ha ha!

I've heard so much ghostly laughter the last week that I'm laughing myself that way now.

There I was. I had the trailer. I had the car to pull it, naturally. I was on my way to meet Monica in Hollywood, where she was living with an aunt from Iowa. And twelve miles west of Albany, the first night out, my brand-new, spic-and-span trailer picks up a hitch-hiking haunt!

But maybe I'd better start at the beginning. It happened this way. I bought the trailer in New England – a Custom Clipper, with chrome and tan outside trim, for $2,998. I hitched it on behind my car and headed westwards, happier than a lark when the dew's on the thorn. I'd been saving up for this day for two years, and I felt wonderful.

I took it easy, getting the feel of the trailer, and so I didn't make very good time. I crossed the Hudson river just after dark, trundled through Albany in a rainstorm, and half an hour later pulled off the road into an old path between two big rocks to spend the night.

The thunder was rolling back and forth overhead, and the lightning was having target practice with the trees. But I'd picked out a nice secluded spot and I made myself comfortable. I cooked up a tasty plate of beans, some coffee, and fried potatoes. When I had eaten I took off my shoes, slumped down in the easy-chair, lit a cigarette, and leaned back.

'Ah!' I said aloud. 'Solid comfort. If only Monica were here, how happy we would be.'

But she wasn't, so I picked up a book.

It wasn't a very good book. I must have dozed off. Maybe I slept for a couple of hours. Maybe three. Anyway, I woke with a start, the echo of a buster of a thunderbolt still rattling the willow pattern tea set in the china cupboard. My hair was standing on end from the electricity in the air.

Then the door banged open, a swirl of rain swept in, and the wind – anyway, I thought it was the wind – slammed the door to. I heard a sound like a ghost – there's no other way to describe it – of a sigh.

'Now this,' said a voice, 'is something like!'

I had jumped up to shut the door, and I stood there with my unread book in my hand, gaping. The wind had blown a whisp of mist into my trailer and the mist, instead of evaporating, remained there, seeming to turn slowly and to settle into shape. It got more and more solid until –

Well, you know. It was a spectre. A haunt. A homeless ghost.

The creature remained there, regarding me in a decidedly cool manner.

'Sit down, chum,' it said, 'and don't look so pop-eyed. You make me nervous. This is my first night indoors in fifteen years, and I wanta enjoy it.'

'Who—' I stammered – 'who—'

'I'm not,' the spectre retorted, 'a brother owl, so don't who-who at me. What do I look like?'

'You look like a ghost,' I told him.

'Now you're getting smart, chum. I *am* a ghost. What *kind* of a ghost do I look like?'

I inspected it more closely. Now that the air inside my trailer had stopped eddying, it was reasonably firm of outline. It was a squat, heavy-set ghost, attired in ghostly garments that certainly never had come to it new. It wore the battered ghost of a felt

hat, and a stubble of ghostly beard showed on his jowls.

'You look like a tramp ghost,' I answered with distaste, and my uninvited visitor nodded.

'Just what I am, chum,' he told me. 'Call me Spike Higgins. Spike for short. That was my name before it happened.'

'Before what happened?' I demanded. The ghost wafted across the trailer to settle down on a bunk, where he lay down and crossed his legs, hoisting one foot encased in a battered ghost of a shoe in the air.

'Before I was amachoor enough to fall asleep riding on top of a truck, and fall off right here fifteen years ago,' he told me. 'Ever since I been forced to haunt this place. I wasn't no Boy Scout, so I got punished by bein' made to stay here in one spot. Me, who never stayed in one spot two nights running before!

'I been gettin' kind of tired of it the last couple of years. They wouldn't even lemme haunt a house. No, I hadda do all my haunting out in th' open, where th' wind an' rain could get at me, and every dog that went by could bark at me. Chum, you don't know what it means to me that you've picked this place to stop.'

'Listen,' I said firmly, 'you've got to get out of here!'

The apparition yawned.

'Chum,' he said, 'you're the one that's trespassin', not me. This is my happy hunting ground. Did I ask you to stop here?'

'You mean,' I asked between clenched teeth, 'that you won't go? You're going to stay here all night?'

'Right, chum,' the ghost grunted. 'Gimme a call for six a.m.' He closed his eyes, and began snoring in an artificial and highly insulting manner.

Then I got sore. I threw a book at him, and it

bounced off the bunk without bothering him in the least. Spike Higgins opened an eye and leered at me.

'Went right through me,' he chortled. 'Instead of me goin' through it. Ha ha! Ha ha ha! Joke.'

'You—' I yelled, in rage. 'You—stuff!'

And I slammed him with the chair cushion, which likewise went through him without doing any damage. Spike Higgins opened both eyes and stuck out his tongue at me.

Obviously I couldn't hurt him, so I got control of myself.

'Listen,' I said, craftily. 'You say you are doomed to haunt this spot for ever? You can't leave?'

'Forbidden to leave,' Spike answered. 'Why?'

'Never mind,' I gritted. 'You'll find out.'

I snatched up my raincoat and hat and scrambled out into the storm. If that ghost was doomed to remain in that spot for ever, I wasn't. I got into the car, got the motor going, and backed out of there. It took a lot of manoeuvring in the rain, with mud underwheel, but I made it. I got straightened out on the concrete and headed westwards.

I didn't stop until I'd covered twenty miles. Then, beginning to grin as I thought of the shock the ghost of Spike Higgins must have felt when I yanked the trailer from underneath him, I parked on a stretch of old, unused road and then crawled back into the trailer again.

Inside, I slammed the door and –

Ha!

Ha ha!

Ha ha ha!

Yes, more bitter laughter. Spike Higgins was still there, sound asleep and snoring.

I muttered something under my breath. Spike Higgins opened his eyes sleepily.

'Hello,' he yawned. 'Been having fun?'

'Listen,' I finally got it out. 'I – thought – you – were – doomed – to – stay – back – there – where – I – found – you – for ever!'

The apparition yawned again.

'Your mistake, chum, I didn't say I was doomed to stay. I said I was forbidden to leave. I didn't leave. You hauled me away. It's all your responsibility and I'm a free agent now.'

'You're a what?'

'I'm a free agent. I can ramble as far as I please. I can take up hoboing again. You've freed me. Thanks, chum. I won't forget.'

'Then—then—' I spluttered. Spike Higgins nodded.

'That's right. I've adopted you. I'm going to stick with you. We'll travel together.'

'But you can't!' I cried out, aghast. 'Ghosts don't travel around! They haunt houses – or cemeteries – or maybe woods. But –'

'What do you know about ghosts?' Spike Higgins' voice held sarcasm. 'There's all kinds of ghosts, chum. Includin' hobo ghosts, tramp ghosts, ghosts with itchin' feet who can't stay put in one spot. Let me tell you, chum, a 'bo ghost like me ain't never had no easy time of it.

'Suppose they do give him a house to haunt? All right, he's got a roof over his head, but there he is, stuck. Houses don't move around. They don't go places. They stay in one spot till they rot.

'But things are different now. You've helped bring in a new age for the brotherhood of spooks. Now a fellow can haunt a house and be on the move at the same time. He can work at his job and still see the country. These trailers are the answer to a problem that's been bafflin' the best minds in th' spirit world for thousands of years. It's the newest thing, the latest and the best. Haunted trailers. I tell you, we'll probably erect a monument to you at our next meeting. The ghost of a monument, anyway.'

Spike Higgins had raised up on an elbow to make his speech. Now, grimacing, he lay back.

'That's enough, chum,' he muttered. 'Talking uses up my essence. I'm going to merge for a while. See you in the morning.'

'Merge with what?' I asked. Spike Higgins was already so dim I could hardly see him.

'Merge with the otherwhere,' a faint, distant voice told me, and Spike Higgins was gone.

I waited a minute to make sure. Then I breathed a big sigh of relief. I looked at my raincoat, at my wet feet, at the book on the floor, and knew it had all been a dream. I'd been walking in my sleep. Driving in it too. Having a nightmare.

I hung up the raincoat, slid out of my clothes and got into a bunk.

I woke up late, and for a moment felt panic. Then I breathed easily again. The other bunk was untenanted. Whistling, I jumped up, showered, dressed, ate and got under way.

It was a lovely day. Blue sky, wind, sunshine, birds singing. Thinking of Monica, I almost sang with them as I rolled down the road. In a week I'd be pulling up in front of Monica's aunt's place in Hollywood and tooting the horn –

That was the moment when a cold draught of air sighed along the back of my neck, and the short hairs rose.

I turned, almost driving into a hay wagon. Beside me was a misty figure.

'I got tired of riding back there alone,' Spike Higgins told me. 'I'm gonna ride up front a while an' look at th' scenery.'

'You—you—' I shook with rage so that we nearly ran off the road. Spike Higgins reached out, grabbed the wheel in tenuous fingers, and jerked us back on to our course again.

'Take it easy, chum,' he said. 'There's enough competition in this world I'm in, without you hornin' into th' racket.'

I didn't say anything, but my thoughts must have been written on my face. I'd thought he was just a nightmare. But he was real. A ghost had moved in with me, and I hadn't the faintest idea how to move him out.

Spike Higgins grinned with a trace of malice.

'Sure, chum,' he said. 'It's perfectly logical. There's haunted castles, haunted palaces and haunted houses. Why not a haunted trailer?'

'Why not haunted ferryboats?' I demanded with bitterness. 'Why not haunted Pullmans? Why not haunted trucks?'

'You think there ain't?' Spike Higgins' misty countenance registered surprise at my ignorance. 'Could I tell you tales! There's a haunted ferryboat makes the crossing at Pough-keepsie every stormy night at midnight. There's a haunted private train on the Atchison, Santa Fé. Pal of mine haunts it. He always jumped trains, but he was a square dealer, and they gave him the private train for a reward.

'Then there's a truck on the New York Central that never gets where it's going. Never has yet. No matter where it starts out for, it winds up some place else. Bunch of my buddies haunt it. And another truck on the Southern Pacific that never has a train to pull it. Runs by itself. It's driven I dunno how many signalmen crazy, when they saw it go past right ahead of a whole train. I could tell you –'

'Don't!' I ordered. 'I forbid you to. I don't want to hear.'

'Why, sure, chum,' Spike Higgins agreed. 'But you'll get used to it. You'll be seein' a lot of me. Because where thou ghost, I ghost. Pun.' He gave a ghostly chuckle and relapsed into silence. I drove along, my mind churning. I had to get rid of him. *Had* to. Before we reached California, at the very latest. But I didn't have the faintest idea in the world how I was going to.

Then, abruptly, Spike Higgins' ghost sat up straight.

'Stop!' he ordered. 'Stop, I say!'

We were on a lonely stretch of road, bordered by old cypresses, with weed-grown marshland beyond. I didn't see any reason for stopping. But Spike Higgins reached out and switched off the ignition. Then he slammed on the emergency brake. We came

squealing to a stop, and just missed going into a ditch.

'What did you do that for?' I yelled. 'You almost ditched us! Confound you, you ectoplasmic, hitch-hiking nuisance! If I ever find a way to lay hands on you –'

'Quiet, chum!' the apparition told me rudely. 'I just seen an old pal of mine. Slippery Samuels. I ain't seen him since he dropped a bottle of nitro just as he was gonna break into a bank in Mobile sixteen years ago. We're gonna give him a ride.'

'We certainly are not!' I cried. 'This is my car, and I'm not picking up any more –'

'It may be your car,' Spike Higgins sneered, 'but I'm the resident haunt, and I got full powers to extend hospitality to any buddy ghosts I want, see? Rule 11, subdivision c. Look it up. Hey, Slippery, climb in!'

A finger of fog pushed through the partly open window of the car at his hail, enlarged, and there was a second apparition on the front seat with me.

The newcomer was long and lean, just as shabbily dressed as Spike Higgins, with a ghostly countenance as mournful as a Sunday School picnic on a rainy day.

'Spike, you old son of a gun,' the second spook murmured, in hollow tones that would have brought gooseflesh to a statue. 'How've you been? What're you doing here? Who's he?' – nodding at me.

'Never mind him,' Spike said disdainfully. 'I'm haunting his trailer. Listen, whatever became of the old gang?'

'Still hoboing it,' the long, lean apparition sighed. 'Nitro Nelson is somewhere around. Pacific Pete and Buffalo Benny are lying over in a haunted jungle somewhere near Toledo. I had a date to join 'em, but

a storm blew me back to Wheeling a couple of days
ago.'

'Mmmm,' Spike Higgins' ghost muttered. 'Maybe
we'll run into 'em. Let's go back in my trailer and do
a little chinning. As for you, chum, make camp any
time you want. Ta ta.'

The two apparitions oozed through the back of the
car and were gone. I was boiling inside, and there
was nothing I could do.

I drove on for another hour, went through Toledo,
then stopped at a wayside camp. I paid my dollar,
picked out a spot and parked.

But when I entered the trailer, the ghosts of Spike
Higgins and Slippery Samuels, the bank robber,
weren't there. Nor had they shown up by the time I
finished dinner. In fact I ate, washed and got into
bed with no sign of them.

Breathing a prayer that maybe Higgins had abandoned me to go back to 'boing it in the spirit world, I
fell asleep. And began to dream. About Monica –

When I woke, there was a sickly smell in the air,
and the heavy staleness of old tobacco smoke.

I opened my eyes. Luckily, I opened them prepared for the worst. Even so, I wasn't prepared well
enough.

Spike Higgins was back. Ha! Ha ha! Ha ha ha! I'll
say he was back. He lay on the opposite bunk, his
eyes shut, his mouth open, snoring. Just the ghost of
a snore, but quite loud enough. On the bunk above
him lay his bank-robber companion. In the easy-
chair was slumped a third apparition, short and
stout, with a round, whiskered face. A tramp spirit,
too.

So was the ghost stretched out on the floor, gaunt
and cadaverous. So was the small, mournful spook in
the bunk above me, his ectoplasmic hand swinging

over the side, almost in my face. Tramps, all of them. Hobo spooks. Five hobo phantoms asleep in my trailer!

And there were cigarette butts in all the ash-trays, and burns on my built-in writing desk. The cigarettes apparently had just been lit and let burn. The air was choking with stale smoke, and I had a headache I could have sold for a fire alarm, it was ringing so loudly in my skull.

I knew what had happened. During the night Spike Higgins and his pal had rounded up some more of their ex-hobo companions. Brought them back. To *my* trailer. Now – I was so angry I saw all five of them through a red haze that gave their ectoplasm a ruby tinge. Then I got hold of myself. I couldn't throw them out. I couldn't harm them. I couldn't touch them.

No, there was only one thing I could do. Admit I was beaten. Take my loss and quit while I could. It was a bitter pill to swallow. But if I wanted to reach Monica, if I wanted to enjoy the honeymoon we'd planned, I'd have to give up the fight.

I got into my clothes. Quietly I sneaked out, locking the trailer behind me. Then I hunted for the owner of the trailer camp, a lanky man, hard-eyed, but well dressed. I guessed he must have money.

'Had sort of a party last night, hey?' he asked me, with a leering wink. 'I seen lights, an' heard singing, long after midnight. Not loud, though, so I didn't bother you. But it looked like somebody was havin' a high old time.'

I gritted my teeth.

'That was me,' I said. 'I couldn't sleep. I got up and turned on the radio. Truth is, I haven't slept a single night in that trailer. I guess I wasn't built for trailer life. That job cost me $2,998 new, just three days ago.

I've got the bill-of-sale. How'd you like to buy it for fifteen hundred, and make two hundred easy profit on it?'

He gnawed his lip, but knew the trailer was a bargain. We settled for thirteen-fifty. I gave him the bill-of-sale, took the money, uncoupled, got into the car and left there.

As I turned the bend in the road, heading westwards, there was no sign that Spike Higgins' ghost was aware of what had happened.

I even managed to grin as I thought of his rage when he woke up to find I had abandoned him. It was almost worth the money I'd lost to think of it.

Beginning to feel better, I stepped on the accelerator, piling up miles between me and that trailer. At least I was rid of Spike Higgins and his friends.

Ha!

Ha ha!

Ha ha ha!

That's what I thought.

About the middle of the afternoon I was well into Illinois. It was open country, and monotonous, so I turned on my radio. And the first thing I got was a police broadcast.

'All police, Indiana and Illinois! Be on the watch for a tan-and-chrome trailer, stolen about noon from a camp near Toledo. The thieves are believed heading west in it. That is all!'

I gulped. It couldn't be! But – it sounded like my trailer, all right. I looked in my rear-vision mirror, aprehensively. The road behind was empty. I breathed a small sigh of relief. I breathed it too soon. For at that moment, round a curve half a mile behind me, something swung into sight and came racing down the road after me.

The trailer.

Ha!

Ha ha!

There it came, a tan streak that zipped round the curve and came streaking after me, zigzagging wildly from side to side of the road, doing at least sixty – without a car pulling it.

My flesh crawled, and my hair stood on end. I stepped on the accelerator. Hard. And I picked up speed in a hurry. In half a minute I was doing seventy, and the trailer was still gaining. Then I hit eighty – and passed a motor-cycle cop parked beside the road.

I had just a glimpse of his pop-eyed astonishment as I whizzed past, with the trailer chasing me fifty yards behind. Then, kicking on his starter, he slammed after us.

Meanwhile, in spite of everything the car would do, the trailer pulled up behind me and I heard the coupling clank as it was hitched on. At once my speed dropped. The trailer was swerving dangerously, and I had to slow. Behind me the cop was coming, siren open wide, but I didn't worry about him because Spike Higgins was materializing beside me.

'Whew!' he said, grinning at me. 'My essence feels all used up. Thought you could give Spike Higgins and his pals the slip, huh? You'll learn, chum, you'll learn. That trooper looks like a tough baby. You'll have fun trying to talk yourself out of this.'

'Yes, but see what it'll get *you*, you ectoplasmic excrescence!' I raged at him. 'The trailer will be stored away in some county garage for months as evidence while I'm being held for trial on the charge of stealing it. And how'll you like haunting a garage?'

Higgins' face changed.

'Say, that's right,' he murmured. 'My first trip for fifteen years, too.'

He put his fingers to his lips, and blew the shrill ghost of a whistle. In a moment the car was filled with cold, clammy draughts as Slippery Samuels and the other three apparitions appeared in the seat beside Higgins.

Twisting and turning and seeming to intermingle a lot, they peered out at the cop, who was beside the car now, one hand on his gun butt, trying to crowd me over to the shoulder.

'All right, boys!' Higgins finished explaining. 'You know what we gotta do. Me an' Slippery'll take the car. You guys take the trailer.'

They slipped through the open windows like smoke. Then I saw Slippery Samuels holding on to the left front bumper, and Spike Higgins holding on to the right, their ectoplasm streaming out horizontal to the road, stretched and thinned by the air rush. And an instant later we began to move with a speed I had never dreamed of reaching.

We zipped ahead of the astonished cop, and the speedometer needle began to climb again. It took the trooper an instant to believe his eyes. Then with a yell he yanked out his gun and fired. A bullet bumbled past; then he was too busy trying to overtake us again to shoot.

The speedometer said ninety now, and was still climbing. It touched a hundred and stuck there. I was trying to pray when down the road a mile away I saw a sharp curve, a bridge and a deep river. I froze. I couldn't even yell.

We came up to the curve so fast that I was still trying to move my lips when we hit it. I didn't make any effort to take it. Instead I slammed on the brakes and prepared to plough straight ahead into a fence, a stand of young poplars and the river.

But just as I braked, I heard Spike Higgins' ghostly

scream, 'Allay-OOP!'

And before we reached the ditch, car and trailer swooped up in the air. An instant later at a height of a hundred and fifty feet, we hurtled straight westwards over the river and the town beyond.

I'd like to have seen the expression on the face of the motorcycle cop then. As far as that goes, I'd like to have seen my own.

Then the river was behind us, and the town, and we were swooping down towards a dank, gloomy-looking patch of woods through which ran an abandoned railway line. A moment later we struck earth with a jouncing shock and came to rest.

Spike Higgins and Slippery Samuels let go of the bumpers and straightened themselves up. Spike Higgins dusted ghostly dust off his palms and leered at me.

'How was that, chum?' he asked. 'Neat, hey?'

'How—' I stuttered – 'how—'

'Simple,' Spike Higgins answered. 'Anybody that can tip tables can do it. Just levitation, 'at's all. Hey, meet the boys. You ain't been introduced yet. This is Buffalo Benny, this one is Toledo Ike, this one Pacific Pete.'

The fat spook, the cadaverous one, and the melancholy little one appeared from behind the car, and smirked as Higgins introduced them. Then Higgins waved a hand impatiently.

'C'm on, chum', he said. 'There's a road there that takes us out of these woods. Let's get going. It's almost dark, and we don't wanna spend the night here. This used to be in Dan Bracer's territory.'

'Who's Dan Bracer?' I demanded, getting the motor going, because I was as anxious to get away from there as Spike Higgins' spook seemed to be.

'Just a railway dick,' Spike Higgins said, with a distinctly uneasy grin. 'Toughest bull that ever kicked a poor 'bo off a freight.'

'So mean he always drank black coffee,' Slippery Samuels put in, in a mournful voice. 'Cream turned sour when he picked up the jug.'

'Not that we was afraid of him—' Buffalo Benny, the fat apparition, squeaked. 'But—'

'We just never liked him,' Toledo Ike croaked, a sickly look on his ghostly features. 'O' course, he ain't active now. He was retired a couple years back, an' jes' lately I got a rumour he was sick.'

'Dyin',' Pacific Peter murmured hollowly.

'Dyin'.' They all sighed the word, looking apprehensive. Then Spike Higgins' ghost scowled truculently at me.

'Never mind about Dan Bracer,' he snapped. 'Let's just get goin' out of here. And don't give that cop no more thought. You think a cop is gonna turn in a report that a car and trailer he was chasin' suddenly sailed up in the air an' flew away like an aeroplane? Not on your sweet life. He ain't gonna say nothing to nobody about it.'

Apparently he was right, because after I had driven out of the woods, with some difficulty, and onto the secondary highway, there was no further sign of pursuit. I headed westwards again, and Spike Higgins and his pals moved back to the trailer, where they lolled about, letting my cigarettes burn and threatening to call the attention of the police to me when I complained.

I grew steadily more morose and desperate as the Pacific Coast, and Monica, came nearer. I was behind schedule, due to Spike Higgins' insistence on my taking a roundabout route so they could see the Grand Canyon, and no way to rid myself of the obnoxious haunts appeared. I couldn't even abandon the trailer. Spike Higgins had been definite on that point. It was better to haul a haunted trailer around than to have one chasing you, he pointed out, and shuddering at the thought of being pursued by a trailer full of ghosts wherever I went, I agreed.

But if I couldn't get rid of them, it meant no Monica, no marriage, no honeymoon. And I was determined that nothing as insubstantial as a spirit was going to interfere with my life's happiness.

Just the same, by the time I had driven over the mountains and into California, I was almost on the point of doing something desperate. Apparently sensing this, Spike Higgins and the others had been on their good behaviour. But I could still see no way of getting rid of them.

It was early afternoon when I finally rolled into Hollywood, haggard and unshaven, and found a trailer camp, where I parked. Heavy-hearted, I bathed and shaved and put on clean clothes. I didn't know what I was going to say to Monica, but I was already several days behind schedule, and I couldn't put off ringing her.

There was a telephone in the camp office. I looked up Ida Bracer – her aunt's name – in the book, then put through the call.

Monica answered. Her voice sounded distraught.

'Oh, Mel,' she exclaimed, as soon as I announced myself, 'where have you been? I've been expecting you for days.'

'I was delayed,' I told her, bitterly. 'Spirits. I'll explain later.'

'Spirits?' Her tone seemed cold. 'Well, anyway, now that you're here at last, I must see you at once. Mel, Uncle Dan is dying.'

'Uncle Dan?' I echoed.

'Yes Aunt Ida's brother. He used to live in Iowa, but a few months ago he was taken ill, and he came out to be with Aunt and me. Now he's dying. The doctor says it's only a matter of hours.'

'Dying?' I repeated again. 'Your Uncle Dan, from Iowa, dying?'

Then it came to me. I began to laugh. Exultantly.

'I'll be right over!' I said, and hung up.

Still chuckling, I hurried out and unhitched my car. Spike Higgins stared at me suspiciously.

'Just got an errand to do,' I said airily. 'Be back soon.'

'You better be,' Spike Higgins' ghost said. 'We

wanta drive around and see those movie stars'
houses later on.'

Ten minutes later Monica herself, trim and lovely,
was opening the door for me. In high spirits, I
grabbed her round the waist, and kissed her. She
turned her cheek to me, then, releasing herself,
looked at me strangely.

'Mel,' she frowned, 'what in the world is wrong
with you?'

'Nothing,' I carolled. 'Monica darling, I've got to
talk to your uncle.'

'But he's too sick to see anyone. He's sinking fast,
the doctor says.'

'All the more reason why I must see him,' I told
her, and pushed into the house. 'Where is he,
upstairs?'

I hurried up, and into the sickroom. Monica's
uncle, a big man with a rugged face and a chin like

the prow of a battleship, was in bed, breathing stertorously.

'Mr Bracer!' I said, breathless, and his eyes opened slowly.

'Who're you?' a voice as raspy as a shovel scraping a concrete floor growled.

'I'm going to marry Monica,' I told him. 'Mr Bracer, have you ever heard of Spike Higgins? Or Slippery Samuels? Or Buffalo Benny, Pacific Pete, Toledo Ike?'

'Heard of 'em?' A bright glow came into the sick man's eyes. 'Ha! I'll say I have. And laid hands on 'em, too, more'n once. But they're dead now.'

'I know they are,' I told him. 'But they're still around. Mr Bracer, how'd you like to meet up with them again?'

'Would I!' Dan Bracer murmured, and his hands clenched in unconscious anticipation. 'Ha!'

'Then,' I said, 'if you'll wait for me in the cemetery the first night after – after – well, anyway, wait for me, and I'll put you in touch with them.'

The ex-railway detective nodded. He grinned broadly, like a tiger viewing its prey, and eager to be after it. Then he lay back, his eyes closed, and Monica, running in, gave a little gasp.

'He's gone!' she said.

'Ha ha!' I chuckled. 'Ha ha ha! What a surprise this is going to be to certain parties.'

The funeral was held in the afternoon, two days later. I didn't see Monica much in the interim. In the first place, though she hadn't known her uncle well, and wasn't particularly grieved, there were a lot of details to be attended to. In the second place, Spike Higgins and his pals kept me on the jump. I had to drive around Hollywood, to all the stars' houses, to Malibou Beach, Santa Monica, Laurel Canyon and the various studios, so they could sightsee.

Then, too, Monica rather seemed to be avoiding me, when I did have time free. But I was too inwardly gleeful at the prospect of getting rid of the ghosts of Higgins and his pals to notice.

I managed to slip away from Higgins to attend the funeral of Dan Bracer, but could not help grinning broadly, and even at times chuckling, as I thought of his happy anticipation of meeting Spike Higgins and the others again. Monica eyed me oddly, but I could explain later. It wasn't quite the right moment to go into details.

After the funeral, Monica said she had a headache, so I promised to come round later in the evening. I returned to the trailer to find Spike Higgins and the others sprawled out, smoking my cigarettes again. Higgins looked at me with dark suspicion.

'Chum,' he said, 'we wanna be hitting the road again. We leave tomorrow, get me?'

'Tonight, Spike,' I said cheerfully. 'Why wait? Right after sunset you'll be on your way. To distant parts. Tra la, tra le, tum tum te tum.'

He scowled, but could think of no objection. I waited impatiently for sunset. As soon as it was thoroughly dark, I hitched up and drove out of the trailer camp, heading for the cemetery where Dan Bracer had been buried that afternoon.

Spike Higgins was still surly, but unsuspicious until I drew up and parked by the low stone wall at the nearest point to Monica's uncle's grave. Then, gazing out at the darkness-shadowed cemetery, he looked uneasy.

'Say,' he snarled, 'watcha stoppin' here for? Come on, let's be movin'.'

'In a minute, Spike,' I said. 'I have some business here.'

I slid out and hopped over the low wall.

'Mr Bracer!' I called. 'Mr Bracer!'

I listened, but a long freight rumbling by half a block distant, where the Union Pacific lines entered the city, drowned out any sound. For a moment I could see nothing. Then a misty figure came into view among the headstones.

'Mr Bracer!' I called as it approached. 'This way!'

The figure headed towards me. Behind me Spike Higgins, Slippery Samuels and the rest of the ghostly crew were pressed against the wall, staring apprehensively into the darkness, and they were able to recognize the dim figure approaching before I could be sure of it.

'Dan Bracer!' Spike Higgins choked, in a high, ghostly squeal.

'It's him!' Slippery Samuels groaned.

'In the spirit!' Pacific Pete wailed. 'Oh oh oh oh OH!'

They tumbled backwards, with shrill squeaks of dismay. Dan Bracer's spirit came forward faster. Paying no attention to me, he took off after the retreating five.

Higgins turned and fled, wildly, with the others at his heels. They were heading towards the railway line, over which the freight was still rumbling, and Dan Bracer was now at their heels. Crowding each other, Higgins and Slippery Samuels and Buffalo Benny swung on to a passing truck, with Pacific Pete and Toledo Ike catching wildly at the rungs of the next.

They drew themselves up to the top of the trucks, and stared back. Dan Bracer's ghost seemed, for an instant, about to be left behind. But one long ectoplasmic arm shot out. A ghostly hand caught the rail of the guard's van, and Dan Bracer swung aboard. A moment later, he was running forward along the tops of the trucks, and up ahead of him, Spike Higgins and his pals were racing towards the engine.

That was the last I saw of them – five phantom figures fleeing, the sixth pursuing in happy anticipation. Then they were gone out of my life, heading east.

Still laughing to myself at the manner in which I had rid myself of Spike Higgins' ghost, and so made it possible for Monica to be married and enjoy our honeymoon trailer trip after all, I drove to Monica's aunt's house.

'Melvin!' Monica said sharply, as she answered my ring. 'What are you laughing about now?'

'Your uncle,' I chuckled. 'He—'

'My uncle!' Monica gasped. 'You—you fiend! You laughed when he died! You laughed all during his funeral! Now you're laughing because he's dead!'

'No, Monica!' I said. 'Let me explain. About the spirits, and how I—'

Her voice broke.

'Forcing your way into the house – laughing at my poor Uncle Dan – laughing at his funeral—'

'But Monica!' I cried. 'It isn't that way at all. I've just been to the cemetery, and—'

'And you came back laughing,' Monica retorted. 'I never want to see you again. Our engagement is broken. And worst of all is the *way* you laugh. It's so—so ghostly! So spooky. Blood-chilling. Even if you hadn't done the other things, I could never marry a man who laughs like that. So here's your ring. And good-bye.'

Leaving me staring at the ring in my hand, she slammed the door. And that was that. Monica is very strong-minded, and what she says, she means. I couldn't even try to explain. About Spike Higgins.

And how I'd unconsciously come to laugh that way through associating with five phantoms. After all, I'd just rid myself of them for good. And the only way Monica would ever have believed my story would have been from my showing her Spike Higgins' ghost himself.

Ha!

Ha ha!

Ha ha ha ha!

If you know anyone who wants to buy a practically unused trailer, cheap, let them get in touch with me.

LET'S PLAY GHOSTS!

Pamela Vincent

ou're talking absolute rot,' said Perry.

'I don't care whether you believe it or not,' shrugged Hugh.

'But we've lived here for years. We'd know if the place were haunted.'

'Not unless you're the sort of people who *feel* these things.'

Perry laughed. 'Oh, feeling! It's easy enough to say you *feel* things, but when have you ever *seen* a ghost?'

'I believe you, Hugh,' said Charlotte, Perry's young sister, when Hugh didn't answer.

'You would,' said her brother, scornfully. '*You* won't even pass a churchyard when it's dark.'

'You don't want to worry about that, Charlie,' Hugh smiled. 'The ones buried in churchyards are all right, they don't need to haunt.'

'But it's creepy with all those funny tombstones,' shivered the little girl.

'It's much creepier in your dining-room,' said Hugh.

'What's creepy about the dining-room?'

They all jumped as Mr Baxter came in and started vaguely looking for something.

'Hugh says it's haunted, Daddy,' replied Charlotte, her eyes shining with excitement.

'Um? Well, suicides often do haunt, don't they?' With relief, Mr Baxter found his tobacco pouch under a cushion, and started to wander away, but—

'What!' exclaimed both his children.

'What are you talking about, Dad?' demanded Perry.

Mr Baxter looked surprised.

'I thought you knew. You were a bit young when we first came here, but I'm sure something was said about someone committing suicide in the house.'

'*Hugh* said it was a n'orrible murder,' said Perry.

'It seemed like that to me,' said Hugh, puzzled.

'No, I'm sure it was suicide,' Mr Baxter frowned, searching his memory.

'Gosh, I thought houses had to be hundreds of years old to have ghosts,' said Charlotte, looking around their cheerful, modern room.

'This was sixty-odd years ago,' grunted her father round the pipe he was now lighting with too many matches. 'Before even your old Dad was born.'

'How did he do it?' asked Perry, with gruesome interest.

'It was a girl,' said Hugh. 'A young girl.'

'That's right,' agreed Mr Baxter. 'She took poison, I think. Don't know why – blighted in love, I expect.'

'No, she was too young for that,' said Hugh.

'Never too young,' said Mr Baxter briskly. 'Look at Charlie here, always in love with someone or other.'

'I'm not!' cried Charlotte.

'You are,' retorted Perry, 'there's that spotty boy in the choir—'

'He's no spottier than you—'

'Shut up kids,' said Mr Baxter, 'I want to talk about Hugh's being psychic—'

'Please, Mr Baxter, I'd rather forget it. I wouldn't have mentioned it, but I felt so bad in the dining-room that the others noticed.'

'But it's so int'resting, Hugh,' said Charlie. 'I wish *I* were psytic.'

Hugh shook his head.

'No, Charlie, it's very uncomfortable.'

'It creates rather a problem,' observed Mr Baxter, thoughtfully. 'We can't have you starving to death while you're staying with us, but you say going into the dining-room upsets you.'

'That's all right, we'll eat in the kitchen,' decided Charlie. 'I'll tell Mummy.'

'She won't like that,' said Perry, 'we always use the dining-room for guests.'

'Hugh'd rather be one of the family – wouldn't you?' smiled Mr Baxter.

'If it's not putting Mrs Baxter to any trouble.'

'It saves bother,' said Charlotte, 'but don't tell your parents we made you eat in the kitchen, will you?'

The holiday was crowded enough for them to forget about the ghost. Hugh's parents were in South America so the two schoolfriends had all summer to spend together, sometimes letting Charlie tag along, sometimes joining up with Baxter cousins of about their own age, Colin and Sue. A fortnight was spent at the seaside – and then they came home to bad weather, with nothing to do but mope indoors.

'D'you know we've got a ghost?' said Perry, bored with sprawling on the floor losing at Monopoly.

Hugh flashed him an annoyed glance and Charlotte exclaimed:

'Oh, Perry, you weren't supposed to say!'

'Why not?' cried Sue. 'We're cousins, we've a right to know.'

'Yes, you must tell us,' said Colin eagerly. Even

winning, he'd had enough Monopoly.

'Hugh, you tell them.'

'Hugh? So *he* was allowed to hear about it,' said Sue indignantly.

'*He* told *us* – oh, Hugh, stop frowning at me like that,' said Perry. 'You might be a sport and let them in on it.'

'Nothing to tell, really, is there? Your father said a young girl took poison about sixty years ago, that's all.'

'It isn't all—what about the ghost?' asked Sue.

'That's why we haven't been eating in the dining-room lately,' said Charlotte helpfully.

'You mean it's in there?' said Colin. 'Why has it only just started haunting, then?'

Perry and Charlotte looked at Hugh, and after a pause he said:

'I'm the only one to feel her presence.'

'What does she look like?' asked Sue.

'I don't know, I can't see her.'

'Then how d'you know she's there?'

'You wouldn't understand unless you felt it too.'

'But why you?' asked Colin. 'You'd think a ghost would be more interested in the people who live in the house.'

'She can't get through to them,' explained Hugh. 'You have to be sort of tuned-in on the right wavelength. Can't we talk about something else?'

'Don't be mean, Hugh,' said Charlotte, gently. 'We're all fascinated.'

'What's she like—what's her name?' Sue was still asking questions.

'I didn't hold a conversation with her. It was as if the thought flashed into my mind: there's a young girl here, someone's poisoned her, it's horrible – and I couldn't stay in the room with it.'

'You said it again, that she was murdered,' Perry

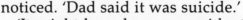

noticed. 'Dad said it was suicide.'

'It might have been an accident, but I don't think she *wanted* to die—' began Hugh.

'That's why she's haunting,' interrupted Sue. 'Hugh, you might be able to help her.'

They all looked at Hugh expectantly.

'I don't see how.'

'Go and ask her,' said Sue.

'You don't know what it's like,' protested Hugh. 'It's like fighting your way through a – through a cloud, something you can't get away from.'

'You're scared,' said Colin.

Hugh fidgeted.

'I think it's mean not to try to help her,' said Sue.

Perry suddenly marched across to the dining-room and flung open the door.

'Come on, ghostie, rattle your chains for us!' he called. 'Give us a fright, too, like poor old Hugh!'

Hugh leapt to his feet.

'All right, I'll try.'

He paused with his hand on the door.

'I'll come with you,' offered Charlie uncertainly. Hugh shook his head, smiling at the little girl.

'It wouldn't work, Charlie – she wouldn't talk to me then.'

He went inside quickly, closing the door behind him. The others crowded nearer.

'I can't hear what they're saying,' complained Charlotte.

'Hugh's talking, but I can't hear anyone else,' said Sue.

'Of course not,' said Perry, 'you don't believe there really is a ghost, do you?'

They strained their ears.

The door opened suddenly and Hugh came out, his face pale. The room beyond looked very dark.

'She's lonely, poor child,' said Hugh. His voice dropped to a horrified whisper. 'She wanted me to stay with her!'

'Come and sit down, Hugh, you look awful,' said Sue.

'I feel awful.'

He sank into a chair and closed his eyes.

'She's drained me of all my energy—'

'We couldn't hear anyone except you,' said Perry flatly.

'No, she was very faint.'

'What did she say?' asked Charlotte.

'That she'd been alone with old people when she was alive, and now she's got nobody.' Hugh's eyes opened, revealing horror as he went on, 'I didn't think she'd let me go!'

'How could she stop you?' asked Colin.

'I don't know, it was like fighting my way out of something clammy and clinging that I couldn't see, and all the time she was begging me not to leave her—'

'Did you find out more about the murder?' asked Perry, practically.

'She said her aunt did it. Her aunt by marriage – the uncle was Lavender's guardian – that's her name, Lavender – and he inherited all her parents' money when she died.'

'How sordid,' said Sue. 'I hope they came to a sticky end, too!'

'It wasn't the uncle's fault. But you're right, the wicked aunt died after a long and painful illness – only it didn't do Lavender any good because she never confessed to the murder and people still thought Lavender had committed suicide.'

'No wonder she's haunting,' said Sue. 'How stupid of everybody, as if a child would take poison on purpose!'

'The aunt made out Lavender had always been a bit strange in the head, and she even had a piece of paper Lavender had scribbled on one day when she was extra unhappy. It said: "I hate my life, why don't I die?" '

'Isn't it sad,' quavered Charlotte, her eyes filling with tears. 'I feel sorry for her.'

'Yes, she needs friends,' said Sue. 'What can we do?'

'Priests used to exorcize ghosts, d'you think they still can?' suggested Colin.

'How do we prove we've got a ghost?' asked Perry. 'We've only got Hugh's word for it.'

'We'll get Daddy to talk to the priest,' said Charlie.

Perry looked at her.

'Poor old Dad, everyone in the neighbourhood thinks he's dotty as it is.'

'Perry, how can you say such an awful thing about your own father?' squeaked Charlie.

'You must admit he's an absent-minded professor type, not exactly in the same world with the rest of us,' Perry pointed out.

The dining-room door closed with a click and they all stared at it.

'I didn't think there was any wind,' said Colin.

'There isn't,' said Perry. 'That's why it's getting so dark, all the clouds are overhead.'

'Where's Sue?' asked Hugh.

Perry glanced at the dining-room door.

'Gone ghost-hunting?' he said.

'But she mustn't!' cried Hugh. 'Perry, get her out of there.'

'Get her yourself,' retorted Perry.

'You two! Who'd imagine you were friends?' declared Colin, flinging the door open. 'Oh! She's not here.'

'Well, we didn't see her go in—' began Perry.

'She *is* in there,' said Hugh, quietly.

'Don't be daft,' said Perry, 'there's nowhere for a mouse to hide.'

He went in and opened the sideboard cupboards, to show their crammed interiors.

'I don't mean she's hiding,' said Hugh, oddly.

Colin stared at him, then understood.

'Come off it, Hugh – Sue's a solid, living human being.'

'Not any more.'

'Oo, it's cold,' shivered Charlie.

The room was *cold*. Very cold. And quite dark now, rain beating against the windows.

'She's somewhere in the house, we'll find her,' said Perry briskly.

But they didn't. They searched everywhere.

'Come on, Sue, you win!' called Colin.

'The joke's gone on long enough,' added Perry.

There was no answer. The only sound was a clock ticking away the time Sue had been missing, and the rain dripping from every ledge outside.

'It's not funny any more,' shouted Perry.

They went back to the sitting-room, which seemed empty in the electric light's glare.

'I think,' said Charlotte, in a small voice, 'Lavender's got a friend now.'

'I'm afraid so, Charlie,' agreed Hugh, sadly.

The little girl burst into tears.

'When are Daddy and Mummy coming home?' she wailed.

'Not till late,' answered Perry.

'Can't we reach them on the telephone?' asked Colin.

'No. Anyway, what could we say? What could *they* do?'

They sank into gloomy silence.

'We didn't tap the walls for secret panels,' said Colin suddenly.

'What have you been reading lately?' scoffed Perry. 'You don't have secret panels in houses like this.'

'It's worth trying.'

'It's no use, Colin,' said Hugh, miserably. 'You know what's happened to Sue.'

'I *don't*,' returned Colin. 'She might have fallen through somewhere and be lying unconscious.'

'There's no room for secret compartments,' insisted Perry.

'*You* didn't know that there was a ghost here,' said Colin reasonably. 'It's worth trying.'

'Well, she's your sister,' shrugged Perry.

They heard Colin thumping the walls, shifting furniture.

And then the door closed with a soft, but firm, click.

Hugh leapt to his feet and raced to open it, then turned to the others, his face stricken.

'She's getting stronger,' he said. 'Lavender's absorbing their energy—'

Colin had gone.

'Those cousins of mine are always up to something,' Perry tried to speak confidently.

He strode over to the window and leaned out.

'Can't see any footprints—'

'But it's raining,' cried Charlie. 'They wouldn't go out there – oh, I'm so frightened.'

Hugh took her hand.

'We'll all stay together, and it'll be all right – Perry, come away from there—'

'Why, do you think I'm going to disappear in front of your very eyes?'

Perry was cross now that he was beginning to feel frightened, too.

'You might.'

Perry shook his wet hair and banged the window shut – and at that moment a door slammed upstairs.

The boys looked at each other, then raced for the stairs.

'Wait for me!' screamed Charlie, fumbling with a loose slipper, but they didn't stop to listen.

'Don't worry about them, Charlie,' Sue spoke from the darkness of the dining-room.

'Sue!'

'Sh! Don't give us away – you come and hide, too.'

'I *knew* you must be somewhere!' cried Charlotte, joyfully, running to join her cousins.

'There's no-one up here,' yelled Perry. 'We've looked all over.'

He and Hugh bounded three steps at a time down to the gloomy hall.

'Charlie? Where've *you* got to now?'

'Oh no, not little Charlie,' groaned Hugh.

'Charlotte, don't fool around,' said Perry, sharply.

Silence.

'She wouldn't be able to keep it up,' said Perry, doubtfully. 'She'd laugh and give the game away—'

He looked at his friend with stricken eyes.

'I'm sorry, Perry,' said Hugh, gently.

'How can we get her back?' asked Perry.

'There's no way back.'

'But—we can't leave her there, wherever she is. She'll be so frightened without me—'

His voice trailed off.

'She likes me,' said Hugh, 'I'll go and look after her.'

'Where?'

Hugh looked towards the dining-room, its door invitingly half-open.

'You can't, Hugh. You said you wouldn't be able to come back.'

'No,' agreed his friend, walking away.

'You mustn't,' cried Perry urgently.

Hugh smiled and went into the darkness. The door closed behind him, looking as if it would never open again.

Perry sank into a chair and looked at his own thoughts, while the house grew colder – and quieter.

'It's all rubbish,' he told himself. 'If Hugh hadn't said anything, we'd have gone on using the dining-room and nothing would have happened. He started it all . . . But *where* have they all disappeared to?"

Slowly Perry became aware that the house was not so quiet as it had been. There were odd shufflings and clicking noises. And wasn't that Charlie's giggle?

He looked towards the dining-room. A line of light showed under the door.

With one bound he had reached it and flung the door open with a crash.

Startled faces turned in his direction.

'Perry! We thought you were never coming!' shrieked Charlotte, running from her seat at the long table to fling her arms around his neck.

'We wondered how long you'd sit there by yourself,' grinned Colin.

'The game's almost over,' said Sue, shaking the dice, 'then you can join in.'

Perry was almost speechless with a mixture of relief and rage.

'You rotten lot! Enjoying yourselves while I've been going dotty in there! I never want to see any of you again!'

He turned to go.

'You haven't been introduced to Lavender yet,' said Hugh.

Perry followed his glance and for the first time noticed a newcomer, a girl not much older than Charlotte, with long, golden hair tied back with a ribbon, and an old-fashioned dress. And the blue eyes shining from a face flushed with happiness.

'Now we're all here,' said Lavender breathlessly, 'we can have fun for ever and ever, can't we?'

NOW YOU SEE IT

David Campton

'm not sure whether this is really a
ghost story, but if a ghost is something that somebody sees but can't
explain, then I suppose it must be.
Anyway, I'm not really trying to tell a story,
just to put down what happened so that I can
look at what I've written and perhaps make
up my own mind whether I believe it myself.

To begin with, Uncle wasn't really my uncle. He
wasn't even my mother's uncle, though she always
called him Uncle. He was just a very old man; but we
had known him so long that he seemed to be part of
the family. We all lived in the same house. It was a
big house at the edge of the town, with a long garden
that stretched right down to the brook. Father looked
after the garden; Mother looked after the house; and
between them they looked after Uncle.

Uncle had moved into the house years before
when he was making a lot of money. He bought and
sold socks, which is not a very exciting way of
getting rich, but it works if you buy and sell enough
socks. At that time the house was in the country,
miles away from the town, and the Hunt had even
been known to sweep through the fields beyond the
brook at the bottom of the garden. Uncle's eyes

would still light up when he recalled the day the house and grounds came up for sale, and he realized he had made enough money from socks to afford it.

The money hadn't lasted for ever, and what there was became worth less and less as the years went by. So in the end all Uncle really had to his name was his house and his pension. Still, Mother and Father stayed on and looked after him and they never mentioned money; though I once overheard Father saying that the house cost more to keep up than it was worth. And Mother answered that if it wasn't for Uncle and me they would move into a bungalow – which would be cheaper to live in and easier to clean. But Uncle loved the old place, and there was no doubt it was just right for a boy to grow up in. Even if Uncle couldn't climb trees any longer, I could. And he cheered me on.

He would also talk for hours about the wild things in the garden. In spite of the houses all around, there were still many creatures at large: a hedgehog for instance, the frogs, and crows nesting at the tops of the trees. I never found a fox there, though, or an owl, or a blindworm, or even a toad. I only heard about them from Uncle.

He talked more as he walked less. He would spend whole days sitting outside in his canvas chair, a rug over his knees even when the sun was shining, because at his age the cold sinks right through to your bones. He talked to anyone who would listen – usually me – and when there was nobody around he would talk to himself. The words he used most often were 'I remember'.

He remembered the time when he saved a fox from the Hunt by letting it into the house through the back door. The fox, which must have known a thing or two, had run upstairs and hidden itself under a bed. The hounds had tried to follow, but had met determined opposition from the people who lived in the house at the time, and who didn't know about their uninvited guest. Uncle never found out how the fox managed to escape from the best bedroom; but he came across a fox some months later, slinking along in the shadow of a hedge. It might have been a different fox, of course, but he swore that this one paused and winked at him.

He remembered the time he found an owl with a broken wing, and looked after it. Afterwards the bird just wouldn't go away. That wasn't so unusual, or even (later) the owl bringing up a family in the lavatory – which wasn't of modern design, but more a draughty shed at the bottom of the yard. When that was done away with in the name of modern progress, the owls went away too. But Uncle always remembered them.

He remembered the blindworm which he saved from other boys who were stoning it. He collected a hiding from coming home that day with a chipped tooth, a black eye, a torn shirt – and a blindworm in a box. A blindworm isn't a worm at all, it's a legless lizard. Nor is it usually blind, though this one was blind in one eye after the stoning incident. It lived on in Uncle's care until it died of old age.

Old age was another subject on which Uncle was an authority. 'The funny thing is,' he said, 'the longer you live, the shorter your life seems to have been. It doesn't seem five minutes since I went home with my bottom wet after sitting down in that brook. I must have been after the toad. It was a sort of toad that was rare even then. I didn't catch it, though. I suddenly didn't want to any more. We just stared at each other. Then I told it to be careful who it tried to make friends with and watched it hop away fast.'

One day Uncle stopped talking. The doctor told us it had been a stroke, hardly surprising in one of such advanced years. The only thing that surprised the doctor was learning that Mother and Father weren't related to him. He seemed to think the arrangement could lead to complications, especially if relatives of Uncle's should turn up. Mother and Father did not think this likely, as in all the years they had known Uncle he had never once mentioned any family. Blindworms, foxes, toads and owls, yes: but brothers or sisters, no.

'We live and learn,' said Mother, when the Vulture Lady arrived one day with a suitcase and announced that she was Uncle's Real Niece.

I think of her as the Vulture Lady because that's what Father called her when he realized what she had come for. 'First time we've had a vulture in these parts,' he grumbled. 'Jackdaws, yes, even cuckoos, but no vultures. It's the smell of death that brings them out. I wonder how many more there'll be. Sharpening their talons to fight over what's left.'

I couldn't understand all that, but agreed with him about the talons. Uncle's Niece had withered brown hands with long pointed nails. In fact in many ways she looked like the picture of a vulture in my bird book.

She made her attitude plain from the moment she set her suitcase down in the hall. Uncle was *her* uncle, even though she hadn't seen him for forty years, and we were the interlopers. From now on Uncle was in her charge, and would we kindly not interfere.

'Blood is thicker than water,' she announced. 'I dropped everything as soon as I heard he was so ill. It's the least one can do for one's own flesh and blood. Blood calls to blood.'

With all that harping on blood she sounded more like a vulture than ever. And I didn't like the idea of Uncle being fed to her. I don't think he wanted her around, but not being able to talk, he couldn't tell her so. If I were ill, she was the last person I'd want to look after me. I didn't see so much of him about this time, because she warned me to stay away from his room.

Before she came I used to sit by his bedside and tell him what was going on outside – where the blackbirds were nesting this year, whether the tits had come back to the house we made for them, and how the biggest hedgehog had been run over while crossing the road. He made grunting noises to show that he understood, and his eyes never left my face. Until the Vulture Lady came in. Then he would sigh, shut his eyes and lie back on the pillow while she hovered.

'Feeling better today?' she would shriek. She had the idea that, because Uncle couldn't talk, he couldn't hear either. Then she would bend over him, peering with her red-rimmed eyes. I think she was hoping he wasn't better, because if anything happened to Uncle, the house would belong to her. I overheard Mother and Father talking about the situation. (I know I shouldn't have listened behind the door, but it's not so easy to tear yourself away from an interesting conversation – and quite impossible to forget it afterwards.)

'A pity he didn't make a will,' said Father. 'Not for us – he could leave the little he's got to a cats' home for all I care. But without a will it must all go to her, and she hasn't so much as sent him a Christmas card for forty years.'

'It beats me how she found out he was so ill,' said Mother.

'Her sort always does,' said Father. 'It's a sort of sixth sense.'

I'm interested in the sixth sense. Some animals and birds are supposed to have it. Here my interest betrayed me, because I put my head round the door to find out more, was spotted, and then sent out into the garden to play.

I met the biggest frog there, and really started something. Uncle had followed the careers of our frogs ever since they were spawn, and here was the chance to show him. I put the frog on his bed. Uncle looked at the frog and the frog looked at Uncle.

'Uh-hu,' said Uncle, which was as much as he could manage.

'Awk-awk,' said the frog, as it usually did.

'*Eeeeeeee!*' screeched the Vulture Lady, who had just come into the bedroom with a basin of gruel.

I tried to explain that Uncle was interested in frogs, and that, as he couldn't get down to the brook any longer, the only way of keeping him in touch was to bring his friends inside to be introduced. But the Vulture Lady didn't listen. She just went on shrieking until Mother came running, and I was led out with instructions to put the frog down the lavatory. I didn't, of course. Instead I restored him to his friends and relations at the bottom of the garden. But the damage had been done. I was ordered to keep away from Uncle's bedroom in future.

I did my best to sneak in to him from time to time, but the Vulture kept a constant watch, and I just couldn't manage it. Once I got as far as opening the bedroom door, and saw him lying with his eyes closed. He reminded me of a bird we once found frozen in the snow. When I whispered 'Uncle', he opened his eyes. There wasn't time for anything else, because something bit my ear. It was the Vulture's bony finger and thumb: and she didn't let go until she had led me downstairs.

She muttered all the way about 'his final hours not being upset by uncouth little yobbos'. I didn't bother much about being called an uncouth little yobbo, but I was worried by the bit about final hours. Mother and Father were worried too. In fact they were so bothered they didn't even look round to see if I was listening.

'At this rate he's not going to last much longer,' said Mother. 'He seems to have lost all interest in living.'

'What has he got to live for?' said Father. 'Lying there with nothing to see, nothing to think about, nobody even to talk to. Except her, and there's no pleasure in that.'

'If only he could have friends in,' suggested Mother.

'He never had many friends,' said Father. 'The few he did make have all passed on. But if any were to come knocking, That One wouldn't allow 'em past the front door. She doesn't want him to get better.'

'You shouldn't say that,' murmured Mother.

'It's the truth, isn't it?' said Father. Then he noticed me, and started to talk about cabbages.

They didn't understand. The fact was, Uncle always had friends, but Mother and Father never recognized animals as such. Which was hardly their fault, because you can't ask a newt to tea, or play cards with a hedgehog. I didn't mention this to anybody, because it might have led to arguments, and wouldn't have done any good. Uncle's Niece wasn't likely to let animals into the house any more than she would have welcomed any other old friends. We'd all seen how she'd behaved over the frog. But I knew Uncle would feel a lot better after being visited by the right sort of company.

I gave a lot of thought to this, usually while sitting under the willow by the brook. I worked out – and discarded – a lot of very elaborate plans, and was just wondering how to persuade robins to nest on Uncle's window-sill, when a fox walked by.

The fox was so sure about what it was doing, that at first I hardly noticed it. 'Oh, there's that old fox again,' and I went on with my thinking. After all, it behaved as if it had every right to stroll up our garden path. At least a couple of minutes went by before I sat up. A fox! Had I really seen a live fox? I'd never even seen a fox before, except stuffed in a museum. And this one certainly knew its way round. Wasting no further time on pointless planning, I pelted up the path.

Mother was in the kitchen making pastry. She received the news quite calmly. She hadn't seen any foxes recently herself, but agreed that one in our house would be something to write to the papers about. On the other hand, when I looked like continuing the search for it, she went on about me finding something else to play at. Quietly. And if I was good, she'd put a piece of pastry in the oven specially for me. I love hot pastry. But that isn't the reason I gave up looking for the fox. No. I could see that the kitchen door was shut. If a fox had come in here, it would be here still. And quite obviously there wasn't a fox here. So I reckoned I must have made a mistake. Perhaps I hadn't seen a fox at all. I've often been told I have more imagination than is good for me.

Uncle was slightly better next day, according to Mother. She helped Uncle's Niece to make the bed, and although the Vulture wanted Uncle all to herself, some jobs call for two pairs of hands.

'His eyes seemed a whole lot brighter,' reported Mother. 'And it seemed as though he was trying to smile a lopsided sort of smile.'

Good news affects different people in different ways. Uncle's Niece cleaned out her bedroom. She demanded dusters and brushes and window-leathers and polish; then attacked the floors and windows and furniture. I suppose she was just working off her temper, but Mother had words with her. Mother cleaned every room in the house at least once a week, and the Vulture's furious activity suggested that the job had not been done properly. Worse, the Vulture insisted there was A Smell in her room.

Mother stood in the middle of her room and sniffed. 'Lavender', she said.

Uncle's Niece sniffed. 'Animal,' she said.

'Foxes can smell their own holes first,' snapped Mother, and left the Vulture to it. Though once she was down in the kitchen again, she wondered whether she ought to have been quite so rude.

I wondered, too. Could the Vulture have smelled fox? And if so, had my fox found its way into the house? I wondered whether Mother might have mentioned my fox; but I needn't have done. She just didn't take my fox seriously. She had to take the next crisis seriously, though.

It was the toad.

I was on my way to bed when the Vulture, who had been taking Uncle his goodnight drink of something awful, began to screech. As I was nearest to Uncle's door, I went in. Mother was quite right about his smile: it had become lopsided, as if one side of his face was frozen. The other side of his face, though, looked ready to laugh. The Vulture had dropped the mug of milky stuff (Mother was not going to be happy about that mess on the rug) and was clutching her skirts. In the space between her and Uncle's bed sat a large toad. Obviously she did not care for toads. And the toad didn't think much of her, either. It eyed her coldly, then stuck its tongue out.

She stopped screaming as soon as I ventured into the room, and started to call me names instead. Some of them I'd never heard before. When she ran out of names she pointed to the visitor.

'It's a toad,' I said.

'Stamp on it,' she ordered.

'I can't do that,' I said. 'That sort of toad is rare. They're dying out.'

'It can't die soon enough for me,' she croaked. 'Kill it. You brought it here. You kill it.'

Naturally I refused. Anybody who kills a rare species these days ought to be locked up, and I told her so.

'You ought to be locked up, you little beast,' she panted. 'Bringing vermin into a respectable house.'

This was quite unfair as I only recognized the toad from pictures I'd seen. I tried to point out that she ought to consider it a privilege to meet one. This did not seem to go down at all well, and the argument might have gone on for some time if the toad hadn't hopped towards her. She gave one more scream, and ran.

I followed her as far as the top of the stairs trying to explain that there was no cause for alarm. However, she had made up her mind what she was going to do, and I was powerless to prevent her. So I turned back into Uncle's room.

He was actually laughing – as much as a man who is so very ill can laugh.

'It's all right,' I assured him. 'I'll make sure it doesn't get hurt.'

That was easier to say than do, because I just couldn't find it. Uncle watched me crawling round his bedroom on my hands and knees, all the time smiling his lopsided smile, as though he were enjoying a private joke. I had my head under his bed when I was hauled out to join in a family row.

It started in whispers, out of respect for a sick man, and got louder and louder the further we went away, until we were almost shouting by the time we were in the living-room. We were Mother, Father and me, until we joined Uncle's Niece. Her usually pallid face was quite flushed, with horrid red blotches on her cheeks, and her creaky voice had become as hoarse as a crow's. She had been doing a lot of shouting too. She started again as soon as she saw me. She wanted Father to belt me, and insisted on watching to make sure he did it properly. Naturally he refused – at least without giving me a fair hearing.

Bringing the frog into the house earlier told against me. Any person who brings a frog into the house is capable of following it up with a toad – even if that particular toad is as rare in these parts as a duckbilled platypus. So my explanations were received with suspicion, if not downright disbelief. In the end, though, I was given the benefit of the doubt; though Father made it clear that there was a lot of doubt.

This did not please the Vulture, who showed another nasty streak along with all her others. She had been looking forward to hearing me yell, and when she was balked she raised her voice even higher and louder. She accused Mother and Father of trying to get rid of her by encouraging me. If that was their attitude, they had better watch out. She knew her rights, and she wasn't going to be cheated of them by scheming servants.

Mother and Father were furious. I'm sure they would have left the house there and then, bag and baggage, if it hadn't been for Uncle. They could hardly leave him to the Vulture; and they told her they would go when he asked them to, and not before.

'We'll see what other people have to say about that,' threatened the Vulture. She started with the doctor.

'What's this I hear about you turning the house into a menagerie, young man?' he asked. He tut-tutted as long as the grownups were within earshot, but talked to me man-to-man as we walked towards his car.

'Did she jump?' he chuckled. 'Just for that minute, I wish I'd been in the old man's place. The incident certainly didn't do him any harm. What does the proverb say? "A merry heart doeth good like medicine." Mind you, I'm not advising you to repeat the dose.' He paused to light his pipe. 'Not too often, anyway.'

He was disappointed by Uncle's progress next time he visited. In fact Uncle seemed to have gone right back and was much weaker. I could have told him what was wrong, but I wasn't allowed to. The Vulture had put her foot down, and none of us was allowed to see Uncle. She even made his bed by herself now, and took up all his meals, such as they were. If I were ill, I wouldn't have wanted the thin slops that she insisted were best for him. So he began to sink again.

'It's all a matter of the will to live,' said the doctor. 'Nothing I can prescribe would be as good as a hearty laugh' (with a sidelong glance at me).

There was nothing I could do about that now, because Uncle's bedroom door was kept locked, except when the Vulture went in. I couldn't even see him, and had to rely on progress reports from the doctor. They got gloomier and gloomier. Why should anybody want to get better when they're kept prisoner with a Vulture for a gaoler?

Instead of devising ways of cheering up Uncle, I took to making plans for getting rid of the Vulture; but as these usually boiled down to kidnapping or murder, which are, strictly speaking, against the law, they had to be abandoned. Although (having read Sherlock Holmes) one of these ideas involved putting a poisonous snake in her bed, I should like to take this opportunity of emphatically denying that I had anything to do with that episode.

I didn't even know that there was anything wrong until I was seized by the scruff of my neck, and practically dragged to the Vulture's bedroom. When she let me go, she was shaking – whether with fright or fury I can't say; but she pointed to her bed with a quivering finger. A wriggling creature lay in the middle of it.

'What is that?' Spit, hiss, spit in my ear.

'A blindworm?' I suggested

'So you know all about it.' More spit in my ear.

This time denials were a waste of breath. I'm sure Father didn't want to do what he did, and he did it with a slipper that made a lot of noise, but didn't hurt much. He explained as well as he could that boys who start by putting snakes in ladies' beds might end by committing worse crimes unless checked. I admit my attempts to put him right by pointing out the differences between a snake and a legless lizard could have been the last straw. It was not the proper time for a lesson on natural history. What really hurt, though, was the Vulture's glee. She was getting her own way at last. One down and one to go. Me today: Uncle tomorrow.

I brooded on the injustice as I lay on my bed, to which I had been banished long before supper. Brooding is a useless way of spending time, but I might have carried on in that way until I fell asleep if I hadn't noticed the owl on my wardrobe.

As it calmly stared at me, my seething resentment died down. It stood out, a ghostly white in the half-light. I ought to have been afraid. Or at least have asked what it was doing there. But I didn't. I had never seen an owl on top of my wardrobe before, but it seemed to belong there. And once I stopped fretting about silly grievances that didn't really matter anyway, my mind began to work properly.

'Are there any more of you?' I asked.

'Who?' said the owl.

'You,' I said. 'I could be wrong, but didn't that lizard have one eye?'

'Oooooh,' said the owl, as though the notion had

just occurred to it.

The conversation stopped as Mother brought me a bowl of bread and milk, which in itself was a sort of punishment, but better than no supper at all.

'Who were you talking to?' she asked.

There are times when telling the truth can be awkward, but this time I decided to risk it. 'The owl on the wardrobe,' I said.

Mother looked at the wardrobe. The owl looked at Mother. Mother looked at me. She didn't know whether to laugh or cry.

'All right,' she said. 'You play whatever you want to play. Just try to keep out of That Woman's way, that's all.'

'But there *is* an owl on the wardrobe,' I insisted.

'If you say so,' said Mother, and kissed me goodnight.

'She couldn't see you,' I told the owl as soon as the door closed behind her.

'No?' said the owl. Or something sounding like that.

I ate my bread and milk while it was still warm; and when I looked up again there was nothing on the top of the wardrobe but a cricket bat, a few old boxes,

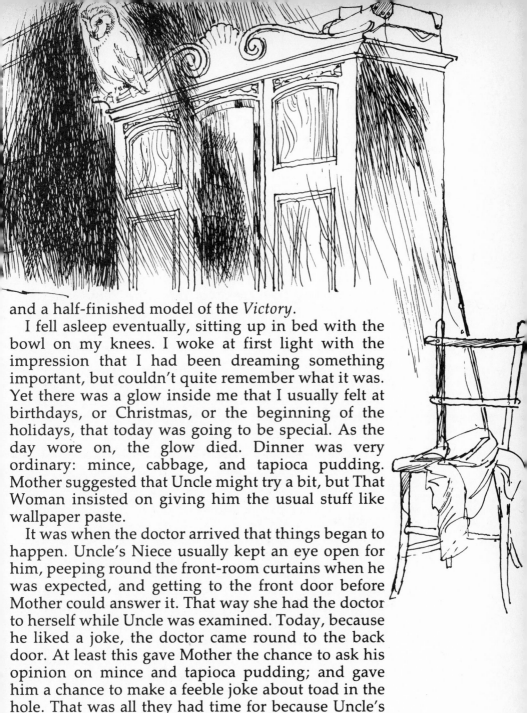

and a half-finished model of the *Victory*.

I fell asleep eventually, sitting up in bed with the bowl on my knees. I woke at first light with the impression that I had been dreaming something important, but couldn't quite remember what it was. Yet there was a glow inside me that I usually felt at birthdays, or Christmas, or the beginning of the holidays, that today was going to be special. As the day wore on, the glow died. Dinner was very ordinary: mince, cabbage, and tapioca pudding. Mother suggested that Uncle might try a bit, but That Woman insisted on giving him the usual stuff like wallpaper paste.

It was when the doctor arrived that things began to happen. Uncle's Niece usually kept an eye open for him, peeping round the front-room curtains when he was expected, and getting to the front door before Mother could answer it. That way she had the doctor to herself while Uncle was examined. Today, because he liked a joke, the doctor came round to the back door. At least this gave Mother the chance to ask his opinion on mince and tapioca pudding; and gave him a chance to make a feeble joke about toad in the hole. That was all they had time for because Uncle's

Niece burst into the kitchen. Eyes glaring, she was panting as though she'd just run a long way very fast.

'Ah!' was all she seemed able to gasp at first. 'Ah. Ah!' She grabbed the doctor by the sleeve, and heaved him towards the stairs. At last she got out, 'Witnesses!' She waved her arms and cried, 'Come on, all of you. I'll show you. You didn't believe me, did you? Now I've got proof.' She stopped outside Uncle's door and fumbled for the key.

'Surely you don't keep that locked,' said the doctor.

'I'm not going to let it escape,' said Uncle's Niece, with a nasty chuckle. 'Not this time. Now you'll see what I've had to put up with. Inside, all of you. Don't let it slip past.'

She hurried us in and slammed the door. Uncle opened his eyes, but otherwise did not show much interest. He was much thinner than when I saw him last. Mother went straight over to him and held his hand. The doctor, though, could see nothing unusual. He glanced quickly round the room, then turned to Uncle's Niece with an eyebrow cocked in a question.

'It's under the bed,' she said. 'Still under the bed. It didn't have a chance to get away. What's more I can smell it.'

We all sniffed. The doctor and Mother went on sniffing, trying to detect an unusual scent. I guessed what it was at once, and dropped down on my hands and knees. Under the bed facing me was a pair of bright eyes and a sharp muzzle. I recognized the fox. So *that* was where it had got to. But surely it couldn't have been there all the time?

The doctor knelt down by the side of me. He looked under the bed; looked at me; then looked under the bed again. Eventually 'What are we supposed to be seeing?' he asked in a heavy whisper.

'It's a fox,' shouted Uncle's Niece. 'Even I know that much.'

'A fox.' The doctor thought about this for a few seconds, then slowly got up, and dusted his trouser knees quite unnecessarily. 'You say there is a fox under this bed.'

'And I know who is responsible,' snapped the Niece. 'Even if I don't know how he managed it. He must have a duplicate key. That boy smuggled it in.'

The owl swooped down and settled on the end of the bed. A light dawned in Uncle's eyes. His Niece shrieked and pointed, 'Like that bird!' she cried.

'And what sort of bird would that be?' said the doctor, patiently.

'You can recognize an owl when you see one, can't you?' snapped the Niece.

'When I see one,' echoed the doctor.

A toad hopped into the middle of the bedside table, only just missing a bottle of eau-de-Cologne.

'You can see it,' whimpered the Niece. 'You must see it.'

'I think you've been overdoing things,' said the doctor. 'I suggest a rest. Get away from here altogether. Leave it all to somebody else.'

As the blindworm began to wriggle over the coverlet towards her, Uncle's Niece began to scream. She was still screaming as the doctor led her away. I watched them go. When I turned back, the room was empty. That is, Mother and Uncle were there; but nothing else.

Mother crossed to me and patted me on the shoulder.

'I'm sorry,' she murmured. 'We never guessed. Tell you what, we'll have tripe and onions for supper to make up for the bread and milk last night.'

Uncle licked his lips. 'Ah,' he said. It wasn't much, but it was a beginning.

THE DOLL'S GHOST

Francis Marion Crawford

t was a terrible accident, and for one moment the splendid machinery of Cranston House got out of gear and stood still. The butler emerged from the retirement in which he spent his elegant leisure, two grooms of the chambers appeared simultaneously from opposite directions, there were actually housemaids on the grand staircase, and those who remember the facts most exactly assert that Mrs Pringle herself positively stood upon the landing.

Mrs Pringle was the housekeeper. As for the head nurse, the under nurse, and the nursery-maid, their feelings cannot be described. The head nurse laid one hand upon the polished marble balustrade and stared stupidly before her, the under nurse stood rigid and pale, leaning against the polished marble wall, and the nursery-maid collapsed and sat down upon the polished marble step, just beyond the limits of the velvet carpet, and frankly burst into tears.

The Lady Gwendolen Lancaster-Douglas-Scroop, youngest daughter of the ninth Duke of Cranston, and aged six years and three months, picked herself up quite alone, and sat down on the third step from the foot of the grand staircase in Cranston House.

'Oh!' ejaculated the butler, and he disappeared again.

'Ah!' responded the grooms of the chambers, as they also went away.

'It's only that doll,' Mrs Pringle was distinctly heard to say, in a tone of contempt.

The under nurse heard her say it. Then the three nurses gathered round Lady Gwendolen and patted her, and gave her unhealthy things out of their pockets, and hurried her out of Cranston House as fast as they could, lest it should be found out upstairs that they had allowed the Lady Gwendolen Lancaster-Douglas-Scroop to tumble down the grand staircase with her doll in her arms. And as the doll was badly broken, the nursery-maid carried it, with the pieces, wrapped up in Lady Gwendolen's little cloak. It was not far to Hyde Park, and when they had reached a quiet place they took means to find out that Lady Gwendolen had no bruises. For the carpet was very thick and soft, and there was thick stuff under it to make it softer.

Lady Gwendolen Douglas-Scroop sometimes yelled, but she never cried. It was because she had yelled that the nurse had allowed her to go downstairs alone with Nina, the doll, under one arm, while she steadied herself with her other hand on the balustrade, and trod upon the polished marble steps beyond the edge of the carpet. So she had fallen, and Nina had come to grief.

When the nurses were quite sure that she was not hurt, they unwrapped the doll and looked at her in turn. She had been a very beautiful doll, very large, and fair, and healthy, with real yellow hair and eyelids that would open and shut over very grown-up dark eyes. Moreover, when you moved her right arm up and down she said 'Pa-pa,' and when you moved the left she said 'Ma-ma' very distinctly.

'I heard her say "Pa" when she fell,' said the under nurse, who heard everything. 'But she ought to have said "Pa-pa".'

'That's because her arm went up when she hit the step,' said the head nurse. 'She'll say the other "Pa" when I put it down again.'

'Pa,' said Nina, as her right arm was pushed down, and speaking through her broken face. It was cracked right across, from the upper corner of the forehead, with a hideous gash, through the nose and down to the little frilled collar of the pale green silk Mother Hubbard frock, and two little three-cornered pieces of porcelain had fallen out.

'I'm sure it's a wonder she can speak at all, being all smashed,' said the under nurse.

'You'll have to take her to Mr Puckler,' said her superior. 'It's not far, and you'd better go at once.'

Lady Gwendolen was occupied in digging a hole in the ground with a little spade, and paid no attention to the nurses.

'What are you doing?' inquired the nursery-maid, looking on.

'Nina's dead, and I'm diggin' her a grave,' replied her ladyship thoughtfully.

'Oh, she'll come to life again all right,' said the nursery-maid.

The under nurse wrapped Nina up again and departed. Fortunately a kind soldier, with very long legs and a very small cap, happened to be there; and as he had nothing to do, he offered to see the under nurse safely to Mr Puckler's and back.

Mr Bernard Puckler and his little daughter lived in

a little house in a little alley, which led out of a quiet little street not very far from Belgrave Square. He was the great doll doctor, and his extensive practice lay in the most aristocratic quarter. He mended the dolls of all sizes and ages, boy dolls and girl dolls, baby dolls in long clothes, and grown-up dolls in fashionable gowns, talking dolls and dumb dolls, those that shut their eyes when they lay down, and those whose eyes had to be shut for them by means of a mysterious wire. His daughter Else was only just over twelve years old, but she was already very clever at mending dolls' clothes, and at doing their hair, which is harder than you might think, though the dolls sit quite still while it is being done.

Mr Puckler had originally been a German, but he had dissolved his nationality in the ocean of London many years ago, like a great many foreigners. He still had one or two German friends, however, who came on Saturday evenings, and smoked with him and played picquet or 'skat' with him for farthing points, and called him 'Herr Doctor', which seemed to please Mr Puckler very much.

He looked older than he was, for his beard was rather long and ragged, his hair was grizzled and thin, and he wore horn-rimmed spectacles. As for Else, she was a thin, pale child, very quiet and neat, with dark eyes and brown hair that was plaited down her back and tied with a bit of black ribbon. She mended the dolls' clothes and took the dolls back to their homes when they were quite strong again.

The house was a little one, but too big for the two people who lived in it. There was a small sitting-room on the street, and the workshop was at the back, and there were three rooms upstairs. But the father and daughter lived most of their time in the workshop, because they were generally at work, even

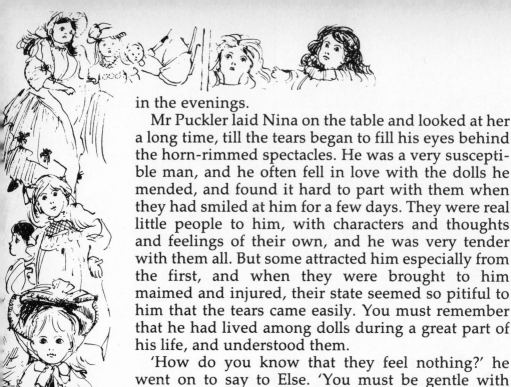

in the evenings.

Mr Puckler laid Nina on the table and looked at her a long time, till the tears began to fill his eyes behind the horn-rimmed spectacles. He was a very susceptible man, and he often fell in love with the dolls he mended, and found it hard to part with them when they had smiled at him for a few days. They were real little people to him, with characters and thoughts and feelings of their own, and he was very tender with them all. But some attracted him especially from the first, and when they were brought to him maimed and injured, their state seemed so pitiful to him that the tears came easily. You must remember that he had lived among dolls during a great part of his life, and understood them.

'How do you know that they feel nothing?' he went on to say to Else. 'You must be gentle with them. It costs nothing to be kind to the little beings, and perhaps it makes a difference to them.'

And Else understood him, because she was a child, and she knew that she was more to him than all the dolls.

He fell in love with Nina at first sight, perhaps because her beautiful brown glass eyes were something like Else's own, and he loved Else first and best, with all his heart. And, besides, it was a very sorrowful case. Nina had evidently not been long in the world, for her complexion was perfect, her hair was smooth where it should be smooth, and curly where it should be curly, and her silk clothes were perfectly new. But across her face was that frightful gash, like a sabre-cut, deep and shadowy within, but clean and sharp at the edges. When he tenderly pressed her head to close the gaping wound, the edges made a fine grating sound, that was painful to hear, and the lids of the dark eyes quivered and trembled as though Nina were suffering dreadfully.

'Poor Nina!' he exclaimed sorrowfully. 'But I shall not hurt you much, though you will take a long time to get strong.'

He always asked the names of the broken dolls when they were brought to him, and sometimes the people knew what the children called them, and told him. He liked 'Nina' for a name. Altogether and in every way she pleased him more than any doll he had seen for many years, and he felt drawn to her, and made up his mind to make her perfectly strong and sound, no matter how much labour it might cost him.

Mr Puckler worked patiently a little at a time, and Else watched him. She could do nothing for poor Nina, whose clothes needed no mending. The longer the doll doctor worked, the more fond he became of the yellow hair and the beautiful brown glass eyes. He sometimes forgot all the other dolls that were waiting to be mended, lying side by side on a shelf, and sat for an hour gazing at Nina's face, while he racked his ingenuity for some new invention by which to hide even the smallest trace of the terrible accident.

She was wonderfully mended. Even he was obliged to admit that; but the scar was still visible to his keen eyes, a very fine light line right across the face, downwards from right to left. Yet all the conditions had been most favourable for a cure, since the cement had set quite hard at the first attempt and the weather had been fine and dry, which makes a great difference in a dolls' hospital.

At last he knew that he could do no more, and the under nurse had already come twice to see whether the job was finished, as she coarsely expressed it.

'Nina is not quite strong yet,' Mr Puckler had

answered each time, for he could not make up his mind to face the parting.

And now he sat before the square deal table at which he worked, and Nina lay before him for the last time with a big brown-paper box beside her. It stood there like her coffin, waiting for her, he thought. He must put her into it, and lay tissue-paper over her dear face, and then put on the lid, and at the thought of tying the string his sight was dim with tears again. He was never to look into the glassy depths of the beautiful brown eyes any more, nor to hear the little wooden voice say 'Pa-pa' and 'Ma-ma'. It was a very painful moment.

In the vain hope of gaining time before the separation, he took up the little sticky bottles of cement and glue and gum and colour, looking at each one in turn, and then at Nina's face. And all his small tools lay there, neatly arranged in a row, but he knew that he could not use them again for Nina. She was quite strong at last, and in a country where there should be no cruel children to hurt her she might live a hundred years, with only that almost imperceptible line across her face, to tell of the fearful thing that had befallen her on the marble steps of Cranston House.

Suddenly Mr Puckler's heart was quite full, and he rose abruptly from his seat and turned away.

'Else,' he said unsteadily, 'you must do it for me. I cannot bear to see her go into the box.'

So he went and stood at the window with his back turned, while Elsie did what he had not the heart to do.

'Is it done?' he asked. 'Then take her away, my dear. Put on your hat, and take her to Cranston House quickly, and when you are gone I will turn round.'

Else was used to her father's queer ways with the

dolls, and though she had never seen him so much moved by a parting, she was not much surprised.

'Come back quickly,' he said, when he heard her hand on the latch. 'It is growing late, and I should not send you at this hour. But I cannot bear to look forward to it any more.'

When Else was gone, he left the window and sat down in his place before the table again, to wait for the child to come back. He touched the place where Nina had laid, very gently, and he recalled the softly-tinted pink face, and the glass eyes, and the ringlets of yellow hair, till he could almost see them.

The evenings were long, for it was late in the spring. But it began to grow dark soon, and Mr Puckler wondered why Else did not come back. She had been gone an hour and a half, and that was much longer than he had expected, for it was barely half a mile from Belgrave Square to Cranston House. He reflected that the child might have been kept waiting, but as the twilight deepened he grew anxious, and walking up and down in the dim workshop, no longer thinking of Nina, but of Else, his own living child, whom he loved.

An undefinable, disquieting sensation came upon him by fine degrees, a chilliness and a faint stirring of his thin hair, joined with the wish to be in any company rather than to be alone much longer. It was the beginning of fear.

He told himself in strong German-English he was a foolish old man, and he began to feel about for the matches in the dusk. He knew just where they should be, for he always kept them in the same place, close to the little tin box that held bits of sealing-wax of various colours, for some kinds of mending. But somehow he could not find the matches in the gloom.

Something had happened to Else, he was sure, and
as his fear increased, he felt as though it might be
allayed if he could get a light and see what time it
was. Then he called himself a foolish old man again,
and the sound of his own voice startled him in the
dark. He could not find the matches.

The window was grey still; he might see what time
it was if he went to close it, and he could go and get
matches out of the cupboard afterwards. He stood
back from the table, to get out of the way of the chair,
and began to cross the board floor.

Something was following him in the dark. There
was a small pattering, as of tiny feet upon the boards.
He stopped and listened, and the roots of his hair
tingled. It was nothing, and he was a foolish old man.
He made two steps more, and he was sure that he
heard the little pattering again. He turned his back to
the window, leaning against the sash so that the

panes began to crack, and he faced the dark. Everything was quiet still, and it smelt of paste and cement and wood-fillings as usual.

'Is that you, Else?' he asked, and he was surprised by the fear in his voice.

There was no answer in the room, and he held up his watch and tried to make out what time it was by the grey dusk that was just not darkness. So far as he could see, it was within two or three minutes of ten o'clock. He had been a long time alone. He was shocked, and frightened for Else, out in London, so late, and he almost ran across the room to the door. As he fumbled for the latch, he distinctly heard the running of the little feet after him.

'Mice!' he exclaimed feebly, just as he got the door open.

He shut it quickly behind him, and felt as though some cold thing had settled on his back and were writhing upon him. The passage was quite dark, but he found his hat and was out in the alley in a moment, breathing more freely, and surprised to find how much light there still was in the open air. He could see the pavement clearly under his feet, and far off in the street to which the alley led he could hear the laughter and calls of children, playing some game out of doors. He wondered how he could have been so nervous, and for an instant he thought of going back into the house to wait quietly for Else. But instantly he felt that nervous fright of something stealing over him again. In any case it was better to walk up to Cranston House and ask the servants about the child. One of the women had perhaps taken a fancy to her, and was even now giving her tea and cake.

He walked quickly to Belgrave Square, and then up the broad streets, listening as he went, whenever there was no other sound, for the tiny footsteps. But he heard nothing, and was laughing at himself when he rang the servants' bell at the big house. Of course, the child must be there.

The person who opened the door was quite an inferior person, for it was a back-door, but affected the manners of the front, and stared at Mr Puckler superciliously under the strong light.

No little girl had been seen, and he knew 'nothing about no dolls'.

'She is my little girl,' said Mr Puckler tremulously, for all his anxiety was returning tenfold, 'and I am afraid something has happened.'

The inferior person said rudely that 'nothing could have happened to her in that house, because she had not been there, which was a jolly good reason why'; and Mr Puckler was obliged to admit that the man ought to know, as it was his business to keep the door and let people in. He wished to be allowed to speak to the under nurse, who knew him; but the man was ruder than ever, and finally shut the door in his face.

When the doll doctor was alone in the street, he steadied himself by the railing, for he felt as though he was breaking in two, just as some dolls break, in the middle of the backbone.

Presently he knew that he must be doing something to find Else, and that gave him strength. He began to walk as quickly as he could through the streets, following every highway and byway which his little girl might have taken on her errand. He also asked several policemen in vain if they had seen her, and most of them answered him kindly, for they saw that he was a sober man and in his right senses, and some of them had little girls of their own.

It was one o'clock in the morning when he went up

to his own door again, worn out and hopeless and broken-hearted. As he turned the key in the lock, his heart stood still, for he knew that he was awake and not dreaming, and that he really heard those tiny footsteps pattering to meet him inside the house along the passage.

But he was too unhappy to be much frightened any more, and his heart went on again with a dull regular pain, that found its way all through him with every pulse. So he went in, and hung up his hat in the dark, and found the matches in the cupboard and the candlestick in its place in the corner.

Mr Puckler was so much overcome and so completely worn out that he sat down in his chair before the worktable and almost fainted, as his face dropped forward upon his folded hands. Beside him the solitary candle burned steadily with a low flame in the still warm air.

'Else! Else!' he moaned against his yellow knuckles. And that was all he could say, and it was no relief to him. On the contrary, the very sound of the name was a new and sharp pain that pierced his ears and his head and his very soul. For every time he repeated the name it meant that little Else was dead, somewhere out in the streets of London in the dark.

He was so terribly hurt that he did not even feel something pulling gently at the skirt of his old coat, so gently that it was like the nibbling of a tiny mouse. He might have thought that it was really a mouse if he had noticed it.

'Else! Else!' he groaned, right against his hands.

Then a cool breath stirred in his thin hair, and the low flame of one candle dropped down almost to a mere spark, not flickering as though a draught were going to blow it out, but just dropping down as if it were tired out. Mr Puckler felt his hands stiffening with fright under his face; and there was a faint rustling sound, like some small silk thing blown in a gentle breeze. He sat up straight, stark and scared, and a small wooden voice spoke in the stillness.

'Pa-pa,' it said, with a break between the syllables.

Mr Puckler stood up in a single jump, and his chair fell over backwards with a smashing noise upon the wooden floor. The candle had almost gone out.

It was Nina's doll-voice that had spoken, and he should have known it among the voices of a hundred other dolls. And yet there was something more in it, a little human ring, with a pitiful cry and a call for help, and the wail of a hurt child. Mr Puckler stood up, stark and stiff, and tried to look round, but at first he could not, for he seemed to be frozen from head to foot.

Then he made a great effort, and he raised one hand to each of his temples, and pressed his own head round as he would have turned a doll's. The candle was burning so low that it might as well have been out altogether, for any light it gave, and the room seemed quite dark at first. Then he saw something. He would not have believed that he could be more frightened than he had been just

before that. But he was, and his knees shook, for he saw the doll standing in the middle of the floor, shining with a faint and ghostly radiance, her beautiful glassy brown eyes fixed on his. And across her face the very thin line of the break he had mended shone as though it were drawn in light with a fine point of white flame.

Yet there was something more in the eyes, too; there was something human, like Else's own, but as if only the doll saw him through them, and not Else. And there was enough of Else to bring back all his pain and to make him forget his fear.

'Else! My little Else!' he cried aloud.

The small ghost moved, and its doll-arm slowly rose and fell with a stiff, mechanical motion.

'Pa-pa,' it said.

It seemed this time that there was even more of Else's tone echoing somewhere between the wooden notes that reached his ears so distinctly, and yet so far away. Else was calling him, he was sure.

His face was perfectly white in the gloom, but his knees did not shake any more, and he felt that he was less frightened.

'Yes, child! But where? Where?' he asked. 'Where

are you, Else?'

'Pa-pa!'

The syllables died away in the quiet room. There was a low rustling of silk, the glassy brown eyes turned slowly away, and Mr Puckler heard the pitter-patter of the small feet in the bronze kid slippers as the figure ran straight to the door. Then the candle burned high again, the room was full of light, and he was alone.

Mr Puckler passed his hand over his eyes and looked about him. He could see everything quite clearly, and he felt that he must have been dreaming, though he was standing instead of sitting down, as he should have been if he had just woken up. The candle burned brightly now. There were the dolls to be mended, lying in a row with their toes up. The third one had lost her right shoe, and Else was making one. He knew that, and he was certainly not dreaming now. He had not been dreaming when he had come in from his fruitless search and had heard the doll's footsteps running to the door. He had not fallen asleep in his chair. How could he possibly have fallen asleep when his heart was breaking? He had been awake all the time.

He steadied himself, set the fallen chair upon its legs, and said to himself again very emphatically that he was a foolish old man. He ought to be out in the streets looking for his child, asking questions, and inquiring at the police-stations, where all accidents were reported as soon as they were known, or at the hospitals.

'Pa-pa!'

The longing, wailing, pitiful little wooden cry rang from the passage, outside the door, and Mr Puckler stood for an instant with white face, transfixed and rooted to the spot. A moment later his hand was on the latch. Then he was in the passage, with the light streaming from the open door behind him.

Quite at the other end he saw the little phantom shining clearly in the shadow, and the right hand seemed to beckon to him as the arm rose and fell once more. He knew all at once that it had not come to frighten him but to lead him, and when it disappeared, and he walked boldly towards the door, he knew that it was in the street outside, waiting for him. He forgot that he was tired and had eaten no supper, and had walked many miles, for a sudden hope ran through and through him, like a golden stream of life.

And sure enough, at the corner of the alley, and at the corner of the street, and out in Belgrave Square, he saw the small ghost flitting before him. Sometimes it was only a shadow, where there was other light, but then the glare of the lamps made a pale green sheen on its little Mother Hubbard frock of silk; and sometimes, where the streets were dark and silent, the whole figure shone out brightly, with its yellow curls and rosy neck. It seemed to trot along like a tiny child, and Mr Puckler could almost hear the pattering of the bronze kid slippers on the pavement as it ran. But it went very fast, and he could only just keep up with it, tearing along with his hat on the back of his head and his thin hair blown by the night breeze, and his horn-rimmed spectacles firmly set upon his broad nose.

On and on he went, and he had no idea where he was. He did not even care, for he knew certainly that he was going the right way.

Then at last, in a wide, quiet street, he was standing before a big, sober-looking door that had two lamps on each side of it, and a polished brass bell-handle, which he pulled.

And just inside, when the door was opened, in the bright light, there was the little shadow, and the pale green sheen of the little silk dress, and once more the small cry came to his ears, less pitiful, more longing.

'Pa-pa!'

The shadow turned suddenly bright, and out of the brightness the beautiful brown glass eyes were turned up happily to his, while the rosy mouth smiled so divinely that the phantom doll looked almost like a little angel just then.

'A little girl was brought in soon after ten o'clock,' said the quiet voice of the hospital doorkeeper. 'I think they thought she was only stunned. She was holding a big brown-paper box against her, and they could not get it out of her arms. She had a long plait of brown hair that hung down as they carried her.'

'She is my little girl,' said Mr Puckler, but he hardly heard his own voice.

He leaned over Else's face in the gentle light of the children's ward, and when he stood there a minute the beautiful brown eyes opened and looked up to his.

'Pa-pa!' cried Else softly, 'I knew you would come!'

Then Mr Puckler did not know what he did or said

for a moment, and what he felt was worth all the fear and terror and despair that had almost killed him that night. But by-and-by Else was telling her story, and the nurse let her speak, for there were only two other children in the room, who were getting well and were sound asleep.

'They were big boys with bad faces,' said Else, 'and they tried to get Nina away from me, but I held on and fought as well as I could till one of them hit me with something, and I don't remember any more, for I tumbled down, and I suppose the boys ran away, and somebody found me there. But I'm afraid Nina is all smashed.'

'Here in the box,' said the nurse. 'We could not take it out of her arms till she came to herself. Should you like to see if the doll is broken?'

And she undid the string cleverly, but Nina was all smashed to pieces. Only the gentle light of the children's ward made a pale green sheen in the folds of the little Mother Hubbard frock.

THROUGH THE DOOR

Ruth Ainsworth

aria was a fortunate little girl, and she knew this herself. Though she was an only child, and therefore a prey to the loneliness an only child experiences, she lived next door to such a large, warm, friendly family that she felt as though she had five brothers and sisters, instead of none.

Her closest friend was Clare, a girl of her own age, but Clare's four older brothers were important too. Mrs Cope, Clare's mother, often included Maria in family outings. She went with them to watch Jimmy in a swimming gala, and she joined in Paul's birthday treat which was a visit to an ice rink. Both Clare and she sometimes accompanied Charles on his bird-watching expeditions.

Charles took no notice of them, provided they lay perfectly still in the ditch, or reed bed, or wherever he had decreed they should freeze into immobility and silence. But they caught Charles' enthusiasm and felt it was all worth while to catch a glimpse of a green woodpecker or hear a grasshopper warbler.

Lance, the eldest, was already a man in Maria's eyes. He went to college, but was as kind-hearted as the rest of the family and he allowed Clare and Maria to sleep on the lawn in his new tent – after he had tried it out himself.

Then, out of the blue, came the terrible news that the Copes were leaving. Their house was up for sale and all was confusion and desolation. When the last furniture van drove off, Maria burst into tears which she had been restraining for weeks. She felt that she would never be happy again. Every day she and Clare had run in and out of each other's house freely. Now all this had come to a dead stop. For ever.

But even weeping must stop at last, and Maria found she could go to bed without the tears starting again. She tried having other friends to tea, but there seemed nothing to do to pass the time. Then her parents gave her a small black kitten and Midge, as he was called, did more than anyone else to make her cheerful. He was a particularly cheerful kitten.

It was many months, not a few weeks as she had hoped, before the first, longed-for, visit to Clare could be arranged, as there had been so much to do to the new house. At last she found herself in a train leaving Liverpool Street for Ipswich, where some of the Cope family would meet her, and drive her the rest of the way. As she settled herself in the corner of the carriage she was very conscious that it was her first long train journey alone, and though she felt excited rather than apprehensive, she was not relaxed as she would have been on a familiar bus ride.

She looked out of the window and tried to remember all she had heard about the new house from conversation or letters. Clare was a writer of long, detailed, many-paged letters that became creased and crumpled with many re-readings.

It had once been a small Elizabethan manor which had been much restored and modernized over the years. 'It's just a shell,' Lance said, 'with massive

chimneys and a few original windows.'

'It's nothing if not old,' said Mrs Cope, 'with uneven floors and draughts, but it seemed to suit us. We liked the views and the garden and it just holds us all when everyone's home.'

'You're to share my bedroom,' Clare had written, 'and it's the best room in the house, with a secret staircase. I won't tell you any more as you'll soon see for yourself. But we can talk as long as we like in bed. No one knows what we are up to. It's a private room, and that's something I've never had before. My last bedroom had a fanlight and someone always noticed if I ever tried to read late.'

The moment she got out of the train at Ipswich, all sense of loss and absence melted away. The Copes were just exactly the same, but even nicer, such of them as had come to meet her. Mrs Cope greeted her as if she were a long-lost daughter, and Clare hugged and kissed her too. It was a real home-coming.

Charles carried her suitcase and told her, seriously, that she might hear a bittern booming if she were lucky. Clare hurried ahead and opened a door.

'We can manage now, Charles. I want to show Maria the rest of the house myself. Look, Maria, these wooden stairs are just for me. They only lead to my bedroom, well, to our bedroom now you're here. They're rather steep and slippery, or so I thought when I first went up them. But they seem ordinary enough now. Take care.'

Maria did find the narrow stairs steep and awkward and she felt inwardly glad that she was not going to sleep by herself, wherever they led. It was all too private, too strange, to her mind.

'All this is my very own,' said Clare triumphantly, as she flung open another narrow door at the top of the stairs. They went into a long, narrow, attic room,

with low beams across the sloping ceiling. It was the
oddest room that Maria had ever seen. Once it must
have been dark and gloomy, a place of shadows and
secrets. Now it had two large windows at floor level,
and two beds with brightly coloured counterpanes
and several pieces of furniture that Maria remembered from the old house. A white painted chest of
drawers. Several white chairs. A red toy box and a
new desk and chair. All this Maria saw in the first
few seconds. Other details she noticed afterwards.

'You've got a new desk. How lovely!'

'Yes. Mummy wanted me to be really comfy and
quiet up here. I can do my prep if I want. Or write to
you. She said the boys and their possessions spread
all over the old house and it was time I had a room of
my own, if I wanted to be out of everybody's way.'

'And do you ever want to be up here alone?'

'Sometimes I do and then it's bliss. Jimmy plays
the same record for hours and hours and nearly
drives us all mad and they all have their friends in
more. That's because we live in the country. But I
often do things downstairs with everyone else. It's
nice being able to choose.

'This is the oldest bit of the house,' she went on.
'Or so Lance says. He knows more about the place
than anyone else. He says this is part of the original
house. Come here. I'll show you.'

Clare opened a door at the end of the room and
Maria peered inside. It was a long, low, oddly shaped
cupboard and would have been pitch dark without a
small, sloping skylight. It was now fitted with hooks
and a rail for coat-hangers. Clare's clothes hung there
looking rather lost.

'There's lots of room for you and spare coat-
hangers. Use what you want when you unpack.'

Maria unpacked and put her clothes in the secret

cupboard. Then the girls went down to tea. The stairs seemed steeper than ever now Maria was going down them. She clung to the handrail every step of the way.

After tea, Maria said she must write a birthday card for her mother, which she had brought with her.

'Write it at my desk,' said Clare. 'You'll find stamps and everything you want.'

'All right. I will.'

Maria liked the idea of using the new desk. She found her way up to the landing and opened the door that led to the stairs. As she went into the room, she was surprised to find she was not alone. She heard no definite sound, but she knew someone had followed her into the attic. She turned round quickly. Close behind her, only a foot or so away, was another girl. This other girl showed no surprise. She seemed so calm and composed that it might have been her room, and Maria the intruder. She was tall and pale, wearing a striped dress, and carrying a pewter plate and mug.

'Who are you?' asked Maria.

'I'm Tabitha.' She offered no apology or explanation for her presence. Maria felt even more like a trespasser.

'What – what are you doing?' She looked at the plate and the mug. Tabitha looked slightly surprised at this obvious question and raised her eyebrows, but she replied gently:

'Taking Father Simon his supper.'

Then, to Maria's horror and amazement, Tabitha and her plate walked right through the solid wooden door of the hanging cupboard, and disappeared. Maria fancied she heard the faint murmur of two voices, Tabitha's clear, childish one, and a man's deeper tone. She did not wait to hear more, but fled to the comfort of the ground floor. She skimmed down the steep stairs as if in a dream, not feeling the wooden treads. Something in her face brought Clare quickly to her side.

'Are you all right? What is it?'

'Can we talk somewhere?' whispered Maria. 'Now.'

'I'll just show Maria the garden,' said Clare loudly, and taking her friend's arm she hurried her out of doors. Maria only waited for the door to close behind them to say urgently:

'Clare, I saw something. I saw a ghost in your room. I know I did. I'm certain.'

'Was it a fair-haired girl?'

Maria's face fell, but she reacted instantly.

'Oh Clare, so you knew all the time. Why ever didn't you tell me if you knew about her? How could you just leave me alone to discover her for myself? We used to share everything.'

Clare squeezed her arm and said warmly:

'It wasn't really a bit like that. Of course I was going to tell you about the ghost – I was longing to – but we've hardly had a minute together since you arrived, without other people milling around. It was rather sad, or so I think now. I once passed a girl with fair hair on the secret staircase. We neither of us said a word. I was far too frightened to speak first. I looked back and saw her reach the door into the attic and just pass through it like air, and disappear.'

'Did you tell anyone?'

'I told Mummy and she told Daddy. They were both very serious and disbelieving. They explained so patiently that I couldn't have seen anything, because there wasn't anything there. When they heard I'd looked back and seen the girl on the stairs they said that proved the whole thing was impossible as it would have been too dark. They went on and on showing me how impossible it was. Then they suggested I swopped rooms with one of the boys if I thought I might feel creepy up there alone.'

'What did you say?' asked Maria.

'Of course I refused. I knew that Jimmy would change with me like a flash, but I wasn't going to give up my lovely bedroom for anything. I said perhaps I'd imagined it and just laid low. I rather think they may have forgotten about it by now.'

'But you haven't forgotten?'

'No, and I never will.'

The girls had a cheerful evening playing a new card game with Jimmy and Paul which involved a great deal of shouting and laughing and slapping down of cards. They went to bed quickly and neither mentioned ghosts. Clare only said as she got into bed:

'The bedside lamp is between us. You just press this to put it on. And the main switch is in the corner.'

'Thanks,' said Maria, snuggling down.

For three days nothing happened that wasn't pleasant and ordinary and like old times. They bird-watched with Charles. Cycled miles down the quiet lanes with Maria on one of the boys' old bicycles. Went shopping. Had a winter picnic. Then, on the third night, Maria woke up and breathed deeply. She smelt a queer unusual smell. In a second she was wide awake.

'Clare, wake up, do! I think the house is on fire.'

She stretched out an arm and shook Clare, screaming in her ear. Clare woke.

'What's wrong? Are you ill?'

'No, just smell. Smell hard. Is it smoke?'

'Let's put the light on.'

They both groped for the button on the lamp, but though it was only a few inches away neither could find it. Maria jumped out of bed and felt for the main switch, but her fingers scrabbled on plain wall. That had vanished too. Choking with terror she found her way to Clare's bed and clung to her. Then came the tinkle of a little bell.

The air cleared and they found the switch for the light. Everything was quiet and normal except for a very faint odour, so faint that it seemed to come and go as they breathed.

'Nothing's on fire,' said Clare comfortingly. She opened the door at the top of the stairs. 'No smell coming up. You poor, poor thing. Did you dream we were being burned alive?'

'There was something peculiar,' insisted Maria. 'It woke me. It nearly choked me. Then, when the little bell rang, it seemed to go. It reminds me of

something.'

They soon fell asleep and in the morning, when Mrs Cope asked if they had a good night, they looked at each other before answering. Then Clare said:

'It would have been good if Maria hadn't dreamed the house was on fire, and shouted in my ear. We soon got off again.'

The next night it was Clare who woke, but not in terror. She touched Maria gently and whispered:

'Open your eyes and keep quiet.'

Maria opened sleepy eyes and saw, at once, that the room was no longer dark. At the far end of the attic, furthest from their beds, was a faint glow. It was the soft, flickering light of several candles. A company of strangely dressed people were gathered in silence before a table spread with a white cloth, with a silver cross above it. Both girls knew it to be an altar. A dark robed priest murmured some words in an unfamiliar tongue. There was the tinkle of a bell. The priest raised his arms. The same queer smell pervaded the room.

'Incense,' breathed Clare.

Maria nodded.

Then came a great thundering outside and a pounding on a wooden door. There was shouting and they heard the words: 'We are betrayed. The Queen's men are at hand.'

At once all was dark. The candles had been blown out instantly. They heard the confused sounds of feet, of furniture being moved, of muffled orders. It was like a rapid scene shifting, well rehearsed. Both girls felt for the switch of the lamp and one of them found it. Light sprang up and they saw, at a glance, that the scene at the far end of the attic had changed. People – candles – altar – silver cross – all had vanished. The dolls' house and the toy chest were back in their places, with the rugs and pictures.

The knocking had stopped and the voices were quiet, but the room still seemed to echo with the thud, thud, on the heavy door.

Though the girls had not been involved in the strange scene, except as spectators, they were both thoroughly disturbed. Their hearts beat quickly and when Clare whispered: 'Let's get out of here,' her voice sounded husky and unnatural, as if her throat were dry. They slid rather than ran down the steep stairs, clinging tightly to the banister, and when they were both safely on the landing, they burst through the nearest door. To Maria it was literally any door as she had not sorted out the various rooms on that floor, and to Clare it meant only that it was the nearest.

It turned out to be Lance's room. He woke at the click of the old-fashioned latch, and switched on his bedside lamp, apparently wide awake in an instant.

'What on earth are you two doing in the middle of the night?' he inquired calmly. 'Have you seen a ghost?'

'Oh Lance,' said Clare thankfully, 'that's just what we have seen. Several ghosts.'

'Both of you?' asked Lance.

'Yes. Both of us together.'

'If two people have seen a ghost it deserves investigation,' went on Lance. 'Serious investigation. And if the ghosts were plural it's even more serious. But we may as well investigate in comfort.'

He turned on the electric fire, and indicated that they were both to sit down on the sofa, and he took his eiderdown off his bed and tucked it cosily over their knees. The warmth and comfort, and Lance's normal, matter-of-fact tone, worked wonders. Someone was taking them seriously, neither panicking nor doubting. Just listening and believing.

'Now tell me everything, every single thing.' Lance ran his fingers through his mop of hair, and sat down opposite, his elbows on his knees, and chin on his clasped hands.

'We smelt a funny smell,' said Maria, 'both of us.'

'It was incense,' corrected Clare, 'though I did not recognize it at first, but it was incense, I'm sure. We woke up, or rather I woke up, and nudged Maria. She woke at once, and we found the room wasn't dark and at the far end a service was going on.'

'It was a Mass,' said Maria. 'They had a priest in white robes and a table made into an altar and a silver cross hanging above.'

'And they rang a little bell,' put in Clare, 'and chanted.'

'It was so secret and solemn,' went on Maria. 'It was beautiful and peaceful till the hammering on the door began, several people hammering with their fists and shouting.'

'It didn't seem to be on our ordinary door, either, not on the one we always use near our beds. It sounded as if it were at the far end of the room,' said Clare. 'What did you think, Maria?'

'Yes, it wasn't close enough to be on our door. You're right. The voices shouting the warning were far away too. A loud voice said: "We are betrayed. The Queen's men are here".'

'Not *here*,' corrected Clare. '*At hand*. The Queen's men are at hand. And then there was more knocking.'

'Yes, you're right, Clare. I remember now.'

Lance listened to every word and when there was a pause, he spoke:

'Queen Elizabeth the First was a Protestant and passed a law forbidding the saying of the Mass. But many Catholic families made elaborate arrangements to worship in secret. There were Catholic carpenters about who, under cover of doing some alterations to the house, devised some secret hiding places where a priest could be concealed. They were called priest holes. Then, usually at night, the priest ventured out to say the forbidden Mass and often neighbours and friends stole through the dark countryside to join them. Attics were sometimes changed into temporary chapels.'

'Where did they make the priest holes?' asked Clare.

'Oh, in secret cupboards and behind panelling and often in the chimney.'

'Wasn't it too hot for the poor priest?' inquired Maria.

'I don't think he *lived* in the chimney. It was a good hiding place if the Queen's men were on the prowl, searching out priests and disobedient Catholics. A man called Thomas Philips, cunning as a fox, led the searches. He could decipher codes and his spies were everywhere, measuring buildings and tapping walls to find secret rooms.'

'What happened when the priests and the Catholics were caught?'

'The priests were often put to death and the Catholics heavily fined. They might be put to death as well.'

'Was my bedroom cupboard a priest hole?' asked Clare, her eyes never leaving Lance's face.

'It might easily have been. They were often built in gables. It might even have had an inner room to deceive the searchers. They wouldn't suspect another secret place if they'd found the first one.'

'Shall we investigate inside my cupboard and see what we can find? Let's start now.' Clare jumped up eagerly.

'Are you both agreed over what you've told me? Did either of you see or hear anything the other didn't?'

They shook their heads.

'Oh no, Lance. We were together so of course we saw the same things. And heard the same things. We were as wide awake as – well, as we are now.'

'Then what happened?' said Lance encouragingly.

'Then they swept everything away like lightning,' said Clare, 'or I suppose that's what they did. They blew out the candles first of all, so we couldn't watch what they were doing. They were so quick that they must have had lots of practice. They must have rehearsed it.'

'I hope they weren't caught,' said Maria. 'They weren't doing any harm. There were some children at the service and Father Simon was like a real father, caring for his family.'

'Who was Father Simon?' asked Lance, quick as a flash. 'You haven't told me about him.'

Clare first, then Maria afterwards, related their earlier meetings with Tabitha, carrying Father Simon's supper.

'You hadn't mentioned Tabitha to Maria before she saw her herself?' asked Lance, addressing Clare.

'No, I told you I hadn't,' said Clare impatiently. 'I was longing to tell her but we hadn't been alone together for a minute. And she was much braver than me. She spoke to Tabitha and found out her name and actually asked her what she was doing.'

'I was a bit puzzled, but she seemed so real and ordinary,' explained Maria, 'except for her old fashioned clothes. I wasn't frightened. It was when she and her supper tray walked right through the cupboard door that I was scared. Then I knew she was someone different. A ghost, in fact.'

'You're lucky girls to see a ghost – lots of ghosts. I wish I'd had the chance,' said Lance. 'Now would you like to finish the night in my bed and I'll go up to the attic, or are you all right?'

The girls looked at each other, but neither wanted to be the first to admit she felt uneasy. Anyhow, there were two of them.

'I'll go back to my own bed, Lance, thank you,' said Clare.

'And so will I,' added Maria.

'O.K.,' said Lance cheerfully. 'You can leave your

bedside lamp on for company, if you like, and I'll
leave my door open. But I don't think you'll see or
hear anything else tonight. If you do, just call and I'll
be up the stairs in a jiffy.'

Though the girls were sure they would lie awake
all night, it was only for a few minutes before sleep
overcame them. They heard nothing more till morning, not even Lance's bare feet as he padded upstairs
to make sure they had dropped off. He, himself,
puzzled and pondered between fitful dozes.

Though Lance and the girls had made no arrangements to keep the night's events to themselves, they
did not mention them to the rest of the family. Lance
had been more impressed than he had shown by
Clare's determination to keep Tabitha's second
appearance from her parents, once she had experi-
enced their sympathetic disbelief, and had realized
that the possession of her bedroom was at stake, the
bedroom she prized so highly. He was also impressed by Maria's attitude. She'd got her head
screwed on the right way, he thought to himself.
Only children aren't all soft and silly. She's a cool
customer, for a start.

During the day, while the younger boys were on
their bicycles and Charles had disappeared with his
binoculars, Lance invited the girls to come to his
room, which was warm and comfortable, though
small. The table was covered with books and papers
as he often studied up there.

'I'll tell you a few facts I've collected about the time
when this house was built. You'll see why, if you
listen.'

They fixed their eyes on him, unwaveringly, and
did not fidget or interrupt. An idea crossed his mind
that he wouldn't mind teaching children, one day, if
they listened like these two, absorbing every syllable.

'Yes, we might take some measurements later on. I don't think Dad would stand for any more walls being pulled down. The alterations have cost too much already. But he couldn't object to peaceful measuring and checking.'

By some mysterious process, never perfectly understood, the other boys were soon caught up in the possibility of there being a priest hole actually in the house, just waiting to be discovered. The children swarmed all over the building with rulers and tape measures, measuring every nook and cranny, and tapping the woodwork like demented woodpeckers, listening for a hollow sound. As they soon found out, many wooden surfaces gave back a hollow note if tapped often enough, with sufficient force. But Lance's respect for the fabric of the house kept them from using tools which could do damage.

'Stick to accurate measuring,' he advised. 'Be scientific. Write it all down. When we get a water-tight case for the existence of a priest hole, then that's the time for the next step. Let's be sure of our facts first.'

A black notebook was produced with PRIEST HOLES written on the cover, and all measurements, scientific or otherwise, were inscribed inside in Lance's spidery writing.

'Whatever the children are doing is keeping them quiet and out of the way,' said Mr Cope with satisfaction.

'It's all Lance,' said his wife. 'I never thought he took much notice of the younger ones, but I was wrong. Clare and Maria never willingly leave him alone. I heard he'd had to lock his door the other day to get some of his own work done.'

'He started the notion of a priest hole and now it's everyone's idea. They are all dead keen on finding one. They talk learnedly about secret Masses and codes and hiding places,' went on Mr Cope. 'Just look at that!' He opened the window and stuck his head out.

'Don't lean out so far, Jimmy,' he shouted, as he looked upward.

'I'm all right, Daddy. Charles has got hold of my feet. I really believe I may be on to something.'

A steel measure waved wildly from a landing window.

'I've dropped it again. You go and fetch it, Charles. I can see it shining in that laurel bush.'

'Fetch it yourself. You let go of it.'

'But I fetched your biro last time you dropped it.'

'Fair's fair.'

Mr Cope withdrew his head and slammed the sitting room window shut.

If they could have listened to a conversation taking place in another part of the house, Mr and Mrs Cope would have been surprised.

'If only we knew that they weren't caught, that night, and that Father Simon wasn't killed,' said Maria. 'But we never shall. I asked Lance if there would be anyone on guard and he said yes, of course. There would always be a look-out. They might have given the warning in time. The sound of distant hoofs – a dog barking – an unexpected light – a little would have been enough to put them on the alert. After all, their lives were at stake.'

There was a pause. Then Clare spoke.

'We shan't see anything again. I know we shan't. It's happened. It won't happen again, ever. I keep wondering why you and I were given that ghostly glimpse of the past. We were so ignorant. So unsuitable.'

'Now I don't agree with you,' contradicted Maria.

'In one way we were very well chosen, apart from being actually on the spot. I think ghosts are often lonely. Tabitha must have felt very drawn to you, as a girl herself, to allow herself to be seen at all. I was too surprised, as it happened, to be really scared so I was able to speak to her. And she replied quietly and naturally. It may have been many years since a living person spoke to her, poor girl. I've heard that ghosts only show themselves to people who believe in them.'

'I'm thankful I was frightened silently,' said Clare, who couldn't forgive herself for being frightened at all. 'You always hear of people screaming and screeching when they see a ghost. Tabitha may have not known that I was petrified,' she went on more cheerfully. 'I didn't utter a word. I do so hope she didn't know, or guess.'

The two girls acquired a good knowledge of priests and priest holes. They read books lent by Lance, and Maria read many more when she got home, helped by a friendly librarian. But she kept discussion of their strange experiences for times, in the holidays, when she and Clare were together and never mentioned it to other friends or even to her parents. Over the years, Tabitha became an intimate and friendly figure in their memories, like someone met on a journey, and never forgotten.

THE EMPTY SCHOOLROOM

Pamela Hansford Johnson

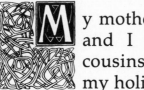y mother and father were in India and I had no aunts, uncles or cousins with whom I could spend my holidays; so I stayed behind in the drab and echoing school to amuse myself as best I could, my only companions the housekeeper, the maid and Mademoiselle Fournier, who also had nowhere else to go.

Our school was just outside the village of Bellançay, which is in the north of France, four or five kilometres from Rouen. It was a tall, narrow house set upon the top of a hill, bare save for the great sweep of beech trees sheltering the long carriage drive. As I look back some twenty-seven years to my life there, it seems to me that the sun never shone, that the grass was always dun-coloured beneath a dun-coloured sky, and that the vast spaces of the lawns were broken perpetually by the scurry of dry brown leaves licked along by a small, bitter wind. This inaccurate impression remains with me because, I suppose, I was never happy at Bellançay. There were twenty or thirty other girls there – French, German or Swiss; I was the only English girl among them. Madame de Vallon, the headmistress, did not love my nation. She could not forget that she had been born in 1815, the year of defeat. With Mademoiselle Maury, the young assistant teacher, I was a little more at ease, for she, even if she did not care for me, had too volatile a nature not to smile or laugh sometimes, even for the benefit of those who were not her favourites.

Mademoiselle Fournier was a dependent cousin of our headmistress. She was in her late fifties, a little woman dry as a winter twig, her face very tight, small and wary under a wig of coarse yellow hair. To pay for her board and lodging she taught deportment; in her youth she had been at the Court of the Tsar, and it was said that at sixteen years of age she was betrothed to a Russian nobleman. There was some sort of mystery here, about which all the girls were curious. Louise de Chausson said her mother had told her the story – how the nobleman, on the eve of his wedding, had shot himself through the head, having received word that certain speculations in which he had for many years been involved had come to light, and that his arrest was imminent . . . 'And from that day,' Louise whispered, her prominent eyes gleaming in the candlelight, 'she began to wither and wither and wither away, till all her beauty was gone . . .' Yes, I can see Louise now, kneeling upon her bed at the end of the vast dormitory, her thick plait hanging down over her nightgown, the little cross with the turquoise glittering at her beautiful and grainy throat. The others believed the story implicitly, except the piece about Mademoiselle Fournier's lost beauty. That they could not stomach. No, she was ugly as a monkey and had always been so.

For myself, I disbelieved in the nobleman; believed in the beauty. I have always had a curious faculty for stripping age from a face, recognizing the structure of the bone and the original texture of the skin beneath the disguisings of blotch, red vein and loosened flesh. When I looked at Mademoiselle Fournier I saw that the pinched and veinous nose had once been delicate and fine; that the sunken eyes had once been almond-shaped and blue; that the small, loose mouth had once pouted charmingly and opened upon romantic words. Why did I not believe in the nobleman? For no better reason than a distrust of Louise's information on any conceivable point. She was a terrible teller of falsehoods.

I was seventeen years old when I spent my last vacation at Bellançay, and knowing that my parents were to return to Europe in the following spring I watched the departure of the other girls with a heart not quite so heavy as was usual upon these occasions. In six months' time I, too, would be welcomed and loved, have adventures to relate and hopes upon which to feed.

I waved to them from a dormer window as they rattled away in fiacre and barouche down the drive between the beech trees, sired and damed, uncled and aunted, their boxes stacked high and their voices high as the treetops. They had never before seemed to me a particularly attractive group of girls – that is, not in the mass. There was, of course, Hélène de Courcey, with her great olive eyes; Madeleine Millet, whose pale red hair hung to her knees; but in the cluster they had no particular charm. That day, however, as, in new bonnets flowered and feathered and gauzed, they passed from sight down the narrowing file of beeches, I thought them all beautiful as princesses, and as princesses fortunate. Perhaps the nip in the air of a grey June made their cheeks rose-red, their eyes bright as the eyes of desirable young ladies in ballrooms.

The last carriage disappeared, the last sound died away. I turned away from the window and went down the echoing stairs, flight after flight to the *salle à manger*, where my luncheon awaited me.

I ate alone. Mademoiselle Fournier took her meals in her own room upon the second floor, reading as she ate, crumbs falling from her lip on to the page. Tonight she and I, in the pattern of all holiday nights, would sit together for a while in the drawing room before retiring.

'You don't make much of a meal, I must say,' Marie, the maid, rebuked me, as she cleared the plates. 'You can't afford to grow thinner, Mademoiselle, or you'll snap in two.' She brought me some cherries, which I would not eat then but preferred to take out with me in the garden. 'I'll wrap them up for you. No! you can't put them in your handkerchief like that; you'll stain it.'

She chattered to me for a while, in her good nature trying to ease my loneliness. Marie, at least, had relations in the village with whom she sometimes spent her evenings. 'What are you going to do with yourself, eh? Read your eyes out as usual?'

'I shall walk this afternoon, unless I find it too chilly.'

'You'll find it raining,' said Marie, cocking a calculating eye towards the high windows, 'in an hour. No, less; in half an hour.'

She busied herself wrapping up my cherries, which she handed to me in a neat parcel with a firm finger-loop of string. 'If it's wet you can play the piano.'

'You've forgotten,' I said, 'we have none now, or shan't have till they send the new one.'

Madame de Vallon had recently sold the instrument, ugly and tinny, and with the money from the sale plus some money raised by parents' subscription had bought a grand pianoforte from Monsieur Oury, the mayor, whose eldest daughter, the musical one, had lately died.

'You can play on Mademoiselle Fournier's,' said Marie, 'she won't mind. You go and ask her.'

'What, is there another piano in the school?' I was amazed. I had been at Belançay for seven years and had fancied no corner of the building unknown to me.

'Ah-ha,' said Marie triumphantly, 'there are still things you don't know, eh? You don't have to do the housework, or you'd be wiser.'

'But where is it?'

'In the empty schoolroom.'

I laughed at her. 'But they're all empty now! Whatever do you mean?'

'The one at the top,' she said impatiently, 'the one up the little flight of four stairs.'

'But that's the lumber room!'

'There's lumber in it. But it was a schoolroom once. It was when my aunt worked here. The piano's up there still, though *she* never plays it now.' Marie jerked her head skywards to indicate Mademoiselle Fournier upstairs.

I was fascinated by this information. We girls had never entered the lumber room because no attraction had been attached to it: to us it was simply a small, grimy door in the attic, locked we imagined, as we had never seen anyone go in or out. All we knew was that old books, valises, crates of unwanted china, were sometimes stacked up there out of the way.

There! I have failed to make my point quite clear. I must try again. *There was no mystery whatsoever attaching to this room*, which is the reason why no girl had ever tried the handle. Schoolgirls are curious and roaming creatures; how better can they be kept from a certain path than by the positive assurance that it is a *cul-de-sac*?

Dismissing Marie, I determined to go and seek permission from Mademoiselle Fournier to play upon her pianoforte. Since the departure of the old one, I had missed my music lessons and above all my practising; most of the girls were delighted to be saved a labour which to me, though I was an indifferent performer, had never been anything but a pleasure.

Mademoiselle had finished her meal and was just coming out upon the landing as I ran up the stairs to find her. I made my request.

She looked at me. 'Who told you about the instrument?'

'Marie.'

She was silent. Her brows moved up and down, moving the wig as they did so. It was a familiar trick with her when she was puzzled or annoyed. At last she said, without expression, 'No, you may not go up there,' and pushing me, hurried on downstairs.

At the turn of the staircase, however, she stopped and looked up. Her whole face was working with some unrecognizable emotion and her cheeks were burning red. 'Is there *no* place one can keep to oneself?' she cried at me furiously, and ducking her head, ran on.

When we sat that evening in the drawing room, in our chairs turned to the fireless grate, she made no reference to the little scene of that afternoon. I thought she was, perhaps, sorry for having spoken so sharply: for she asked me a few personal questions of a kindly nature and just before bed time brought out a tin box full of sugared almonds, which she shared with me.

She rose a little before I did, leaving me to retire when I chose. I stayed for perhaps half an hour in that vast, pale room with its moth-coloured draperies and its two tarnished chandeliers hanging a great way below the ceiling. Then I took up my candle and went to bed.

Now I must insist that I was a docile girl, a little sullen, perhaps, out of an unrealized resentment against my parents for (as I thought) deserting me; but obedient. I never had a bad conduct report from any of our teachers. It is important that this fact should be realized, so the reader shall know that what I did was not of my own free will.

I could not sleep. I lay open-eyed until my candle burned halfway down and the moon shifted round into the window-pane, weaving the golden light with its own blue-silver. I had no thought of any importance. Small pictures from the day's humdrum events flashed across my brain. I saw the neatly-looped parcel of cherries, the currant stain at the hem of Marie's apron, the starch-blue bird on the bonnet of Louise de Chausson, who had left Bellançay to marry an elderly and not very rich nobleman of Provence. I saw the leaves scurrying over the grey lawns, saw a woodpecker rapping at the trunk of the tree behind the house. What I did not see was the face of Mademoiselle Fournier upturned from the stairway. She never entered my thoughts at all.

And so it is very strange that just before dawn I rose up, put on my dressing gown and sought about the room until I found a pair of gloves my father had had made for me in India, fawn-coloured, curiously stitched in gold and dark green thread. These I took up, left the room and made my way silently up through the quiet house till I came to the door of the lumber room – or, as Marie had called it, the empty schoolroom. I paused with my hand upon the latch and listened. There was no sound except the impalpable breathing of the night, compound perhaps of the breathings of all who sleep, or perhaps of the movement of the moon through the gathered clouds.

I raised the latch gently and stepped within the room, closing the door softly behind me.

The chamber ran halfway across the length of the house at the rear of it, and was lighted by a ceiling window through which the moonrays poured lavishly down. It was still a schoolroom, despite the lumber stacked at the far end, the upright piano standing just behind the door. Facing me was a dais, on which stood a table and a chair. Before the dais were row upon row of desks, with benches behind. Everything was very dusty. With my finger I wrote DUST upon the teacher's table, then scuffed the word out again.

I went to the pianoforte. Behind the lattice-work was a ruching of torn red silk; the candle stumps in the sconces were red also. On the rack stood a piece of music, a Chopin nocturne simplified for beginners.

Gingerly I raised the lid and a mottled spider ran across the keys, dropped on hasty thread to the floor and ran away. The underside of the lid was completely netted by his silk; broken strands waved in the disturbed air and over the discoloured keys. As a rule I am afraid of spiders. That night I was not afraid. I laid my gloves on the keyboard, then closed the piano lid upon them.

I was ready to go downstairs. I took one glance about the room and for a moment thought I saw a shadowy form sitting upon one of the back benches, a form that seemed to weep. Then the impression passed away, and there was only the moonlight painting the room with its majesty. I went out, latched the door and crept back to my bed where, in the first colouring of dawn, I fell asleep.

Next day it was fine. I walked to the river in the morning, and in the afternoon worked at my *petit-point* upon the terrace. At teatime an invitation came for me. The mayor, Monsieur Oury, wrote to Mademoiselle Fournier saying he believed there was a young lady left behind at school for the holidays, and that if she would care to dine at his house upon the following evening it would be a great pleasure to him and to his two young daughters. 'We are not a gay house these days,' he wrote, 'but if the young lady cares for books and flowers there are a great number of both in my library and conservatory.'

'Shall I go?' I asked her.

'But of course! It is really a great honour for you. Do you know who the mayor's mother was before her marriage? She was a Uzès. Yes. And when she married Monsieur Oury's father, a very handsome man, her family cut her off with nothing at all and never spoke to her again. But they were very happy. You must wear your best gown and your white hat. Take the gown to Marie and she will iron it for you.'

The day upon which I was to visit Monsieur Oury was sunless and chilly. Plainly the blue dress that Marie had so beautifully spotted and pressed would not do at all. I had, however, a gown of fawn-coloured merino, plain but stylish, with which my brown straw hat would look very well.

Mademoiselle Fournier left the house at four o'clock to take tea with the village priest. She looked me over before she went, pinched my dress, tweaked it, pulled out the folds, and told me to sit quite still until the mayor's carriage came for me at half past six. 'Sit like a mouse, mind, or you will spoil the effect. Remember, Monsieur Oury is not nobody.'

She said suddenly, 'Where are your gloves?'

I had forgotten them.

'Forgetting the very things that make a lady look a lady! Go and fetch them at once. Marie!'

The maid came in.

'Marie, see Mademoiselle's gloves are nice, and brush her down once more just as you see the carriage enter the drive. I mustn't wait now. Well, Maud, I wish you a pleasant evening. Don't forget you must be a credit to us.'

When she had gone Marie asked for my gloves. 'You'd better wear your brown ones with that hat, Mademoiselle.'

'Oh!' I exclaimed, 'I can't! I lost one of them on the expedition last week.'

'Your black, then?'

'They won't do. They'd look dreadful with this gown and hat. I know! I have a beautiful Indian pair that will match my dress exactly! I'll go and look for them.'

I searched. The reader must believe that I hunted all over my room for them anxiously, one eye upon the clock, though it was not yet twenty minutes past four. Chagrined, really upset at the thought of having my toilette ruined, I sat down upon the edge of the bed and began to cry a little. Tears came very easily to me in those lost and desolate days.

From high up in the house I heard a few notes of the piano, the melody of a Chopin nocturne played fumblingly in the treble, and I thought at once, 'Of course! The gloves are up there, where I hid them.'

The body warns us of evil before the senses are half awakened. I knew no fear as I ran lightly up towards the empty schoolroom, yet as I reached the door I felt a wave of heat engulf me, and knew a sick, nauseous stirring within my body. The notes, audible only to my ear (not to Marie's, for even at that moment I could hear her calling out some inquiry or gossip to the housekeeper), ceased. I lifted the latch and looked in.

The room appeared to be deserted, yet I could see the presence within it and know its distress. I peeped behind the door.

At the piano sat a terribly ugly, thin young girl in a dunce's cap. She was half turned towards me, and I saw her pig-like profile, the protruding teeth, the spurt of sandy eyelash. She wore a holland dress in the fashion of twenty years ago, and lean yellow streamers of hair fell down over her back from beneath the paper cone. Her hands, still resting on the fouled keyboard, were meshed about with the spider's web; beneath them lay my Indian gloves.

I made a movement towards the girl. She swivelled sharply and looked me full in the face. Her eyes were

all white, red-rimmed, but tearless.

To get my gloves I must risk touching her. We looked at each other, she and I, and her head shrank low between her hunching shoulders. Somehow I must speak to her friendlily, disarm her while I gained my objective.

'Was it you playing?' I asked.

No answer. I closed my eyes. Stretching out my hands as in a game of blind man's buff, I sought for the keyboard.

'I have never heard you before,' I said.

I touched something: I did not know whether it was a glove or her dead hand.

'Have you been learning long?' I said. I opened my eyes. She was gone. I took my gloves, dusted off the webs and ran, ran so fast down the well of the house that on the last flight I stumbled and fell breathless into Marie's arms.

'Oh, I have had a fright! I have had a fright!'

She led me into the drawing room, made me lie down, brought me a glass of wine.

'What is it, Mademoiselle? Shall I fetch the house-keeper? What has happened?'

But the first sip of wine had made me wary. 'I thought I saw someone hiding in my bedroom, a man. Perhaps a thief.'

At this the house was roused. Marie, the house-keeper and the gardener, who had not yet finished his work, searched every room (the lumber room, too, I think) but found nothing. I was scolded, petted, dosed, and Marie insisted, when the housekeeper was out of the way, on a *soupcon* of rouge on my cheeks because, she said, I could not upset Monsieur le Maire by looking like a dead body – he, poor man, having so recently had death in his house!

I recovered myself sufficiently to climb into the

carriage, when it came, to comport myself decently on the drive, and to greet the mayor and his two daughters with dignity. Dinner, however, was a nightmare. My mind was so full of the horror I had seen that I could not eat – indeed I could barely force my trembling hand to carry the fork to my lips.

The mayor's daughters were only children, eleven and thirteen years old. At eight o'clock he bade them say good night to me and prepare for bed. When they had left us I told him I thought I had stayed long enough: but with a very grave look he placed his hand upon my arm and pressed me gently back into my chair.

'My dear young lady,' he said, 'I know your history, I know you are lonely and unhappy in France without your parents. Also I know that you have suffered some violent shock. Will you tell me about it and let me help you?'

The relief of his words, of his wise and kindly gaze, was too much for me. For the first time in seven years I felt fathered and in haven. I broke down and cried tempestuously, and he did not touch me or speak to me till I was a little more calm. Then he rang for the servant and told her to bring some lime-flower tea. When I had drunk and eaten some of the sweet cake that he urged upon me I told him about the empty schoolroom and of the horror which sat there at the webbed piano.

When I had done he was silent for a little while. Then he took both my hands in his.

'Mademoiselle,' he said, 'I am not going to blame you for the sin of curiosity; I think there was some strange compulsion upon you to act as you did. Therefore I mean to shed a little light upon this sad schoolroom by telling you the story of Mademoiselle Fournier.'

I started.

'No,' he continued restrainingly, 'you must listen quietly; and what I tell you you must never repeat to a soul save your own mother until both Mademoiselle Fournier and Madame de Vallon, her cousin, have passed away.'

I have kept this promise. They have been dead some fourteen years.

Monsieur Oury settled back in his chair. A tiny but comforting fire was lit in the grate, and the light of it was like a ring of guardian angels about us.

'Mademoiselle Fournier,' he began, 'was a very beautiful and proud young woman. Although she had no dowry, she was yet considered something of a *partie*, and in her nineteenth year she became affianced to a young Russian nobleman who at that time was living with his family upon an estate near Arles. His mother was not too pleased with the

match, but she was a good woman, and she treated Charlotte – that is, Mademoiselle Fournier – with kindness. Just before the marriage Charlotte's father, who had been created a marquis by Bonaparte and now, by tolerance, held a minor government post under Louis Philippe, was found to have embezzled many thousands of francs.'

'Her father!' I could not help but exclaim.

Monsieur Oury smiled wryly. 'Legend has the lover for villain, eh? No; it was Aristide Fournier, a weak man, unable to stomach any recession in his fortunes. Monsieur Fournier shot himself as the gendarmes were on their way to take him. Charlotte, her marriage prospects destroyed, came near to lunacy. When she recovered from her long illness her beauty had gone. The mother of her ex-fiancé, in pity, suggested that a friend of hers, a lady at the Court of the Tsar, should employ Charlotte as governess to her children, and in Russia Charlotte spent nine years. She returned to France to assist her cousin with the school at Bellançay that Madame de Vallon had recently established.'

'Why did she return?' I said, less because I wished to know the answer than because I wished to break out of the veil of the past he was drawing about us both, and to feel myself a reality once more, Maud Arlett, aged seventeen years and nine months, brown hair and grey eyes, five foot seven and a half inches tall.

I did not succeed. The veil tightened, grew more opaque. 'Nobody knows. There were rumours. It seems not improbable that she was dismissed by her employer . . . why, I don't know. It is an obscure period in Charlotte's history.'

He paused, to pour more tea for me.

'It was thought at first that Charlotte would be of

great assistance to Madame de Vallon, teach all subjects and act as Madame's secretary. It transpired, however, that Charlotte was nervous to the point of sickness, and that she would grow less and less capable of teaching young girls. Soon she had no duties in the school except to give lessons in music and deportment.

'The music room was in the attic, which was then used as a schoolroom also. The pianoforte was Charlotte's own, one of the few things saved from the wreck of her home.'

Monsieur Oury rose and walked out of the ring of firelight. He stood gazing out of the window, now beaded by a thin rain, and his voice grew out of the dusk as the music of waves grew out of the sea. 'I shall tell you the rest briefly, Mademoiselle. It distresses me to tell it to you at all, but I think I can help you in no other way.

'A young girl came to the school, a child; perhaps twelve or thirteen years of age. Her mother and father were in the East, and she was left alone, even during the vacations –'

'Like myself!' I cried.

'Yes, like yourself; and I have an idea that that is why she chose you for her . . . *confidante.*'

I shuddered.

He seemed to guess at my movement for, turning from the window, he returned to the firelight and to me.

'In one way, however, she was unlike you as can possibly be imagined. Mademoiselle.' He smiled with a faint, sad gallantry. 'She was exceedingly ugly.

'From the first, Charlotte took a dislike to her, and it grew to mania. The child, Thérèse Dasquier, was never very intelligent; in Charlotte's grip she became almost imbecile. Charlotte was always devising new

punishments, new humiliations. Thérèse became the mock and the pity of the school.'

'But Madame de Vallon, couldn't she have stopped it?' I interrupted indignantly.

'My dear,' Monsieur Oury replied sadly, 'like many women of intellect – she is, as you know, a fine teacher – she is blind to most human distress. She is, herself, a kind woman: she believes others are equally kind, cannot believe there could be . . . suffering . . . torment . . . going on beneath her very nose. Has she ever realized *your* loneliness, Mademoiselle, given you any motherly word, or . . .? I thought not. But I am digressing, and that I must not do. We have talked too much already.

'One night Thérèse Dasquier arose quietly, crept from the dormitory and walked barefooted a mile and a half in the rain across the fields to the river, where she drowned herself.'

'Oh, God,' I murmured, my heart cold and heavy as a stone.

'God, I think,' said Monsieur Oury, 'cannot have been attentive at that time . . .' His face changed. He added hastily, 'And God forgive me for judging Him. We cannot know – we cannot guess . . .' he continued rapidly, in a dry, rather high voice oddly unlike his own. 'There was scandal, great scandal. Thérèse's parents returned to France and everyone expected them to force the truth to light. They turned out to be frivolous and selfish people, who could scarcely make even a parade of grief for a child they had never desired and whose death they could not regret. Thérèse was buried and forgotten. Slowly, very slowly, the story also was forgotten. After all, nobody *knew* the truth, they could only make conjecture.'

'Then how did you know?' I cried out.

'Because Madame de Vallon came to me in bitter

distress with the tale of the rumours and besought me to clear Charlotte's name. You see, she simply could not believe a word against her. And at the same time the aunt of Marie, the maid, came to me swearing she could prove the truth of the accusations . . . Three days afterwards she was killed in the fire which destroyed the old quarter of Bellançay.'

I looked my inquiry into his face.

'I knew which of the women spoke the truth,' he replied, answering me, 'because in Madame de Vallon's face I saw concern for her own blood. In the other woman's I saw concern for a child who to her was nothing.'

'But still, you *guessed!*' I protested

He turned upon me his long and grave regard. 'You,' he said, '*you* do not know the truth? Even you?'

I do not know how I endured the following weeks in that lonely school. I remember how long I lay shivering in my bed, staring into the flame of the candle because I felt that in the brightest part of it alone was refuge, how the sweat jumped out from my brow at the least sound in the stillness of midnight, and how, towards morning, I would fall into some morose and terrible dream of dark stairways and locked doors.

Yet, as day by day, night by night, went by with no untoward happening, my spirit knew some degree of easing and I began once more to find comfort in prayer – that is, I dared once again to cover my face while I repeated 'Our Father', and to rise from my knees without fear of what might be standing patiently at my shoulder.

The holidays drew to an end. 'Tomorrow,' said Mademoiselle Fournier, folding her needlework in preparation for bed, 'your companions will be back with you once more. You'll like that, eh?'

Ever since my request and her refusal, she had been perfectly normal in her manner – I mean, she had been normally sour, polite, withdrawn.

'I shall like it,' I sighed, 'only too well.'

She smiled remotely. 'I am not a lively companion for you, Maud, I fear. Still, I am as I am. I am too old to change myself.'

She went on upstairs, myself following, our candles smoking in the draught and our shadows prancing upon the wall.

I said my prayers and read for a little while. I was unusually calm, feeling safety so nearly within my reach that I need be in no hurry to stretch out my hand and grasp it tight. The bed seemed softer than usual, the sheets sweet-smelling, delicately warm and light. I fell into a dreamless sleep.

I awoke suddenly to find the moon full on my face. I sat up, dazzled by her light, a strange feeling of energy tingling in my body. 'What is it,' I whispered, 'that I must do?'

The moon shone broadly on the great surfaces of gleaming wood, on the bureau, the tallboy, the wardrobe, flashed upon the mirror, sparkled on the spiralling bedposts. I slipped out of bed and in my nightgown went out into the passage.

It was very bright and still. Below me, the stairs fell steeply to the tessellated entrance hall. To my right the passage narrowed to the door behind which Mademoiselle Fournier slept, her wig upon a candlestick, her book and her spectacles lying on the rug at her side – so Marie had described her to me. Before me the stairs rose to the turn of the landing, from which a further flight led to the second floor, the third floor and the attics. The wall above the stair rail was white with the moon.

I felt the terror creeping up beneath my calm, though only as one might feel the shadow of pain while in the grip of a drug. I was waiting now as I had been instructed to wait, and I knew for what. I stared upwards, my gaze fastened upon the turn of the stairs.

Then, upon the moonlit wall, there appeared the shadow of a cone.

She stood just out of sight, her fool's-capped head nodding forward, listening even as I was listening.

I held my breath. My forehead was ice-cold.

She came into view then, stepping carefully, one hand upholding a corner of her skirt, the other feeling its way along the wall. As she reached me I closed my eyes. I felt her pass by, knew she had gone along the passage to the room of Mademoiselle Fournier. I heard a door quietly opened and shut.

In those last moments of waiting my fear left me, though I could move neither hand nor foot. My ears were sharp for the least sound.

It came: a low and awful cry, tearing through the quiet of the house and blackening the moonlight itself. The door opened again.

She came hastening out, and in the shadow of the cap she smiled. She ran on tiptoe past me, up the stairs.

The last sound? I thought it had been the death cry of Mademoiselle Fournier; but there was yet another.

As Marie and the housekeeper came racing down, white-faced, from their rooms (they must have passed her as she stood in the shade) I heard very distinctly the piping voice of a young girl:

'Tiens, Mademoiselle, je vous remercie beaucoup!'

We went together, Marie, the housekeeper and I, into the room of Charlotte Fournier, and only I did not cry out when we looked upon the face.

'You see,' said Monsieur Oury, on the day I left Bellançay for ever to join my parents in Paris, 'she did make you her *confidante*. She gave to you the privilege of telling her story and publishing her revenge. Are you afraid of her now, knowing that there was no harm in her for *you*, knowing that she has gone for ever, to trouble no house again?'

'I am not afraid,' I said, and I believed it was true; but even now I cannot endure to awaken suddenly on moonlit nights, and I fling my arms about my husband and beg him to rouse up and speak with me until the dawn.

THE UNQUIET SPIRIT

Jean Stubbs

At Christmas, every year, Caroline suffered and was in ecstasy because of Robert. Christmas was the only holiday he spent wholly at Beeches. At Easter and in the summer he went away to places like Yugoslavia and Greece; during term time he studied archaeology at Cambridge. He was an untidy young man with a delightful smile and a need for company. Beeches became a lively house when Robert was home. His guardian, the Reverend Cyril Mackie, padded out of his study to greet him, and said:

'A touch of Bacchus about you, my boy! Inherited from your father!'

Then, shaking his head, remembering a personal golden age, he retreated chuckling.

'Mrs Welch, Mrs Welch,' he called to his housekeeper, 'the prodigal has returned. Spread the festal board and crown him with vine leaves!'

Crown him with vine leaves, thought Caroline, peering through the banisters and hoping he would notice her. All her thirteen years she had adored Robert and he had been kind to her. At one time she hoped to grow fast enough to catch him up, but ten years is not easily bridged and he remained tantalizingly ahead of her. Even Mrs Welch was fond of Robert, sensible, faithful, strict Mrs Welch, who removed Caroline's orange lipstick and forbade her a black taffeta party dress.

Oh, Robbie Mack, I love you, thought Caroline, and inched her way down the stairs. He was temporarily alone while they fussed around his luggage, and he turned.

'How's Queen Caroline?' he cried, and swung her off her feet. 'Here, duckie!'

She accepted the chocolate and smuggled it into her dressing gown pocket. She wished it had been something more exotic and mysterious.

'Is anyone else coming?' she asked, knowing Robert's weakness for an *entourage*.

'Tomorrow afternoon,' he said, already turning away from her. 'Five of the bunch. You know them, apart from Venetia. You'll like Venetia, duckie.'

I shall loathe Venetia, thought Caroline, I bet that isn't her real name either. She'll have long black hair and orange lipstick, like all Robbie's girls, and she'll patronize me.

'Back to bed, chicken,' said Robert and patted her behind absently, and walked out to help Mrs Welch and the odd-job man with the bags.

'Good night,' said Caroline, with dignity, but half-way up the stairs she put both hands over her heart to prevent it from breaking.

The three young men and four young girls sat reasonably upright in their tall chairs beneath the eyes of Mrs Welch. There was a formality about the dining-room at Beeches which quelled the most heretic soul. For over forty years the Reverend Cyril had dined at eight precisely, beginning with soup and ending with brandy. Through that time had passed, briefly and beautifully, his wife; his house-keeper, after his wife's death; and Robert and Caroline, children of his brother. He was a kind man, shy but gracious, a scholar and a traditionalist. Now, presiding over the rosewood table, his gentle humour blossomed.

'Robert tells me,' he said to Venetia, 'that the day of the ghost is over. I understand, my dear young lady, that in the midst of your studies you have discovered time to be a ghost-hunter for the sole purpose, one feels, of providing they are out of date. Am I correct?'

She smiled and put aside a long swinging lock of black hair. Her teeth were white and even against the orange lipstick.

'Dear Mr Mackie,' she said, and you could tell she liked him and was being as well-mannered as she could, 'I've found no ghosts to hunt, as yet. But Robert tells me you have an apparition at Beeches.'

Cyril Mackie put his spoon slowly into the crème caramel. As he grew older he found he had much more time than when he was young.

'Aha!' he said, and complimented Mrs Welch on her cooking with a lift of a white eyebrow. '*Our* apparition has no appearance whatsoever. It is merely a distressed series of noises. We have good acoustics in the house and the sound carries quite well, from a small room on the first floor. You should have an opportunity of hearing it while you are with us. Our ghostly tenant finds the winter a sad season.'

Caroline had decided this evening to sit next to Robert. She could never make up her mind whether it was better to sit opposite and watch him, or sit

beside him and feel his presence. Mrs Welch had discovered a trace of powder just before dinner, and sent Caroline off to wash her face. So she shone like an apple while Venetia and the other girls glowed like peaches.

'I'm a shockingly factual person,' said Venetia, in her gay voice, with her nice little shade of deference to the Reverend Cyril. 'I shall think you're teasing me until I actually do hear it. What does it do? Clank its chains?'

'Gracious me, no!' said her host, and wiped his mouth on the damask napkin.

'Have you tried to exorcise it, sir?' asked Stephen.

'Has anyone investigated it, sir?'

'Someone must be hoaxing you, Mr Mackie, surely?'

'It's Rob, with a gramophone, Mr Mackie!'

'Can you record it on tape?'

'If your acoustics are so good,' said Venetia, 'it may very well be the wind in the chimney. Do you believe in ghosts, Mrs Welch?' she added, and turned prettily to the housekeeper.

'I believe in what I hear, Miss Johnson,' said Mrs Welch, 'and I have heard this noise for many years.'

The Reverend Cyril was trying to say something. They hushed each other and looked at him respectfully.

'I was about to answer *one* of the questions,' he said, and cleared his throat. 'I think it was Stephen who asked me if I had tried to exorcise the spirit. No – my bell, book and candle friend –' they all laughed politely '– I have done no such thing. Such an *uncivil* business. My attitude has been one of academic interest and *laissez-faire!* I have discovered some little history of the sound. I am something of a student in my retirement. Perhaps you will allow me to tell you

a little of it – over coffee?'

At this signal Mrs Welch caught the eye of each lady present, and rose. The decanter of brandy was mirrored in the surface of the dining table.

'Caroline,' said Mrs Welch, 'it is half past nine, dear!'

'Good night, everybody,' said Caroline.

She kissed her guardian on his bald spot, which sat pink and neat between his white wings of hair. She kissed Mrs Welch just by her dark grey eyebrow. She touched Robert on the cheek and he gave her a hug and a dab. She nodded slightly to the guests, and went quietly before them from the room.

'She's a dear little person, isn't she?' said Venetia.

Caroline ran up the stairs so that she should not hear any more, and missed a remark from her guardian. He measured the brandy into four glasses that squatted balloon-like on the rosewood surface.

'I am reminded constantly of her mother,' he said. 'Caroline possesses all the old-fashioned graces which one so rarely sees nowadays. She is thoughtful, unobtrusive and deeply affectionate. I am her great admirer.'

And he warmed his glass in the palm of his hand, raised it slightly, and sipped.

'Would any of you gentlemen care for a cigar?' he said courteously. 'I can recommend them.'

Over the fine white coffee cups, with their band of black and gold, Mrs Welch presided in dark blue velvet.

'What sort of noise does it make?' asked Venetia, but the housekeeper had sat through many similar dinner parties and was reticent.

'Mr Mackie has his own way of telling a story,' she said. 'It isn't for me to speak out of turn!'

And would say no more, until the gentlemen joined them. The Reverend Cyril was warm, fed and expansive. He took out a gold fob watch from his waistcoat pocket, and checked on the hour.

'A quarter after ten,' he said. 'May I interrupt your ritual, Mrs Welch, while our guests listen?'

She inclined her head, aware of every move. He beckoned them to the door and put a plump forefinger to his lips. The young people crowded around him, rapt and intent.

And into the twentieth century, into the reassurance of fire and candlelight and Fortnum and Mason's coffee, came a wail which set their scepticism aside. The sound caught at their nerves and played on them. Up and down and around came the sob and cry, the ebb and flow of sorrow, the uncomforted plaint. Then, silence.

He closed the door and ushered them into comfortable seats.

'It's a baby,' said Venetia. 'You didn't tell me it was a baby! Are you absolutely *sure* it's a ghost?'

'Yes, indeed,' said Cyril Mackie, smiling and accepting his coffee. 'Beeches is completely detached, and in any case we could hardly keep up a constant supply of hidden babies for nearly a century! That sound,' he said to their startled faces, 'is exactly ninety-eight years old. It comes from the small bedroom at the end of the corridor on the first floor. We keep it as a type of storeroom, now. And I assure you I have been in that room and heard the sound at my elbow. There is a set pattern of noise. One could say that the summer months never bring it. In the spring and autumn it is infrequent. But in winter, particularly in the coldest months, we can pretty well count upon it – can't we, Mrs Welch?'

'Yes, indeed,' said the housekeeper, and refilled

their cups.

'You will hear it again during the early hours,' said Cyril Mackie, 'but there is no need for alarm, my dear young ladies. It is simply a motherless sound. It does not walk or haunt or play the spectre. One could call it an unquiet spirit, crying for comfort.'

Mrs Welch opened a box of mint chocolates and passed them around. Cyril Mackie settled to his tale.

'Beeches is a rather nice example of early Victorian architecture. The family who built it were remotely connected to me. A branch line, as you may say. The Papa made his fortune in trade and thought to set up a little dynasty for himself. I have the family Bible somewhere . . .'

He looked about him vaguely, but this was pure theatre. The Bible was three yards behind a glass-fronted bookcase. Mrs Welch produced it, as a lawyer produces evidence for the benefit of the judge. Six young heads bent over the page, hypnotized.

In copper-plate, brown with age, was set down a family record. First the marriage, between Maria Jane Acton, spinster, and George Joseph Webley, bachelor. Church, time and minister were carefully noted. On the following page, ruled like a ledger, the children numbered one to nine.

No. 1. At three minutes after five in the morning of the Fourth of December, 1851, a son, Richard George Webley, by the Grace of God. Both well.

The children came at eighteen-month intervals until the last entry.

No. 9 At ten minutes to seven on the evening of the Twenty First of November, 1863, my dear wife and companion, Maria Jane Webley, was brought to bed of a daughter and died at a half after eight in spite of all our ministrations. The child, being immediately baptized Ann Maria, survived her mother by only five hours.

The Lord giveth and the Lord taketh away,
Blessed be the name of the Lord.

'George Webley sold the house and furniture and pretty well everything in it, to my grandfather,' said Cyril Mackie. 'He went as though he had been struck by lightning. He was an unassuming man, in spite of a sharp head for business, and he loved his wife too much for his own good. The eldest daughter, of course, took the family under her wing. She was younger than Caroline, but the same breed: full of heart and kindness. They did it in those days, you know. "Mothers" at eleven – hardly had time enough to be children themselves. The family did well in later life. George Webley never married again. When they were off his hands he died.'

'And is this the baby?' said Venetia, pointing to the last entry.

'That is what seems evident to me,' said Cyril Mackie. 'I have various old housekeeping books and letters and diaries which belonged to my mother and grandmother. I believe they, too, are somewhere about . . .'

He looked vaguely around him again, and Mrs Welch supplied more evidence from the bookcase. He turned the leaves of a notebook.

'The first instance was in the November of the following year,' he said. 'A housemaid heard the baby crying at her elbow as she placed a warming-pan in the bed. She ran out of the room in her terror and fell down a short flight of stairs, occasioning grievous injury to her right leg. Gracious! Quite a pandemonium it must have caused!'

He traced the history for a little longer and then took out his gold watch.

'You will excuse me, I beg,' he said. 'I never stay later than a quarter after eleven.'

'Oh but, Mr Mackie,' cried Venetia, jumping up, 'can I try to rid you of your ghost, please? I haven't had any opportunity of putting theory into practice, you see!'

'I will have no bell, book and candle business!' he said firmly.

'No, no, no,' said Venetia. 'I just want to try to photograph it, and put it on a tape-recorder!'

He chuckled and shook his head.

'You can try as much as you like,' he said, 'but I don't think you'll make a particle of difference, my dear young lady!'

'I think,' said Caroline to Mrs Welch, as she helped her to make the mince pies on Christmas Eve, 'that

Robert is going to marry Venetia.'

'What makes you think that?' said Mrs Welch. 'Don't put so much sugar on top, Caroline, it goes dark brown in the oven!'

'It's the way he looks at her,' said Caroline, 'and they've been hours in the storeroom, trying to catch the ghost.'

Mrs Welch raised her eyebrows and said nothing, rolling out pastry.

'It's still crying, too,' said Caroline.

'Well, of course it's crying,' said the housekeeper. 'It's an unquiet spirit, as Mr Mackie says. You don't get rid of an unquiet spirit by taking its photograph.'

'I hadn't thought of that,' said Caroline. 'Mrs Welch, do *you* think that Robert will marry Venetia?'

'He's got to marry sometime, I suppose,' said the housekeeper evasively. 'Don't put so much mince-meat in, Caroline, they'll boil over in the oven!'

'He *is* going to marry her,' said Caroline, and put down the small pastry top and left the kitchen.

Of course, she had known for years that it was hopeless to love Robert as much as she did. He was her brother, for one thing, which made it pretty certain that she was going to lose him. But he had been so many other things as well, since their parents had died eight years ago, that she had become twined up in him. She sat for a long time on the side of her bed, clutching her handkerchief and crying, and then she bathed her eyes and went downstairs to see out the rest of the evening.

She was awake at once, hearing the wail, and looked at the luminous hands and figures on her bedside clock. Nearly three in the morning. She turned over again, and shut her eyes. Venetia's camera and tape-recorder seemed to be cold things with which to comfort an unquiet spirit, and at this notion she was wide awake once more.

At the foot of her bed bulged a pillowcase full of parcels, but she noticed them only in passing. For the first time the cry occurred to her as belonging to something. It was not just a story to tell after dinner, nor a family ghost to be exhibited, nor an investigation case, it was a sound that needed comforting. She lay for a long time, trying to think of another idea, and then slid out of bed and put on her dressing gown. She picked up her pillow and eiderdown and her hot bottle and took them with her. The crying had stopped and she listened at the storeroom door to make quite certain that Venetia was not there with her ghost-hunting equipment, then she went inside and closed the door behind her.

The moon shone through the curtainless window, which was a help, and the small room was stacked with racks of apples. They smelled of September and Caroline sniffed at them, reassured. She made herself into a nice bundle on the floor and clutched her hot bottle, waiting.

The wail was all about her, echoing through the rows and rows of silver apples, lost in its own wilderness. But this time at least it would be answered. Caroline stretched out her arm, offering a little circle of warmth and sympathy to the desolate sound at her side. She wanted to make amends, to atone for nearly a century of neglect, to wonder what it must have thought of them all; and she fell asleep.

Mrs Welch woke her up, as near to worried as Caroline had ever seen her.

'You're a naughty girl on a Christmas morning,' said Mrs Welch. 'Thank goodness I'm an early riser or you'd have had the house by the ears. Come along and see your presents and I'll make you a cup of tea!'

My word! There's been more than enough of this ghost-hunting!'

The remembrance of the day before smote Caroline, and then faded. She felt unaccountably light-hearted, light-hearted enough to tell a fib to Mrs Welch. She put her arms around the housekeeper's neck.

'I was trying to catch the ghost,' she said, 'but it never came!'

At breakfast-time the air was full of excitement. Robert and Venetia pulled crackers, stolen from beneath the Christmas tree in the drawing-room, and threw the torn scraps of paper at each other afterwards . . . Everyone made a great fuss of Caroline, who was the youngest and therefore the likeliest candidate for a child's Christmas. She caught the housekeeper and the Reverend Cyril glancing at her once or twice and she knew that they were wondering if they should say something, or not. After a light lunch, for Cyril Mackie preferred to have his turkey in state in the evening, Caroline knocked on the door of his study.

He was asleep, mouth awry, a book open on his lap. Noiselessly she found a pen and paper, and wrote on it in her best hand.

Darling Uncle Cyril, Please don't worry about Robert and Venetia being engaged. I am very glad.
                        Love from your Caroline
She found Mrs Welch in the kitchen, supervising the washing-up.

'I know about Robert and Venetia,' she said, 'and I'm very pleased, really.'

Mrs Welch took a long sideways look at her, then was as brisk as ever.

'They plan to announce it this evening,' she said.

'Mr Mackie's got two bottles of champagne and you're to have a glass. Did you like your presents?'

'Yes, thank you,' said Caroline, and stuck out a finger to take up chestnut stuffing, illicitly.

'None of that!' said the housekeeper, quick as a lizard. 'And what on earth have you put on your eyebrows, for heaven's sake?'

Caroline went, sighing, to the bathroom to wash it off. Mrs Welch followed her, arms folded.

'What do you think about going away to school?' she asked casually.

Caroline recognized the oblique approach as an accomplished fact.

'When?' she asked

'For the summer term, in another four months, if you want to. Mr Mackie won't have you going under orders, so's to speak.'

'Whose idea was it, Mrs Welch?'

The housekeeper tapped her lips, thinking.

'It was mine,' she said, matter-of-fact and objective as always. 'I thought you were lonely. I thought it was time you had a bit of life. Stuck here from one end of the year to the next. No young company.'

Caroline dried her eyebrows, divided in her feelings on the subject.

'It'll be your turn, then, to bring a party of people home,' said Mrs Welch, 'won't it?'

'Like Robbie Mack?' said Caroline, and the idea burst over her.

For a moment she was filled with a desire to tell the housekeeper about the baby ghost, but she withheld it and hugged her hard instead.

'I'm not saying you won't be a bit strange at first, away from home,' said Mrs Welch, 'but you can always write me a line, and I'll do my best to put things in the right light for you.'

'Oh, I *love* you, Mrs Welch,' said Caroline. 'I love you, and the *whole world!*'

They stood round the silver Christmas tree, glasses in hand, and wished all happiness to Robert and Venetia. The champagne made Caroline's nose prick and she sneezed. They all laughed, and she laughed with them and Robert gave her a smacking great kiss and swung her up above his head.

'Caroline the Great will be our first guest, won't she?' he said to Venetia.

'You're taking everything away, then?' said the Reverend Cyril. 'Yourself and Venetia and Caroline, even, if Venetia has been successful, my noisy young friend upstairs – who seems to be very quiet this evening!'

'What will you do, sir, without a good ghost story for the dinner table?' said Stephen, ebullient.

Cyril Mackie raised his glass to Venetia.

'I shall first of all, with the aid of the necessary documents, tell the tale of the Webley ghost,' he said, mocking at himself. 'And then I shall tell another tale: the story of Robert bringing home a young lady who had already conquered *him* and was looking for *further* conquests!'

They were all very amiable and happy, talking of nothing. Mrs Welch caught Caroline's eyes.

'Good night, everybody,' said Caroline obediently.

She kissed her uncle on the top of his head, Mrs Welch on her dark cheek, Robert, and – after a second's hesitation – Venetia.

Upstairs, the blessed silence spread with such insistency that Caroline pushed open the door of the storeroom and went inside.

Racks of apples gleamed ghostly in the moonlight. Clouds sailed, remote and beautiful as ships passing that will never come to harbour. The window-frame slanted its shadow across the smooth bare boards. Nothing else. Caroline unfastened the window and rested her arm on the sill, sharing the peace and fulfillment.

A ghost, she reasoned, was only a human being without a body. One should not, as Cyril Mackie said, be uncivil to it. Like all unquiet spirits, whether alive or dead, it required only a little comforting.

THE WELL

W. W. Jacobs

wo men stood in the billiard-room of an old country house, talking. Play, which had been of a half-hearted nature, was over, and they sat in the open window, looking out over the park stretching away beneath them, conversing idly.

'You're time's nearly up, Jem,' said one at length, 'this time six weeks you'll be yawning out the honeymoon and cursing the man – woman I mean – who invented them.'

Jem Benson stretched his long limbs in the chair and grunted in dissent.

'I've never understood it,' continued Wilfred Carr, yawning. 'It's not in my line at all; I never had enough money for my own wants, let alone for two. Perhaps if I were as rich as you or Croesus I might regard it differently.'

There was just sufficient meaning in the latter part of the remark for his cousin to forbear to reply to it. He continued to gaze out of the window and to smoke slowly.

'Not being as rich as Croesus – or you,' resumed Carr, regarding him from beneath lowered lids, 'I paddle my own canoe down the stream of Time, and, tying it to my friends' doorposts, go in to eat their dinners.'

'Quite Venetian,' said Jem Benson, still looking out of the window. 'It's not a bad thing for you, Wilfred, that friends' doorposts, go in to eat their dinners.'

Carr grunted in his turn. 'Seriously though, Jem,' he said, slowly, 'you're a lucky fellow, a very lucky fellow. If there is a better girl above ground than Olive, I should like to see her.'

'Yes,' said the other, quietly.

'She's such an exceptional girl,' continued Carr, staring out of the window. 'She's so good and gentle. She thinks you are a bundle of all the virtues.'

He laughed frankly and joyously, but the other man did not join him.

'Strong sense of right and wrong, though,' continued Carr, musingly. 'Do you know, I believe that if she found out that you were not –'

'Not what?' demanded Benson, turning upon him fiercely. 'Not what?'

'Everything that you are,' returned his cousin, with a grin that belied his words, 'I believe she'd drop you.'

'Talk about something else,' said Benson, slowly; 'your pleasantries are not always in the best taste.'

Wilfred Carr rose and taking a cue from the rack, bent over the board and practised one or two favourite shots. 'The only other subject I can talk about just at present is my own financial affairs,' he said slowly, as he walked round the table.

'Talk about something else,' said Benson again, bluntly.

'And the two things are connected,' said Carr, and dropping his cue he sat on the table and eyed his cousin.

There was a long silence. Benson pitched the end

of his cigar out of the window, and leaning back closed his eyes.

'Do you follow me?' inquired Carr at length.

Benson opened his eyes and nodded at the window.

'Do you want to follow my cigar?' he demanded.

'I should prefer to depart by the usual way for your sake,' returned the other, unabashed. 'If I left by the window all sorts of questions would be asked, and you know what a talkative chap I am.'

'So long as you don't talk about my affairs,' returned the other, restraining himself by an obvious effort. You can talk yourself hoarse.'

'I'm in a mess,' said Carr, slowly, 'a devil of a mess. If I don't raise fifteen hundred by this day fortnight, I may be getting my board and lodging free.'

'Would that be any change?' questioned Benson.

'The quality would,' retorted the other. 'The address also would not be good. Seriously, Jem, will you let me have the fifteen hundred?'

'No,' said the other, simply.

Carr went white. 'It's to save me from ruin,' he said, thickly.

'I've helped you till I'm tired,' said Benson, turning and regarding him, 'and it is all to no good. If you've got into a mess, get out of it. You should not be so fond of giving autographs away.'

'It's foolish, I admit,' said Carr, deliberately. 'I won't do so any more. By the way, I've got some to sell. You needn't sneer. They're not my own.'

'Whose are they?' inquired the other.

'Yours.'

Benson got up from his chair and crossed over to him. 'What is this?' he asked, quietly. 'Blackmail?'

'Call it what you like,' said Carr. 'I've got some letters for sale, price fifteen hundred. And I know a man who would buy them at that price for the mere chance of getting Olive from you. I'll give you first offer.'

'If you have got any letters bearing my signature, you will be good enough to give them to me,' said Benson, very slowly.

'They're mine,' said Carr, lightly; 'given to me by the lady you wrote them to. I must say that they are not all in the best possible taste.'

His cousin reached forward suddenly, and catching him by the collar of his coat, pinned him down on the table.

'Give me those letters.'

'They're not here,' said Carr, struggling, 'I'm not a fool. Let me go, or I'll raise the price.'

The other man raised him from the table in his powerful hands, apparently with the intention of dashing his head against it. Then suddenly his hold relaxed as an astonished-looking maid-servant entered the room with letters. Carr sat up hastily.

'That's how it was done,' said Benson, for the girl's benefit as he took the letters.

'I don't wonder at the other man making him pay for it, then,' said Carr blandly.

'You will give me those letters,' said Benson, suggestively, as the girl left the room.

'At the price I mentioned, yes,' said Carr; 'but so sure as I am a living man, if you lay your clumsy hands on me again, I'll double it. Now, I'll leave you for a time while you think it over.'

He took a cigar from the box and lighting it carefully quitted the room. His cousin waited until the door had closed behind him, and then turning to the window sat there in a fit of fury as silent as it was terrible.

The air was fresh and sweet from the park, heavy

with the scent of new-mown grass. The fragrance of a cigar was now added to it, and glancing out he saw his cousin pacing slowly by. He rose and went to the door, and then, apparently altering his mind, he returned to the window and watched the figure of his cousin as it moved slowly away into the moonlight. Then he rose again, and, for a long time, the room was empty.

It was empty when Mrs Benson came in some time later to say goodnight to her son on her way to bed. She walked slowly round the table, and pausing at the window gazed from it in idle thought, until she saw the figure of her son advancing with rapid strides towards the house. He looked up at the window.

'Goodnight,' said she.

'Goodnight,' said Benson, in a deep voice.

'Where is Wilfred?'

'Oh, he has gone,' said Benson.

'Gone?'

'We had a few words; he was wanting money again, and I gave him a piece of my mind. I don't think we shall see him again.'

'Poor Wilfred!' sighed Mrs Benson. 'He is always in trouble of some sort. I hope that you were not too hard upon him.'

'No more than he deserved,' said her son, sternly. 'Goodnight.'

The well, which had long ago fallen into disuse, was almost hidden by the thick tangle of undergrowth which ran riot at that corner of the old park. It was partly covered by the shrunken half of a lid, above which a rusty windlass creaked in company with the music of the pines when the wind blew strongly. The full light of the sun never reached it, and the ground surrounding it was moist and green when other parts of the park were gaping with the heat.

Two people walking slowly round the park in the fragrant stillness of a summer evening strayed in the direction of the well.

'No use going through the wilderness, Olive,' said Benson, pausing on the outskirts of the pines and eyeing with some disfavour the gloom beyond.

'Best part of the park,' said the girl briskly; 'you know it's my favourite spot.'

'I know you're very fond of sitting on the coping,' said the man slowly, 'and I wish you wouldn't. One day you will lean back too far and fall in.'

'And make the acquaintance of Truth,' said Olive lightly. 'Come along.'

She ran from him and was lost in the shadow of the pines, the bracken crackling beneath her feet as she ran. Her companion followed slowly, and emerging from the gloom saw her poised daintily on the edge of the well with her feet hidden in the rank grass and nettles which surrounded it. She motioned her companion to take a seat by her side, and smiled softly as she felt a strong arm passed about her waist.

'I like this place,' said she, breaking a long silence, 'it is so dismal – so uncanny. Do you know I wouldn't dare to sit here alone, Jem. I should imagine that all sorts of dreadful things were hidden behind the bushes and trees, waiting to spring out on me. Ugh!'

'You'd better let me take you in,' said her companion tenderly; 'the well isn't always wholesome, especially in the hot weather. Let's make a move.'

The girl gave an obstinate little shake, and settled herself more securely on her seat.

'Smoke your cigar in peace,' she said quietly. 'I am settled here for a quiet talk. Has anything been heard of Wilfred yet?'

'Nothing.'

'Quite a dramatic disappearance, isn't it?' she continued. 'Another scrape, I suppose, and another letter for you in the same old strain; "Dear Jem, help me out." '

Jem Benson blew a cloud of fragrant smoke into the air, and holding his cigar between his teeth brushed away the ash from his coat sleeves.

'I wonder what he would have done without you,' said the girl, pressing his arm affectionately. 'Gone under long ago, I suppose. When we are married, Jem, I shall presume upon the relationship to lecture him. He is very wild, but he has his good points, poor fellow.'

'I never saw them,' said Benson, with startling bitterness. 'God knows I never saw them.'

'He is nobody's enemy but his own,' said the girl, startled by this outburst.

'You don't know much about him,' said the other,

sharply. 'He was not above blackmail; not above ruining the life of a friend to do himself a benefit. A loafer, a cur, and a liar!'

The girl looked up at him soberly but timidly and took his arm without a word, and they both sat silent while evening deepened into night and the beams of the moon, filtering through the branches, surrounded them with a silver network. Her head sank upon his shoulder, till suddenly with a sharp cry she sprang to her feet.

'What was that?' she cried breathlessly.

'What was what?' demanded Benson, springing up and clutching her fast by the arm.

She caught her breath and tried to laugh. 'You're hurting me, Jem.'

His hold relaxed.

'What is the matter?' he asked gently. 'What was it startled you?'

'I was startled,' she said, slowly, putting her hands on his shoulder. 'I suppose the words I used just now are ringing in my ears, but I fancied that somebody behind us whispered, *"Jem, help me out."* '

'Fancy,' repeated Benson, and his voice shook; 'but these fancies are not good for you. You – are frightened – at the dark and gloom of these trees. Let me take you back to the house.'

'No, I am not frightened,' said the girl, reseating herself, 'I should never be really frightened of anything when you were with me, Jem. I'm surprised at myself for being so silly.'

The man made no reply but stood, a strong, dark figure, a yard or two from the well, as though waiting for her to join him.

'Come and sit down, sir,' cried Olive, patting the brickwork with her small, white hand, 'one would think that you did not like my company.'

He obeyed slowly and took a seat by her side, drawing so hard at his cigar that the light of it shone upon his face at every breath. He passed his arm, firm and rigid as steel, behind her, with his hand resting on the brickwork, beyond.

'Are you warm enough?' he asked tenderly, as she made a little movement.

'Pretty fair,' she shivered; 'one oughtn't to be cold at this time of the year, but there's a cold, damp air comes up from the well.'

As she spoke a faint splash sounded from the depths below, and for her the second time that evening, she sprang from the well with a little cry of dismay.

'What is it now?' he asked in a fearful voice. He stood by her side and gazed at the well, as though half expecting to see the cause of her alarm emerge from it.

'Oh, my bracelet,' she cried in distress, 'my poor mother's bracelet. I've dropped it down the well.'

'Your bracelet!' repeated Benson, dully. 'Your bracelet? The diamond one?'

'The one that was my mother's,' said Olive. 'Oh, we can get it back surely. We must have the water drained off.'

'Your bracelet!' repeated Benson, stupidly.

'Jem,' said the girl in terrified tones, 'dear Jem, what is the matter?'

For the man she loved was standing regarding her with horror. The moon which touched it was not responsible for all the whiteness of the distorted face, and she shrank back in fear to the edge of the well. He saw her fear and by a mighty effort regained his composure and took her hand.

'Poor little girl,' he murmured, 'you frightened me. I was not looking when you cried, and I thought that you were slipping from my arms, down – down –'

His voice broke, and the girl throwing herself into his arms clung to him convulsively.

'There, there,' said Benson, fondly, 'don't cry, don't cry.'

'Tomorrow,' said Olive, half-laughing, half-crying, 'we will all come round the well with hook and line and fish for it. It will be quite a new sport.'

'No, we must try some other way,' said Benson. 'You shall have it back.'

'How?' asked the girl.

'You shall see,' said Benson. 'Tomorrow morning at latest you shall have it back. Till then promise me that you will not mention your loss to anyone. Promise.'

'I promise,' said Olive, wonderingly. 'But why not?'

'It is of great value, for one thing, and – But there – there are many reasons. For one thing it is my duty to get it for you.'

'Wouldn't you like to jump down for it?' she asked mischievously. 'Listen.'

She stooped for a stone and dropped it down.

'Fancy being where that is now,' she said, peering into the blackness; 'fancy going round and round like a mouse in a pail, clutching at the slimy sides, with the water filling your mouth, and looking up to the little patch of sky above.'

'You had better come in,' said Benson, very quickly. 'You are developing a taste for the morbid and horrible.'

The girl turned, and taking his arm walked slowly in the direction of the house; Mrs Benson, who was sitting in the porch, rose to receive them.

'You shouldn't have kept her out so long,' she said chidingly. 'Where have you been?'

'Sitting on the well,' said Olive, smiling, 'discussing our future.'

'I don't believe that place is healthy,' said Mrs Benson, emphatically. 'I really think it might be filled in, Jem.'

'All right,' said her son, slowly. 'Pity it wasn't filled in long ago.'

He took the chair vacated by his mother as she entered the house with Olive, and with his hands hanging limply over the sides sat in deep thought. After a time he rose, and going upstairs to a room which was set apart for sporting requisites selected a sea fishing line and some books and stole softly downstairs again. He walked swiftly across the park in the direction of the well, turning before he entered the shadow of the trees to look back at the lighted windows of the house. Then having arranged his line he sat on the edge of the well and cautiously lowered it.

He sat with his lips compressed, occasionally looking about him in a startled fashion, as though he half expected to see something peering at him from the belt of trees. Time after time he lowered his line until at length in pulling it up he heard a metallic tinkle against the side of the well.

He held his breath then, and forgetting his fears drew the line in inch by inch, so as not to lose its precious burden. His pulse beat rapidly, and his eyes were bright. As the line came slowly in he saw the catch hanging to the hook, and with a steady hand drew the last few feet in. Then he saw that instead of the bracelet he had hooked a bunch of keys.

With a faint cry he shook them from the hook into the water below, and stood breathing heavily. Not a sound broke the stillness of the night. He walked up and down a bit and stretched his great muscles; then he came back to the well and resumed his task.

For an hour or more the line was lowered without result. In his eagerness he forgot his fears, and with eyes bent down the well fished slowly and carefully. Twice the hook became entangled in something and was with difficulty released. It caught a third time, and all his efforts failed to free it. Then he dropped the line down the well, and with head bent walked towards the house.

He went first to the stables at the rear, and then retiring to his room for some time paced restlessly up and down. Then without removing his clothes he flung himself upon the bed and fell into a troubled sleep.

Long before anybody else was astir he arose and stole softly downstairs. The sunlight was stealing in at every crevice, and flashing in long streaks across the darkened rooms. The dining-room into which he looked struck chill and cheerless in the dark yellow light which came through the lowered blinds. He remembered that it had the same appearance when his father lay dead in the house; now, as then, everything seemed ghastly and unreal; the very chairs standing as their occupants had left them the night before seemed to be indulging in some dark communication of ideas.

Slowly and noiselessly he opened the hall door and passed into the fragrant air beyond. The sun was shining on the drenched grass and trees, and a slowly vanishing white mist rolled like smoke about the grounds. For a moment he stood, breathing deeply the sweet air of the morning, and then walked slowly in the direction of the stables.

The rusty creaking of a pump-handle and a spatter

of water upon the red-tiled courtyard showed that somebody else was astir, and a few steps farther he beheld a brawny, sandy-haired man gasping wildly under severe self-infliction at the pump.

'Everything ready, George?' he asked quietly.

'Yes, sir,' said the man, straightening up suddenly and touching his forehead. 'Bob's just finishing the arrangements inside. It's a lovely morning for a dip. The water in the well must be just icy.'

'Be as quick as you can,' said Benson, impatiently.

'Very good, sir,' said George, burnishing his face harshly with a very small towel which had been hanging up over the top of the pump. 'Hurry up, Bob.'

In answer to his summons a man appeared at the door of the stable with a coil of stout rope over his arm and a large metal candlestick in his hand.

'Just to try the air, sir,' said George, following his

master's glance, 'a well gets rather foul sometimes, but if a candle can live down it, a man can.'

His master nodded, and the man, hastily pulling up the neck of his shirt and thrusting his arms into his coat, followed him as he led the way slowly to the well.

'Beg pardon, sir,' said George, drawing up to his side, 'but you are not looking over and above well this morning. If you'll let me go down I'd enjoy the bath.'

'No, no,' said Benson, peremptorily.

'You ain't fit to go down, sir,' persisted his follower. 'I've never seen you look so before. Now if –'

'Mind your business,' said his master curtly.

George became silent and the three walked with swinging strides through the long wet grass to the well. Bob flung the rope on the ground and at a sign from his master handed him the candlestick.

'Here's the line for it, sir,' said Bob, fumbling in his pockets.

Benson took it from him and slowly tied it to the candlestick. Then he placed it on the edge of the well, and striking a match, lit the candle, and began slowly to lower it.

'Hold hard, sir,' said George, quickly, laying his hand on his arm, 'you must tilt it or the string'll burn through.'

Even as he spoke the string parted and the candlestick fell into the water below.

Benson swore quietly.

'I'll soon get another,' said George, starting up.

'Never mind, the well's all right,' said Benson.

'It won't take a moment, sir,' said the other over his shoulder.

'Are you master here, or am I?' said Benson

hoarsely.

George came back slowly, a glance at his master's face stopping the protest upon his tongue, and he stood by watching him sulkily as he sat on the well and removed his outer garments. Both men watched him curiously, as having completed his preparations he stood grim and silent with his hands by his sides.

'I wish you'd let me go, sir,' said George, plucking up courage to address him. 'You ain't fit to go, you've got a chill or something. I shouldn't wonder it's the typhoid. They've got it in the village bad.'

For a moment Benson looked at him angrily, then his gaze softened. 'Not this time, George,' he said, quietly. He took the looped end of the rope and placed it under his arms, and sitting down threw one leg over the side of the well.

'How are you going about it, sir?' queried George, laying hold of the rope and signing to Bob to do the same.

'I'll call out when I reach the water,' said Benson; 'then pay out three yards more quickly so that I can get to the bottom.'

'Very good, sir,' answered both.

Their master threw the other leg over the coping and sat motionless. His back was turned towards the men as he sat with his head bent, looking down the shaft. He sat for so long that George became uneasy.

'All right, sir?' he inquired.

'Yes,' said Benson, slowly. 'If I tug at the rope, George, pull up at once. Lower away.'

The rope passed steadily through their hands until a hollow cry from the darkness below and a faint splashing warned them that he had reached the water. They gave him three yards more and stood with relaxed grasp and strained ears, waiting.

'He's gone under,' said Bob in a low voice.

The other nodded, and moistening his huge palms took a firm grip of the rope.

Fully a minute passed, and the men began to exchange uneasy glances. Then a sudden tremendous jerk followed by a series of feebler ones nearly tore the rope from their grasp.

'Pull!' shouted George, placing one foot on the side and hauling desperately. 'Pull! pull! He's stuck fast; he's not coming; P–U–LL!'

In response to their terrific exertions the rope came slowly in, inch by inch, until at length a violent splashing was heard, and at the same moment a scream of unutterable horror came echoing up the shaft.

'What a weight he is!' panted Bob. 'He's stuck fast or something. Keep still, sir, for heaven's sake, keep still.'

For the taut rope was being jerked violently by the struggles of the weight at the end of it. Both men with grunts and sighs hauled it in foot by foot.

'All right, sir,' cried George, cheerfully.

He had one foot against the well, and was pulling manfully; the burden was nearing the top. A long pull and a strong pull, and the face of a dead man with mud in his eyes and nostrils came peering over the edge. Behind it was the ghastly face of his master; but this he saw too late, for with a great cry he let go his hold of the rope and stepped back. The suddenness overthrew his assistant, and the rope tore through his hands. There was a frightful splash.

'You fool!' stammered Bob, and ran to the well helplessly.

'Run!' cried George. 'Run for another line.'

He bent over the coping and called eagerly down as his assistant sped back to the stables shouting wildly. His voice re-echoed down the shaft but all else was silence.

CHILDREN ON THE BRIDGE

Kenneth Ireland

Mr Fulwood was delighted with the village in which he had bought a cottage for his retirement. He had always fancied living in such a pretty place, had dreamed of a village just like this during his whole working life, out of the hubbub and hurry of the town. Now that he had retired, his dream, he was sure, had come true.

Mr Fulwood was a bachelor, well used to managing by himself. With his pension from work, plus his State pension, he would be able to manage very nicely, and the cottage had come up for sale at just the right time. Not that the village was isolated – he would not have liked that – because it had a regular bus service into the nearest market town, and that was part of the attraction. He was now able to live in the countryside, yet within a bus ride of the conveniences of a town. Just the right sort of combination.

And the village really was pretty. It had a shallow river running through it with meadows on either side, at one point passing underneath a little bridge which carried the main road through the village; it had an ancient church with old houses clustered round it as if for protection; there was a scattering of farms; a real old-fashioned village inn; a general village shop and friendly people. What more could he want?

Even the children were friendly, far different from the preoccupied, surly ones he had encountered living in towns. He noticed some on his first morning out, down to the village shop. They were sitting on the low wall of the bridge as he passed, five of them he counted, all looking clean, fresh and bright.

'Good morning,' said the first of them.

'Good morning,' he responded cheerily, then they all called the same back to him again . . . not shouted after him, but just called a greeting.

On his way back from the shop they were still sitting there in a row, all about the same age it seemed to him, except that the tallest one who sat at the end, who had spoken to him first, was perhaps a year older or thereabouts.

'Got everything you wanted?' the nearest to him asked, noticing his carrier bag.

'Yes, thanks,' said Mr Fulwood, and smiled at all of them.

'Be seeing you,' he heard as he passed.

Every day he made a point of going to the shop for some small thing, at first because the short walk was good for him – the fact that he had retired was no excuse for just pottering around his cottage in his bedroom slippers, he had decided. But then he had another motive, which was to have the pleasure of seeing these delightful children.

They would either be sitting on the wall and swinging their legs, or they would be down by the river. Or if the day was warm, they would be playing in the river with their shoes and socks off. They were all boys, he noticed; not a girl among them. But that was understandable, he supposed, because at their age boys and girls tended to play separately. He knew that was how it was when he had been their age. Every time they saw him, they would either call out to him, or if they were down by the river they would turn and wave, and he would wave back. He began to enjoy their company.

'Come down and join us,' the tallest one called to Mr Fulwood one afternoon. They were down at the river-side.

'How do I get down?' he asked.

'Just climb over the fence at the side of the bridge, and then come down. It's easy.'

He had not climbed a fence for a good thirty years, but he found that this low wooden one presented no problem. He smiled to himself, at the thought of what his friends in the city would say if they could see him now, not only climbing over a fence obviously placed there to keep people out, but in his oldest clothes as well. In the city, just a few weeks before, he would never have dreamed of appearing in public in anything but a suit. This country life was just the thing, he was thinking, as he almost ran down the grass of the meadow to where these boys were waiting for him.

'This is Charlie,' said the tallest boy, introducing that one to him, 'and this is Trevor, and this is Mark, and this is Darren, and I'm Errol.'

'How do you do?' returned Mr Fulwood politely. 'I'm Mr Fulwood.'

'We know,' said Charlie. 'We know the names of everybody in the village.'

'Of course you would,' said Mr Fulwood. In such a small village, everyone would know everybody else. He was expecting to discover the names of most of the other people living in the village before long. He was learning every time he called into the village shop, because the shopkeeper always addressed the customers by name.

All the boys had their shoes and socks off.

'Do you want to come in with us?' asked Trevor.

'In where with you?' asked Mr Fulwood jovially.

'The water, of course,' said Errol. 'You can if you like. It's not very deep. There are only tiddlers in there, but you can catch one in your hands if you're careful. You only have to paddle.'

'Paddle? At my age?' Mr Fulwood was amused at the thought.

'Why not?' demanded Darren. He was the smallest, with a cheeky face. He was the one who had once asked if Mr Fulwood had everything that he wanted.

'All right,' said Mr Fulwood after a moment's hesitation. 'I will! Why not?'

He took his shoes and socks off, rolled his trousers up to the knee, and followed them into the water, which felt delightfully cool to his feet and ankles.

'We sometimes go right in,' confided Darren, 'but not when anyone's around. We've got no trunks, you see.'

'We've got no trunks when we decide to go right in,' corrected Errol. Mr Fulwood could see no reason for the correction.

'That's right. Not when we decide to go right in. You wouldn't want to join us then.'

'No, I think I'd better not then,' said Mr Fulwood hastily.

'Show you how to catch a tiddler,' said the one who had been called Charlie.

Mr Fulwood had a thoroughly enjoyable time trying to catch tiddlers. He didn't quite manage it, and once he almost fell full-length in the attempt, to be rescued immediately by two or three of the boys who seemed to be keeping a careful watch on him.

To be honest with himself, he did not see why these children should want to be friendly with an elderly man like himself. He had to admit that he would not have selected himself for company at their age. But perhaps it was part of their nature to be friendly, he decided. They recognized him as one who needed a few friends, no doubt, he having just moved in amongst strangers, and so were doing their bit to make him feel at home in the best way they knew. And very pleasant it was too, he also had to admit.

Then he looked at his watch.

'Good heavens,' he said, 'it's well past tea time and I ought to be going.'

'Aw, you don't have to,' said Trevor.

'Oh yes I do,' said Mr Fulwood. 'Um . . .' he looked around. 'How do I dry my feet?'

He had forgotten all about having to do that.

'We use our hankies,' said Errol.

'Good idea,' said Mr Fulwood, and sat on the grass, took out his handkerchief and dried himself properly before putting on his shoes and socks again.

'Come and join us – any time,' one of them called as he walked back up to the fence, climbed over and set off along the road for home.

'I will,' replied Mr Fulwood.

Every day when it was fine the children were there by the bridge over the river. It took a long time for him to realize something.

'Don't you go to school?' he asked suddenly one morning, when he was just sitting on the grass watching them play.

'Not now,' said Mark. He was the one who spoke least as a rule.

'Holidays, is it?'

'Sort of,' said Mark.

They were playing tig at the time, so at that point he had to run off again.

'Do you want to play tig, Mr Fulwood?' asked Charlie.

'At my age?' he laughed.

'Can if you want to. We enjoy having you with us.'

So he did play tig, and the next time he went down there he took along a tennis ball which he had bought in the village specially for the occasion and taught them how to play hot rice. It seemed they didn't know how to play that, but he remembered how from years ago, when he had been at school. It was surprising how quickly it all came back to him.

The road through the village was never very busy, but every now and then one or other of the villagers would walk past and look at Mr Fulwood curiously as he sat on the wall or played with the boys on the meadow, or waded about in the shallow river. They would never say anything to him when he was there. Probably they thought he was a rather strange old man to be playing with little kids at his age, but he didn't mind. He was happy.

One did say something to him once about it, actually. It was one of the really old men who lived in the village, hobbling along with the aid of a stick past his cottage as Mr Fulwood was just emerging from his gate.

'Morning, Mr Fulwood,' said the old man, then stopped.

'Good morning, Mr Cooper,' greeted the other breezily.

Mr Cooper, however, stood still, leaning on his stick, instead of walking on. 'I ought to tell you,' he said slowly, 'because many round here won't. You ought to keep away from that bridge.'

'Oh, that's all right, Mr Cooper, it's perfectly innocent,' replied Mr Fulwood.

'That may be,' said the old man solemnly, 'but you ought to take warning before it's too late.'

Then he hobbled on towards his own house further along the road, and would say no more. Indignantly Mr Fulwood set off towards the village, waving to the boys who were clearly expecting him to pass, and telling them that he would be back presently, after he had been to the shop.

Mrs Guffy, the shopkeeper, was for once alone in the shop when he entered. He was still rather disturbed at old man Cooper's comments about those innocent children. It had almost sounded as if he had no liking for them at all, and he couldn't understand such an attitude. He looked around the shop after he had made his small purchases, and his eyes lighted on some bags of boiled sweets.

'And I'll have a bag of those,' he added, 'and the boys can share them among themselves.'

'What boys?' asked Mrs Guffy sharply, looking up.

'Errol and Charlie and the other boys I see every time I come across the bridge,' he explained. 'Is there something wrong?' For Mrs Guffy's face was definitely registering almost horror of some kind.

'You've been with them?' she asked.

'Well – yes.'

'You've spoken to them?'

'I chat with them quite a lot,' he said. 'They seem to like me to join them.' He didn't like to say that he actually played games with them, but Mrs Guffy was already ahead of him.

'So that's why you bought that ball the other day,' she said.

'Why, yes.'

Mrs Guffy leaned forward over the counter earnestly. 'Mr Fulwood, don't you have anything more to do with them. Don't you go buying them sweets, nor balls, nor anything else. You just keep away from that bridge, for a long time. Look, I'll have Mr Guffy deliver what you want in the evenings, if you'd like, just so's you don't have to come across that bridge.'

Mr Fulwood was flabbergasted. 'But why?' he asked.

'Because otherwise they won't leave you alone until they've got what they want,' she said. 'You take care, Mr Fulwood.'

'I'm sure you're exaggerating,' he said, paid for his groceries and left, but not with a bag of sweets. Mrs Guffy simply wouldn't sell one to him.

After a day or so, he began to understand something of what she might have meant. He had been seeing these thoroughly nice boys twice a day, and at the end of that afternoon, as he left, one of them called after him: 'See you later, then, Mr Fulwood.' It was Errol who had called, he thought.

He had not realized that they had meant later that night. He was just watching the television when he heard them outside his back door.

'Mr Fulwood,' he heard a boy's voice call, and recognized it at once as Trevor's.

He went to the kitchen window and opened it. Outside they were all there, all five of them.

'Hello, Trevor. Hello,' he said to the others. 'What do you want? Is something wrong?'

'No, Mr Fulwood, we just wondered if you would like to join us.' That was Errol.

'What, now?'

'Yes.'

'No, I don't think so, not just now.'

But they just stood there, saying nothing.

'No, not just now,' he said again. 'I'll see you tomorrow, no doubt.'

They left, but twice again they came that night, calling him either at the front door or the back, and the last time was at just after half-past ten, just before he went to bed. He was upstairs in his bedroom at the time, so he opened the window and looked down.

'No, I'm going to bed,' he said firmly, 'where you should be going at this time of night. I'll see you tomorrow. Now go home, or your parents will be worried.'

He didn't like the gentle laughter which arose after that last remark, but closed the window anyway, and they went away. He decided that he had better have a quiet word with them in the morning. This sort of thing could get him a bad name with the neighbours,

if the calling had disturbed them. People went to bed early in the village, he knew that.

But the next day they all seemed so happy to have him with them that he had not the heart to tell them off. Instead, he merely mentioned casually that they should not make a noise which might annoy the neighbours at night, and they looked so contrite that he knew he would not have to speak to them about it again.

That afternoon he could not see them, for he had to pay a visit to the town on the bus in order to collect his money from the bank, and the bus did not take him over the bridge but in the opposite direction. When he returned home, he found the vicar waiting on his doorstep. That was a surprise.

'Come in, vicar,' he said, unlocking his door. 'Shall I make you a cup of tea?'

'No thank you, Mr Fulwood,' said the vicar. For some reason he looked decidedly uncomfortable, and once he had sat down came straight to the point.

'I understand you have been seeing some children on the bridge,' he said, without any preamble.

'Well, everyone knows that,' said Mr Fulwood. 'What's wrong with that? You're the third person to mention them to me, with some kind of warning.'

'Errol, Charlie, Trevor, Mark, Darren – is that right?'

'Well, yes, they are their names. Five of them. But what's wrong?'

'They are evil, Mr Fulwood, that's what is wrong.' The vicar was so serious that Mr Fulwood was startled.

'I just can't believe it. They're so – well, such a joy to be with. They're so lively and well-behaved with it, too. There's no evil there, I assure you.'

'So you intend to go on seeing them, and talking to

them, and have them ask you to join them, eh?'

'I don't see why not.'

'When they call tonight, then, I beg you not to open your door to them.'

Now how on earth did the vicar know that they had called at his house? Somebody must have told him. He could not possibly have heard their voices calling him from as far away as the vicarage.

'And then, *not having opened your door to them tonight*, I want you to go over the bridge as usual in the morning, but this time count them.'

'Count them?' Mr Fulwood was astonished. There were five of them, he knew that for certain.

'You might find that tomorrow there will be six. If you find that there are six, come away at once and see me. At once, Mr Fulwood,' the vicar emphasized.

Then he left Mr Fulwood's cottage without further explanation. He simply would not give one. All the vicar would say was that if he would not believe that the boys were evil, if tomorrow there were six of them he might be able to convince him.

That night, they did come again. It was almost as if they were circling the house, and they were calling to him plaintively: 'Mr Fulwood, won't you join us? . . . Mr Fulwood, do come and join us . . . We like your company, Mr Fulwood, so why won't you join us?'

It was somewhat unnerving, and at the same time like ignoring good friends, but nevertheless he remained inside the house with the curtains drawn, not moving until the voices faded and they had gone. They made no attempt to try the door, he noticed. Of course, they were too polite for that, he knew. In the morning he would pretend that he had fallen asleep and had not heard them.

That was his intention as he set out for his regular walk across the bridge and into the main part of the village, but when he reached the bridge they were all seated on the low parapet swinging their legs and with such smiling, welcoming looks on their faces that he thought that he would just walk by. Then he happened to notice that there was an extra boy sitting with them, and almost stopped in his tracks. Mr Fulwood had seen him somewhere around before, but for the moment could not quite place him. Then he noticed several marks scratched deep into the solid stonework of the bridge.

'A lorry ran into it yesterday afternoon while you were out of the village,' Errol explained, seeing where he was gazing.

'Well, I can't stop just now. I'm in a bit of a hurry.' And he walked on quickly into the village but instead of going to the shop went straight to the vicarage and rang the doorbell. The vicar answered the door almost at once.

'There were six?' he asked.

'Yes,' said Mr Fulwood. 'Now tell me how you knew that there would be.'

'Come inside,' advised the vicar. Then: 'Describe the sixth boy, would you?'

'Well, he had dark hair, was pleasant-looking – as all of them are – he was wearing a blue jumper, jeans, some sort of sandals on his feet. Oh, and he had a little scar on the tip of his nose. Not much to say about him, really.'

'Tommy Stokes,' snapped the vicar. His tone was almost vicious. 'You are in great danger, Mr Fulwood. I would advise you to leave the village as soon as possible, today if you can, but tomorrow at the latest. Go away – anywhere. Take a holiday, if you like, but stay away for two or three weeks. But whatever you decide to do, don't mention anything about it to any of these boys.'

'Now look here, vicar,' said Mr Fulwood, 'you don't take me for a complete fool, do you? Then perhaps you'll be so kind as to tell me just what is going on!'

The vicar seemed quite calm now. 'Those delightful children all attended the school here in the village at one time, but they were not delightful at all. It was only discovered what they had been up to when a body was dug up in the middle of the night from the churchyard, and in the morning found draped across the altar of the church, together with other indications that some kind of black magic rite had taken place.

'From then on, things went from bad to worse. Of course, it was discovered who had been involved, but they were held then to be too young to be prosecuted, so nothing was done. Then there was no stopping them. Their last of many activities was to persuade the driver of a van to stop outside the village on some pretext, and give them a lift. On the way, just before the bridge, they attempted to kill the driver. It seems that they hoped to force him to drive straight at the bridge, while at the same time escaping themselves, just in time. Unfortunately for

them, the rear doors of the van jammed and they were unable to escape.

'The van crashed, right enough, but the survivor was the driver, not the boys. He was able to tell the story – not all the details, you realise, but enough for everyone to know exactly what had been planned. He was permanently crippled, and now has an artificial leg. You've met him – Mr Cooper.'

'But –' Mr Fulwood was slowly beginning to realize the implication of what the vicar was telling him.

'Yes, Mr Fulwood, I'm afraid so. We know that they are there. We, who have lived in this village for years, know how to avoid them. Your great problem is – you have *seen* them.'

The vicar must have been having him on. It must be some sort of joke! Mr Cooper must be getting on for eighty. What was he doing driving a van?

'It was about thirty years ago. Now do you see? Tommy Stokes also saw them. He was killed in an accident with a lorry yesterday afternoon. He had told his mother only the day before that they had asked him to join them. People who saw the accident said the driver simply seemed to lose all control, and by the time he had recovered, Tommy Stokes was

dead under his wheels. The funeral is on Friday. Now do you see, Mr Fulwood? Tommy Stokes was also new to the village, so he didn't know any better, either.

'Pack your things and go at once, Mr Fulwood. Next week, I intend to exorcise that bridge, in hopes that we can at last get rid of them. Come back to your cottage in two or three weeks, and then you should be safe.'

Mr Fulwood almost ran out of the vicarage and back towards his own home. He could hear the vicar calling after him: 'Whatever you do, don't stop on the way!'

He didn't need the advice. By now he was convinced. When he came within sight of the bridge he broke into a gentle trot, then calmed down and determined to walk past as if nothing was wrong.

The children were no longer sitting on the bridge, but standing across the road. They were not exactly in a line as if to prevent his passing, but they were *there*.

'Can't stop now,' he said as cheerily as he could.

The new boy was standing right in front of him. 'Come on, Tommy,' he said, not stopping. 'I'll talk to you later.'

He realized his mistake at once.

'He knows!' shouted Errol.

Now they did form a line like a barricade, to prevent him from moving further. He began to push through them, in a panic. He got through, then began to run. The boys began to run after him. To the house, he was thinking. They don't come into the house. Once there I'll be safe. He ran faster, and looked behind to see if they were still chasing, but they were not any longer. In fact, they were no longer there at all.

The car coming round the bend in the road hit him almost before he saw it, and then they were all round him again, looking at him as he lay on the ground. Charlie helped him to his feet, and Trevor and Mark took hold of his hands to help steady him. They were never evil children, he was convinced of that now. That vicar ought to be in a lunatic asylum. He had heard of vicars like that, who went mad.

The driver of the car was climbing, rather shaken, out of his vehicle and coming towards him. There seemed to be something lying on the ground in front of the car, and the driver stopped and bent down over it. Then Mr Fulwood realized that it was his own body lying there. He shook himself free of the helping hands and stared at the boys wildly.

'You were too late, Mr Fulwood,' said Errol calmly, with a most attractive smile on his face. 'Now you've joined us properly.'

THE WOODSEAVES GHOSTS

Catherine Gleason

he only snag about staying at Woodseaves,' said David Mitchell, 'is the library.'

'Yes,' his sister Sally agreed. 'Do you remember how frightened we were when we first saw it? We were sure there were ghosts about, hiding in the corners!'

'I'm not so sure that it isn't haunted,' said David, with an air of mystery. Sally was two years younger than him and she usually believed every word he said.

Her eyes grew big as saucers. 'You don't really think so, do you? What do you mean?'

'Well, you remember reading in that local history book about the boy and girl who were supposed to have disappeared in there? It was exactly a hundred and fifty years ago that they vanished. So they might turn up again.' His voice dropped to a whisper. 'One of these Fridays, when we're in the library doing our school work, the air will turn cold and the door will slowly start to open . . . creeeak . . .'

'Oh, stop it!' cried Sally. 'You're making me shiver!'

'And then,' continued David in a creepy voice,

'something dressed in a long white gown will glide in . . . and – grab you!'

Sally gave a little shriek and covered her ears, while David burst out laughing. 'Only teasing you, silly.'

'You are horrid, David,' said Sally, giggling in spite of herself. 'You're just trying to scare me because we have to do some work in there tonight. Well, I'm not afraid!'

'Neither am I, really,' said David. 'Come on, slowcoach, we're going to be late for tea. Where's Max?'

The heavy golden labrador lumbered up to them and they made their way back through Woodseaves Park to the Hall.

Great-Uncle Timothy Mitchell owned the Hall, and lived there with his housekeeper Martha and, of course, Max. Like his house, Uncle Tim was rather Victorian and rambling, but David and Sally were very fond of him and loved spending their summer holidays at Woodseaves.

This was the first year their parents hadn't been with them, because their father had taken a job in America that summer and Mrs Mitchell had gone with him.

Martha was very neat and motherly and precise, and she had been Uncle Tim's housekeeper for donkey's years. She was only ever strict about one thing, and that was their doing an hour or so's work in the library on the subjects they hadn't done very well in at school. This, as David said, was the one snag about staying there, but then it wasn't much of a disadvantage, considering all the other things that Woodseaves had to offer. Midway between the town and the country, everything was within easy reach, from riding stables to a cinema.

'What did you do with yourselves today, children?'
Uncle Tim asked them over tea.

He and Martha had always called David and Sally
'children', and David suspected that they always
would, no matter how big they grew.

'We fed the goldfish in the pond, and then David
climbed a tree and nearly fell in the stream, and then
the Smithson twins took us over to South Meadow to
see the lambs,' said Sally. 'They're getting quite big
now.'

'What, the Smithsons?' The old man looked startled.

'No, Uncle, the lambs,' giggled Sally. Uncle Tim
was so vague at times.

'I was reading about ghosts in a local history book,'
said David. 'Do you know there are supposed to be
two of them here at Woodseaves?'

'That's right.' Uncle Tim chuckled. 'A brother and
his young sister, about the same ages as you two.
They were said to have been murdered by their
wicked step-mother, or some such nonsense.'

'Why?' demanded Sally, who had more than her
fair share of curiosity.

'The stepmother wanted Woodseaves for her own
sons, and the other two were in the way, I suppose.'

'Really, Mr Timothy, you shouldn't be filling the
children's heads with such stories,' said Martha
reprovingly. 'We've lived here more years than we
care to remember, and we've never seen any ghosts.'

'That's probably because there aren't any such
things,' suggested David.

'Exactly. Ghosts don't exist.'

Sally wasn't so sure.

'There. Finished at last.' David threw down his
pen thankfully and stretched, pushing back his chair.
It had taken him nearly an hour to plough through

his French exercise.

'Well, hang on a minute,' said Sally crossly. She was struggling with a maths problem.

'O.K.' Idly, David glanced around the library. All the other rooms at Woodseaves were light and modern-furnished, but even in the height of summer the library looked gloomy, damp and ancient. Hundreds of old books, some very valuable, were shut into the dark, glass-fronted cases against the walls, and the firelight cast weird dancing reflections on to them.

'Nearly finished now,' said Sally, one hand stroking Max, who shifted restlessly beside her. The big dog always seemed uneasy in the library. Suddenly he jumped up and ran over to the window, barking furiously.

'Max! Come and lie down,' ordered David.

Max slunk reluctantly away from the window, tail down, to the opposite corner of the room. He made a funny sort of noise, halfway between a whine and a howl, and scratched at the door, looking back at them with piteous eyes. David opened the door for him and the dog shot out of the room as if something was after him.

'That's strange,' said Sally. 'Maybe he saw a cat outside?'

'I don't think so.' David peered out of the window at the dusky night. 'Perhaps he –'

Suddenly all the lights went out, and, except for the glowing fire, the room was plunged into darkness. Sally gave a little scream.

'It's all right,' said David calmly, sitting by the fire. 'The lights have fused, that's all. I expect Uncle will have them on again in a minute.'

'I hope so,' said Sally. 'It's rather scary in here with – oh!' She broke off with a cry of astonishment.

David swung round and followed her gaze to the window. His mouth dropped open in sheer amazement as he saw two strange figures, hand in hand, passing straight through the window into the library!

David and Sally clutched each other in terror. But the figures did not look terrifying; they were a boy and a girl, dressed in old-fashioned clothes.

'Do not be afraid. We are not come to harm you,' said the boy.

'What . . . who are you?' asked David in a quavery voice.

'My name is Lucretia, and this is my brother, Comus,' said the girl, with a slight bow.

'Er . . . how do you do,' said Sally, a little unsteadily.

'May we sit down? We have been wandering for many years, and we are somewhat fatigued,' the boy introduced as Comus said politely.

Sally rubbed her eyes and stared. The ghostly figures sat quite calmly in the two leather armchairs opposite and, through their outlines, she could see the chairs quite clearly.

'David,' she whispered, 'do you think we're dreaming?'

'No,' said David excitedly. 'I think they're the two who were murdered here – don't you remember Uncle Tim's story? – and they've come back to the – to the scene of the crime,' he finished lamely.

'Indeed, you are right,' said Lucretia in her sweet, light voice. 'Our lives were cut short very much against our wills, one hundred and fifty years ago this very evening.'

David nodded. 'Uncle Tim told us about you.'

Sally wriggled in her chair. Half of her was scared enough to dash straight out of the library, shrieking for Uncle Tim, but the other half was full of inquisitiveness. After a short struggle, curiosity won.

'How did it happen?' she asked finally. 'Your being murdered, I mean.'

'Yes, how?' David, too, was still a little frightened, and spoke rather more aggressively than he intended. 'Our uncle said you were killed by a wicked stepmother, like people in a fairy tale, and it all sounds very fishy to me.'

Comus and Lucretia looked at each other in a puzzled way.

'It had nothing to do with fish,' said Comus. 'It was poisoned veal, as I remember.'

'That is right,' said Lucretia. 'You see, our mama died when we were a little younger than you are now, and Papa married again, almost straight away. He was a very good man, and he wished to secure a second mother for us.'

'But his second wife, our stepmother, was a most wicked woman,' continued Comus. 'She was widowed too, so she married Papa in order to provide for her own baby sons. Really, you know, she did not care a rap for him or for us. She only wanted her children to have Woodseaves, and we stood in the way, because Woodseaves would have been ours when we were old enough to inherit it.'

'At first, we did not realize the extent of her malice,' Lucretia resumed, 'though we did consider it odd when she told us that deadly nightshade was good for us, and to eat as much as we could if ever we found it growing wild.'

'And she was always suggesting that we go for a bathe in the deepest part of the river,' added Comus. 'After we told her repeatedly that we could not swim!'

'Yet she was always very pleasant to us,' Lucretia

sighed. 'We hardly believed she could wish us any harm. Then, one evening, she served us a dish of veal here in the library where we were reading, and that was that.'

'You were poisoned?' asked Sally, round-eyed.

'Yes – we fell asleep, and awoke like this.' Comus held up a transparent hand.

'And what happened to your stepmother?' asked David.

'She died of the consumption shortly afterwards, and confessed on her deathbed to having poisoned us. Her sons did not long survive her, and so it was all a wasted effort, really.' Lucretia looked sadly into the fire.

'What a shame!' cried the warm-hearted Sally indignantly. 'I think it's terrible that you should have had such short, unhappy lives. Honestly, David, we don't know how lucky we are, do we?'

'You're right,' agreed David seriously. 'We do have marvellous parents, when you come to think about it. None of this wicked-stepmother stuff at all.'

Comus and Lucretia exchanged glances of something like envy.

'Your parents, then, are very kind?' asked Comus wistfully.

'Oh, yes! They couldn't be nicer,' said Sally eagerly. 'I wish we could help you,' she added to their phantom visitors.

'Perhaps you can,' said Comus at once. 'For we have come here tonight to offer you a proposition.'

'What kind of proposition?' David asked suspiciously.

'We wish to change places with you,' said Comus simply. 'If you are agreeable to our suggestion, we would become you, and you would become –'

'Ghosts?' said Sally faintly.

'Er . . . I don't think we'd like that very much, thank you,' said David. 'Anyway, why us?'

'Why, because you are here at Woodseaves,' said Lucretia. 'And you are about the same ages as we are. Being a ghost can be great fun, you know,' she added mischievously. 'Watch me!'

And before their eyes, she vanished. David and Sally watched breathlessly as a heavy vase rose into the air, apparently by itself, and flew across the room. 'Catch!' came a gleeful cry from nowhere, and David had to go into a quick rugby dive to save the vase before it hit the ground.

There was a tinkling laugh and Lucretia appeared again. 'There! You see? Some very naughty ghosts do that sort of thing all the time.'

'I don't think we'd want to drift about chucking vases around, actually,' said Sally, as David rubbed his bruised elbows.

'Oh, dear!' sighed Lucretia.

'Perhaps you would prefer to reside in the celestial regions?' suggested Comus.

'What do you mean?' asked Sally. 'You do talk oddly, you know!'

'Everybody talked like that a hundred and fifty years ago,' David reminded her.

'Precisely. I beg your pardon,' Comus apologized to Sally. 'I meant to say, how about Heaven?'

And just then, the door opened.

'Are you still in here, children?' Martha fiddled with the light switch. 'Have both of the light bulbs gone? What a nuisance!' She came into the firelit room, glancing straight at the ghostly figures in the armchairs.

'We were just talking, Martha,' said Sally.

'Well, don't stay too long, dears. Bed in half an hour, you know.'

'Why didn't Martha see you?' asked David, as soon as she had gone.

'We did not wish her to,' said Comus.

'What was that you said about Heaven?' Sally demanded impatiently.

'My brother wondered if you would care to go there,' said Lucretia carelessly.

'Have you really been to Heaven? I don't believe it!' said David.

'Indeed we have,' said Lucretia, with indignation. 'We might have stayed there, too, but that we kept on hankering after life on earth, and THEY do not like it if you are half-hearted about Heaven. And so we came back. Won't you change places with us, please?' she asked imploringly. 'THEY wouldn't mind, you know.'

David and Sally did not ask who THEY were; they rather thought they knew already.

'Well, really, I don't think . . .' began David doubtfully, but Sally was overcome with curiosity and cut in with:

'What's it really like in Heaven? Do tell us all about it.'

'Oh, it is a wonderful place, of course, but much

depends on whereabouts you go. There are many different sections,' explained Comus.

'How do you mean?' Sally was puzzled. Heaven was Heaven, wasn't it?

'Well,' said Lucretia, 'there is one part where all the soldiers go who have been killed in battle. They feast and drink all the time, and have their wounds bandaged. I found it monotonous – dull, you know,' she added, wrinkling her nose and tossing back her light brown ringlets. 'All of their conversation concerns war and battles. It is messy too, with all that blood and iodine.'

'Valhalla!' cried David excitedly. 'I've heard about that at school – it's the Heaven of the Vikings. Do all the Chinese Kung Fu fighters who get beaten go there as well?'

Comus looked puzzled. 'I have never heard of this Kung Fu,' he confessed. 'The Eastern people generally seem to go to Nirvana, where they do nothing but sit and think all the time. They call it meditation. Now that really is dull.'

'The Mount Olympus one is quite pleasant,' said Lucretia doubtfully. 'If you like hatching plots and chasing fauns through forests, that is. I believe they

have a few unicorns and winged horses there, too.'

'Really? Winged horses?' Sally was thrilled. She was pony-mad.

'Yes. And there is ordinary Heaven as well, where you walk on clouds and wear haloes,' said Comus. 'A great many Royal Air Force pilots seem to end up there. I think they really mean to go to Valhalla, but they cannot resist the wings, you see.'

'It also helps if you play a musical instrument,' added Lucretia. 'Won't you change places with us? I am sure you would like it very much.'

'How could you do that?' asked David curiously.

'Oh! That is very simple,' said Comus. 'We hold your hands for a second, and concentrate very hard and our minds would change places with yours. You see? It is extremely easy.'

'Well – I'm really very sorry,' said David, 'but I'm afraid we can't.'

'No,' said Sally regretfully. 'It's our parents, you see. They would miss us terribly.'

'Ah, but they would never know,' argued Comus. 'After all, we would look exactly the same as you. It's just that we should have swapped minds. Within a few weeks we could learn to talk as you do, and then nobody at all would be able to tell the difference.'

'I'm afraid it's impossible,' said David slowly.

There was a sad little pause. Comus looked very downcast, and Lucretia dabbed her eyes with a transparent lace handkerchief. Sally thought longingly about unicorns and winged horses, and David tried very hard not to think of Valhalla.

'Well!' Comus said finally. 'Then there is nothing more to be said. We had better be going.'

'I'm sorry we couldn't help,' said Sally, 'and it's been simply marvellous talking to you.'

'It has been our pleasure,' said Comus and Lucretia

politely. 'We wish you goodnight.' And they put out their hands in farewell.

'Goodbye,' said Sally and David, and without thinking they shook hands with the ghostly pair.

'Now then, children!' Martha pushed open the library door. 'It really is getting late. Oh, good, the lights are working again. I've cooked you some fish fingers for a suppertime snack – come along to the kitchen before they get cold.' And she bustled out again.

They looked at each other and smiled.

'What on earth can fishes' fingers look like, Sister? Evidently a new variety of fish has been discovered.'

'Indeed; when we were here last, fish did not even have hands, let alone fingers. Let us go and try them!'

Hand in hand, they walked out of the library to find the kitchen.

THE VIOLET CAR

E. Nesbit

o you know the downs – the wide windy spaces, the rounded shoulders of the hills leaned against the sky, the hollows where farms and homesteads nestle sheltered, with trees round them pressed close and tight as a carnation in a button-hole?

On long summer days it is good to lie on the downs, between short turf and pale, clear sky, to smell the wild thyme, and hear the tiny tinkle of the sheep-bells and the song of the skylark. But on winter evenings when the wind is waking up to its work, spitting rain in your eyes, beating the poor, naked trees and shaking the dusk across the hills like a gray pall, then it is better to be by a warm fireside, in one of the farms that lie lonely where shelter is, and oppose their windows glowing with candlelight and firelight to the deepening darkness, as faith holds up its love-lamp in the night of sin and sorrow that is life.

I am unaccustomed to literary effort, and I feel that I shall not say that what I have to say, or that it will convince you, unless I say it very plainly. I thought I could adorn my story with pleasant words, prettily arranged. But as I pause to think of what really happened, I see that the plainest words will be the best. I do not know how to weave a plot, nor how to embroider it. It is best not to try. These things happened. I have no skill to add to what happened; nor is any adding of mine needed.

I am a nurse – and I was sent for to go to Charlestown – a mental case. It was November and the fog was thick in London, so that my cab went at a foot's pace, so I missed the train by which I should have gone. I sent a telegram to Charlestown, and waited in the dismal waiting room at London Bridge. The time was passed for me by a little child. Its mother, a widow, seemed too crushed to be able to respond to its quick questionings. She answered briefly, and not, as it seemed, to the child's satisfaction. The child itself presently seemed to perceive that its mother was not, so to speak, available. It leaned back on the wide, dusty seat and yawned. I caught its eye, and smiled. It would not smile, but it looked. I took out of my bag a silk purse, bright with beads and steel tassels, and turned it over and over. Presently, the child slid along the seat and said, 'Let me.' After that all was easy. The mother sat with eyes closed. When I rose to go, she opened them and thanked me. The child, clinging, kissed me. Later, I saw them get into a first class carriage in my train. My ticket was a third class one.

I expected, of course, that there would be a conveyance of some sort to meet me at the station, but there was nothing. Nor was there a cab or a fly to be seen. It was by this time nearly dark, and the wind was driving the rain almost horizontally along the unfrequented road that lay beyond the door of the station. I looked out, forlorn and perplexed

'Haven't you engaged a carriage?' It was the widow lady who spoke.

I explained.

'My motor will be here directly,' she said, 'you'll let me drive you? Where is it you are going?'

'Charlestown,' I said, and as I said it, I was aware of a very odd change in her face. A faint change, but quite unmistakable.

'Why do you look like that?' I asked her bluntly. And, of course, she said, 'Like what?'

'There's nothing wrong with the house?' I said, for that, I found, was what I had taken that faint change to signify; and I was very young, and one has heard tales. 'No reason why I shouldn't go there, I mean?'

'No – oh no –' she glanced out through the rain, and I knew as well as though she had told me that there was a reason why *she* should not wish to go there.

'Don't trouble,' I said, 'it's very kind of you but it's probably out of your way and . . .'

'Oh, but I'll take you – of *course* I'll take you,' she said, and the child said, 'Mother, here comes the car.'

And come it did, though neither of us heard it till the child had spoken. I know nothing of motor cars, and I don't know the names of any of the parts of them. This was like a brougham – only you got in at the back, as you do in a waggonette; the seats were in the corners, and when the door was shut there was a little seat that pulled up, and the child sat on it between us. And it moved like magic, or like a dream of a train.

We drove quickly through the dark. I could hear the wind screaming, and the wild dashing of the rain against the windows, even through the whirring of the machinery. One could see nothing of the country, only the black night, and the shafts of light from the lamps in front.

After, as it seemed, a very long time, the chauffeur

got down and opened a gate. We went through it, and after that the road was very much rougher. We were quite silent in the car, and the child had fallen asleep.

We stopped, and the car stood pulsating, as though it were out of breath, while the chauffeur hauled down my box. It was so dark that I could not see the shape of the house, only the lights in the downstairs windows, and the low-walled front garden faintly revealed by their light and the light of the motor lamps. Yet I felt that it was a fair-sized house, that it was surrounded by big trees, and that there was a pond or river close by. In daylight next day I found that all this was so. I have never been able to tell how I knew it that first night, in the dark, but I did know it. Perhaps there was something in the way the rain fell on the trees and on the water. I don't know.

The chauffeur took my box up a stone path, whereon I got out, and said my goodbyes and thanks.

'Don't wait, please, don't,' I said. 'I'm all right now. Thank you a thousand times!'

The car, however, stood pulsating till I had reached the doorstep, then it caught its breath, as it were, throbbed more loudly, turned, and went.

And still the door had not opened. I felt for the knocker, and rapped smartly. Inside the door I was sure I heard whispering. The car light was fast diminishing to a little distant star, and its panting sounded now hardly at all. When it ceased to sound at all, the place was quiet as death. The lights glowed redly from curtained windows, but there was no other sign of life. I wished I had not been in such a hurry to part from my escort, from human companionship, and from the great, solid, competent presence of the motor car.

I knocked again, and this time I followed the knock by a shout.

'Hullo!' I cried. 'Let me in. I'm the nurse!'

There was a pause, such a pause as would allow time for whisperers to exchange glances on the other side of the door.

Then a bolt ground back, a key turned, and the doorway framed no longer cold, wet wood, but light and welcoming warmth – and faces.

'Come in, oh, come in,' said a voice, a woman's voice, and the voice of a man said: 'We didn't know there was anyone there.'

And I had shaken the very door with my knockings!

I went in, blinking at the light, and the man called a servant, and between them they carried my box upstairs.

The woman took my arm and led me into a low, square room, pleasant, homely, and comfortable, with solid mid-Victorian comfort – the kind that expressed itself in rep and mahogany. In the lamplight I turned to look at her. She was small and thin, her hair, her face, and her hands were of the same tone of greyish yellow.

'Mrs Eldridge?' I asked.

'Yes,' said she, very softly. 'Oh! I am so glad you've come. I hope you won't be dull here. I hope you'll stay. I hope I shall be able to make you comfortable.'

She had a gentle, urgent way of speaking that was very winning.

'I'm sure I shall be very comfortable,' I said; 'but it's I that am to take care of you. Have you been ill long?'

'It's not me that's ill, really,' she said, 'It's him –'

Now, it was Mr Robert Eldrige who had written to engage me to attend on his wife, who was, he said, slightly deranged.

'I see,' said I. One must never contradict them; it only aggravates their disorder.

'The reason . . .' she was beginning, when his foot sounded on the stairs, and she fluttered off to get candles and hot water.

He came in and shut the door – a fair bearded, elderly man, quite ordinary.

'You'll take care of her,' he said. 'I don't want her to get talking to people. She fancies things.'

'What form do the illusions take?' I asked, prosaically.

'She thinks I'm mad,' he said, with a short laugh.

'It's a very usual form. Is that all?'

'It's about enough. And she can't hear things that I can hear, see things that I can see, and she can't smell things. By the way, you didn't see or hear anything of a motor as you came up, did you?'

'I came up *in* a motor car,' I said shortly. 'You never sent to meet me, and a lady gave me a lift.' I was going to explain about my missing the earlier train, when I found that he was not listening to me. He was watching the door. When his wife came in, with a steaming jug in one hand and a flat candlestick in the other, he went towards her, and whispered eagerly. The only words I caught were: 'She came in a real motor.'

Apparently, to these simple people a motor was as great a novelty as to me. My telegraph, by the way, was delivered next morning.

They were very kind to me; they treated me as an honoured guest. When the rain stopped, as it did late the next day, and I was able to go out, I found that Charlestown was a farm, a large farm, but even to my inexperienced eyes it seemed neglected and unprosperous. There was absolutely nothing for me to

do but to follow Mrs Eldridge, helping her where I could in her household duties, and to sit with her while she sewed in the homely parlour. When I had been in the house a few days, I began to put together the little things that I had noticed singly, and the life at the farm seemed suddenly to come into focus, as strange surroundings do after a while.

I found that I had noticed that Mr and Mrs Eldridge were very fond of each other, and that it was a fondness, and their way of showing it was a way that told that they had known sorrow, and had borne it together. That she showed no sign of mental derangement, save in the persistent belief of hers that *he* was deranged. That the morning found them fairly cheerful; that after the early dinner they seemed to grow more and more depressed; that after the 'early cup of tea' – that is just as dusk was falling – they always went for a walk together. That they never asked me to join them in this walk, and that it always took the same direction – across the downs towards the sea. That they always returned from this walk pale and dejected; that she sometimes cried afterwards alone in their bedroom, while he was shut up in the little room they called the office, where he did his accounts, and paid his men's wages, and where his hunting-crops and guns were kept. After supper, which was early, they always made an effort to be cheerful. I knew that this effort was for my sake, and I knew that each of them thought it was good for the other to make it.

Just as I had known before they showed it to me that Charlestown was surrounded by big trees and had a great pond beside it, so I knew, and in as inexplicable a way, that with these two fear lived. It looked at me out of their eyes. And I knew, too, that this fear was not her fear. I had not been two days in the place before I found that I was beginning to be fond of them both. They were so kind, so gentle, so ordinary, so homely – the kind of people who ought not to have known the name of fear – the kind of people to whom all honest, simple joys should have come by right, and no sorrows but such as come to us all, the death of old friends, and the slow changes of advancing years.

They seemed to belong to the land – to the downs, and the copses, and the old pastures, and the lessening cornfields. I found myself wishing that I, too, belonged to these, that I had been born a farmer's daughter. All the stress and struggle of cram and exam, of school, and college, and hospital, seemed so loud and futile, compared with these open secrets of the down life. And I felt this the more, as more and more I felt that I must leave it all – that there was, honestly, no work for me here such as for good or ill I had been trained to do.

'I ought not to stay,' I said to her one afternoon, as we stood at the open door. It was February now, and the snowdrops were thick in tufts beside the flagged path. 'You are quite well.'

'I am,' she said.

'You are quite well, both of you,' I said. 'I oughtn't to be taking your money and doing nothing for it.'

'You're doing everything,' she said, 'you don't know how much you're doing.'

'We had a daughter of our own once,' she added vaguely, and then, after a very long pause, she said very quietly and distinctly:

'He has never been the same since.'

'How not the same?' I asked, turning my face up to the thin February sunshine.

She tapped her wrinkled, yellow-grey forehead, as country people do.

'Not right here,' she said.

'How?' I asked. 'Dear Mrs Eldridge, tell me; perhaps I could help somehow.'

Her voice was so sane, so sweet. It had come to this with me, that I did know which of those two was the one who needed my help.

'He sees things that no one else sees, and hears things no one else hears, and smells things that you can't smell if you're standing there beside him.'

I remembered with a sudden smile his words to me on the evening of my arrival:

'She can't see, or hear, or smell.'

And once more I wondered to which of the two I owed my service.

'Have you any idea why?' I asked. She caught at my arm.

'It was after our Bessie died,' she said – 'the very day she was buried. The motor that killed her – they said it was an accident – it was on the Brighton Road. It was a violet colour. They go into mourning for queens with violet, don't they?' she added; 'and my Bessie, she was a queen. So the motor was violet. That was all right, wasn't it?'

I told myself now that I saw that the woman was not normal, and I saw why. It was grief that had turned her brain. There must have been some change in my look though I ought to have known better, for she said suddenly, 'No I'll not tell you any more.'

And then he came out. He never left me alone with her for very long. Nor did she ever leave him for very long alone with me.

I did not intend to spy upon them, though I am not sure that my position as nurse to one mentally afflicted would not have justified such spying. But I did not spy. It was chance. I had been to the village to get some blue sewing silk for a blouse I was making, and there was a royal sunset which tempted me to prolong my walk. That was how I found myself on the high downs where they slope to the broken edge of England – the sheer, white cliffs against which the English Channel beats for ever. The furze was in flower, and the skylarks were singing, and my thoughts were with my own life, my own hopes and dreams. So I found that I had struck a road, without knowing when I had struck it. I followed it towards the sea, and quite soon it ceased to be a road, and merged in the pathless turf as a stream sometimes disappears in sand. There was nothing but turf and furze bushes, the song of the skylarks, and beyond the slope that ended at the cliff's edge, the booming of the sea. I turned back, following the road, which defined itself again a few yards back, and presently sank to a lane, deep-banked and bordered with brown hedge stuff. It was there that I came upon them in the dusk. And I heard their voices before I saw them, and before it was possible for them to see me. It was her voice that I heard first.

'No, no, no, no, no,' it said.

'I tell you yes,' that was his voice; 'there – can't you hear it, that panting sound – right away – away? It must be at the very edge of the cliff.'

'There's nothing, dearie,' she said, 'indeed there's nothing.'

'You're deaf – and blind – stand back I tell you, it's close upon us.'

I came round the corner of the lane then, and as I came, I saw him catch her arm and throw her against the hedge – violently, as though the danger he feared were indeed close upon them. I stopped behind the turn of the hedge and stepped back. They had not seen me. Her eyes were on his face, and they held a world of pity, love, agony – his face was set in a mask of terror, and his eyes moved quickly as though they followed down the lane the swift passage of something – something that neither she nor I could see. Next moment he was cowering, pressing his body into the hedge – his face hidden in his hands, and his whole body trembling so that I could see it, even from where I was a dozen yards away, through the light screen of the overgrown hedge.

'And the smell of it!' he said, 'do you mean to tell me you can't smell it?'

She had her arms round him.

'Come home, dearie,' she said. 'Come home! It's all your fancy – come home with your old wife that loves you.'

They went home.

Next day I asked her to come to my room to look at the new blue blouse. When I had shown it to her I told her what I had seen and heard yesterday in the lane.

'And now I know,' I said, 'which of you it is that wants care.'

To my amazement she said very eagerly, 'Which?'

'Why, he – of course,' I told her, 'there was nothing there.'

She sat down in the chintz-covered armchair by the window, and broke into wild weeping. I stood by her and soothed her as well as I could.

'It's a comfort to know,' she said at last, 'I haven't known what to believe. Many a time, lately, I've wondered whether after all it could be me that was mad, like he said. And there was nothing there? There always *was* nothing there – and it's on him the judgment, not on me. On him. Well, that's something to be thankful for.'

So her tears, I told myself, had been more of relief at her own escape. I looked at her with distaste, and forgot that I had been fond of her. So that her next words cut me like little knives.

'It's bad enough for him as it is,' she said – 'but it's nothing to what it would be for him, if I was really to go off my head and him left to think he'd brought it on me. You see, now I can look after him the same as I've always done. It's only once in the day it comes over him. He couldn't bear it, if it was all the time – like it'll be for me now. It's much better it should be him – I'm better able to bear it than he is.'

I kissed her then and put my arms round her, and said, 'Tell me what it is that frightens him so – and it's every day, you say?'

'Yes – ever since. I'll tell you. It's a sort of comfort to speak out. It was a violet-coloured car that killed our Bessie. You know our girl that I've told you about. And it's a violet-coloured car that he thinks he sees – every day up there in the lane. And he says he hears it, and that he smells the smell of the machinery – the stuff they put in it – you know.'

'Petrol?'

'Yes, and you can *see* he hears it, and you can *see* he sees it. It haunts him, as if it was a ghost. You see, it was he that picked her up after the violet car went over her. It was that that turned him. I only saw her as he carried her in, in his arms – and then he'd covered her face. But he saw her just as they'd left her, lying in the dust . . . you could see the place on the road where it happened for days and days.'

'Didn't they come back?'

'Oh yes . . . they came back. But Bessie didn't come back. But there was a judgment on them. The very night of the funeral, that violet car went over the cliff – dashed to pieces – every soul in it. That was the man's widow that drove you home the first night.'

'I wonder she uses a car after that,' I said. I wanted something commonplace to say.

'Oh,' said Mrs Eldridge, 'it's all what you're used to. We don't stop walking because our girl was killed on the road. Motoring comes as natural to them as walking to us. There's my old man calling – poor old dear. He wants me to go out with him.'

She went, all in a hurry, and in her hurry slipped on the stairs and twisted her ankle. It all happened in a minute and it was a bad sprain.

When I had bound it up, and she was on the sofa, she looked at him, standing as if he were undecided, staring out of the window with his cap in his hand. And she looked at me.

'Mr Eldridge mustn't miss his walk,' she said. 'You go with him, my dear. A breath of air will do you good.'

So I went, understanding as well as though he had told me, that he did not want me with him, and that he was afraid to go alone, and that he yet had to go.

We went up the lane in silence. At that corner he stopped suddenly, caught my arm, and dragged me back. His eyes following something that I could not see. Then he exhaled a held breath, and said, 'I thought I heard a motor coming.' He had found it hard to control his terror, and saw beads of sweat on his forehead and temples. Then we went back to the house.

The sprain was a bad one. Mrs Eldridge had to rest, and again next day it was I who went with him to the corner of the lane.

This time he could not, or did not try to, conceal what he felt. 'There – listen!' he said. Surely you can hear it?'

I heard nothing.

'Stand back,' he cried shrilly, suddenly, and we stood back close against the hedge.

Again the eyes followed something invisible to me, and again the held breath exhaled.

'It will kill me one of these days,' he said, 'and I don't know that I care how soon – if it wasn't for her.'

'Tell me,' I said, full of that importance, that conscious competence, that one feels in the presence of other people's troubles. He looked at me.

'I will tell you, by God,' he said. 'I couldn't tell *her*. Young lady, I've gone so far as wishing myself a Roman, for the sake of a priest to tell it to. But I can tell *you*, without losing my soul more than it's lost already. Did you ever hear tell of a violet car that got smashed up – went over the cliff?'

'Yes,' I said. 'Yes.'

'The man that killed my girl was new to the place. And he hadn't any eyes – or ears – or he'd have known me, seeing we'd been face to face at the inquest. And you'd have thought he'd have stayed at home that one day, with the blinds drawn down. But not he. He was swirling and swivelling all about the country in his cursed violet car, the very time we were burying her. And at dusk – there was a mist coming up – he comes up behind me on this very lane, and I stood back, and he pulls up, and he calls out, with his damned lights full in my face:

"Can you tell me the way to Hexham, my man?" says he.

'I'd have liked to show him the way to hell. And that was the way for me, not him. I don't know how I came to do it. I didn't mean to do it. I didn't think I was going to – and before I knew anything, I'd said it. "Straight ahead," I said; "keep straight ahead." Then the motor-thing panted, chuckled, and he was off. I ran after him to try to stop him – but what's the use of running after these motor-devils? And he kept straight on. And every day since then, every dear day, the car comes by, the violet car that nobody can see but me – and it keeps straight on.'

'You ought to go away,' I said, speaking as I had been trained to speak. 'You fancy these things. You probably fancied the whole thing. I don't suppose you ever *did* tell the violet car to go straight ahead. I expect it was all imagination, and the shock of your poor daughter's death. You ought to go right away.'

'I can't,' he said earnestly. 'If I did, someone else would see the car. You see, somebody *has* to see it every day as long as I live. If it wasn't me, it would be someone else. And I'm the only person who *deserves* to see it. I wouldn't like any one else to see it – it's too horrible. *It's* much more horrible than you think,' he added slowly.

I asked him, walking beside him down the quiet lane, what it was that was so horrible about the violet car. I think I quite expected him to say that it was splashed with his daughter's blood . . . What he did say was, 'It's too horrible to tell you,' and he shuddered.

I was young then, and youth always thinks it can move mountains. I persuaded myself that I could cure him of his delusion by attacking – not the main fort – that is always, to begin with, impregnable, but one, so to speak, of the outworks. I set myself to persuade him not to go to that corner in the lane, at that hour in the afternoon.

'But if I don't, someone else will see it.'

'There'll be nobody there *to* see it,' I said briskly.

'Someone will be there. Mark my words, someone will be there – and then they'll know.'

'Then I'll be the someone,' I said. 'Come – you stay at home with your wife, and *I'll* go – and if I see it I'll promise to tell you, and if I don't – well, then I will be able to go away with a clear conscience.'

'A clear conscience,' he repeated.

I argued with him in every moment when it was possible to catch him alone. I put all my will and all my energy into my persuasions. Suddenly, like a door that you've been trying to open, and that has resisted every key till the last one, he gave way. Yes – I should go to the lane. And he would not go.

I went.

Being, as I said before, a novice in the writing of stories, I perhaps haven't made you understand that it was quite hard for me to go – that I felt myself at once a coward and a heroine. This business of an imaginary motor that only one poor old farmer could see, probably appears to you quite commonplace and ordinary. It was not so with me. You see, the idea of this thing had dominated my life for weeks and months, had dominated it even before I knew the nature of the domination. It was this that was the fear that I had known with these two people, the fear that shared their bed and board, that lay down and rose up with them. The old man's fear of this and his fear of his fear. And the old man was terribly convincing. When one talked with him, it was quite difficult to believe that he was mad, and that there wasn't, and couldn't be, a mysteriously horrible motor that was visible to him, and invisible to other people. And when he said that, if he were not in the lane, someone else would see it – it was easy to say 'Nonsense,' but to think 'Nonsense' was not so easy, and to *feel* 'Nonsense' quite oddly difficult.

I walked up and down the lane in the dusk, wishing not to wonder what might be the hidden horror in the violet car. I would not let blood into my thoughts. I was not going to be fooled by thought transference, or any of those transcendental follies. I was not going to be hypnotized into seeing things.

I walked up the lane – I had promised him to stand near that corner for five minutes, and I stood there in the deepening dusk, looking up towards the downs and the sea. There were pale stars. Everything was very still. Five minutes is a long time. I held my watch in my hand. Four – four and a half – four and three-quarters. Five. I turned instantly. And then I saw that *he* had followed me – he was standing a dozen yards away – and his face was turned from me. It was turned towards a motor car that shot up the lane – it came very swiftly, and before it came to where he was, I knew that it was very horrible. I crushed myself back into the crackling bare hedge, as I should have done to leave room for the passage of a real car – though I knew that this one was not real. It looked real – but I knew it was not.

As it neared him, he started back, then suddenly he cried out. I heard him. 'No, no, no, no – no more, no more,' was what he cried, with that he flung

himself down on the road in front of the car, and its great tyres passed over him. Then the car shot past me and I saw what the full horror of it was. There was no blood – that was not the horror. The colour of it was, as she had said, violet.

I got to him and got his head up. He was dead. I was quite calm and collected now, and felt that to be so was extremely creditable to me. I went to a cottage where a labourer was having tea – he got some men and a hurdle.

When I had told his wife, the first intelligible thing she said was: 'It's better for him. Whatever he did he's paid for now –' So it looks as though she had known – or guessed – more than he thought.

I stayed with her till her death. She did not live long.

You think perhaps that the old man was knocked down and killed by a real motor, which happened to come that way of all ways, at that hour of all hours, and happened to be, of all colours, violet. Well, a real motor leaves its mark on you where it kills you, doesn't it? But when I lifted up that old man's head from the road, there was no mark on him, no blood, no broken bones, his hair was not disordered, nor his dress. I tell you there was not even a speck of mud on him, except where he had touched the road in falling. There were no tyre-marks in the mud.

The motor car that killed him came and went like a shadow. As he threw himself down, it swerved a little so that both its wheels should go over him.

He died, the doctor said, of heart-failure. I am the only person to know that he was killed by a violet car, which, having killed him, went noiselessly away towards the sea. And that car was empty – there was no one in it. It was just a violet car that moved along the lanes swiftly and silently, and was empty.

THE WOMAN IN THE GREEN DRESS

Joyce Marsh

lison Temple stood at her kitchen sink washing up. It was always the first chore of her day, and with the ease of long practice she flicked her cloth around the cups and across the saucers and plates. It was not a job that required much concentration and only half her mind was on what she was doing, for the 8.03 from Sutton Street was due at any moment and she was listening for the first sounds of its approach.

Below her and less than fifty yards away the shining bright ribbon of the track snaked away towards Caitham Junction a quarter of a mile or so down the line. Most of her neighbours in the flats complained of the noise, dirt and inconvenience of living so close to the railway line – but not Alison. Even at the age of thirty-six she had never outgrown her childhood pleasure in watching the trains go by.

The huge engines of her childhood days, belching clouds of smoke and steam, had given way to sleek, gleaming diesel locomotives which throbbed with speed as they hurtled over their unending miles of track. There was a tremendous excitement in their monstrous power, but her romantic imagination was, and always had been, most deeply stirred by the passengers briefly glimpsed as they sped on to distant places where she herself had never been. These anonymous travellers fascinated her; without past or future, their lives touched her own for one split second and then were gone, as if they had never existed until that moment and never would again.

She could hear the train now, and by leaning forward and slightly craning her neck she could just see the yellow-nosed diesel coming down the line. It was travelling quite fast, but as usual it began to slow down before reaching her flat and by the time the engine was opposite her window she could see into the carriage quite plainly. The train was not crowded and she gave each carriage a long, concentrated stare. Suddenly out of the corner of her eye she caught a flash of bright green, and she turned her head sharply.

In the second to last carriage a woman wearing a vivid green dress was leaning far out of the window. Her arms waved frantically and her head was strained far back as if someone inside the carriage were pulling at her hair. The train rolled on toward Alison's house, slowly, calmly, and the woman in the green dress struggled desperately against some unseen force.

The carriage came abreast of the window and Alison was looking straight into the woman's eyes. The desperate, urgent fear in those eyes flung across the dividing space until Alison felt it herself in the tightening of the muscles of her throat and the fearful pounding of her heart.

Then with a violent effort the woman in green jerked her head free and throwing herself even further forward she began to struggle with the

outside handle of the carriage door. In a brief
moment she had succeeded and the door swung
open. The horrified watcher at the window saw her
gather herself to leap out, but the unseen person in
the carriage violently pulled her back, and she was
gone from sight. The train passed by the window
and only by pressing her face against the glass was
Alison able to see the open swinging door – and
then, just before it passed out of sight, an arm, a
man's arm, reach out to pull it shut.

Alison stood quite still, her face remaining pressed
against the cool glass. Every detail of the scene she
had just witnessed was sharply etched on her mind.
In a few seconds, the first numbing shock had
passed, and as the last carriage finally disappeared
from view she moved swiftly. She had to warn the
station ahead; the train would pull into Caitham
Junction in a few minutes and could pull out again
before anyone knew of the woman's desperate
plight.

The rainbow soap suds still glistened on her hands
as Alison fumbled urgently with the telephone
directories. The dampness on them made it difficult
to turn the pages and with a quick impatient gesture
she flung the books on the floor. The police – dial 999
– that was the quickest way.

'Which service do you require?'

'The police and please, this is very urgent.'

In less than a minute she was connected to the
police. Forcing herself to be very calm, for a wild,
incoherent rush of words would only delay the
necessary action, Alison gave her name and address
first and then, speaking clearly and carefully, briefly
explained her call. And that, for the moment, was all
she could do for the woman in the green dress.

It was little more than an hour later when the

police constable called on her. He was a courteous young man but inclined to be slow and ponderous as he checked the details of her statement. Alison answered carefully, controlling her impatience as best she could until at last she could bear it no longer.

'What about the woman? Were you in time – is she all right?'

The disjointed questions were hurled at him urgently. He looked at her curiously and for what seemed a particularly long time before he answered.

'Madam, there was no trace of a woman answering your description, neither was there any sign of a disturbance in any of the carriages.'

Alison stared at him unbelievingly. Then she said, 'But there must have been, perhaps you searched the wrong train.'

'No, Madam, it was the right train and she was not there. Possibly the lady had left the station by the time we got there.'

'She couldn't have done, she wouldn't have just walked away, not after what I saw happening to her. I tell you that woman was being violently attacked, I saw it all from the window.'

Alison waved her hand vaguely in the direction of the kitchen window. The policeman made no move to check her view-point but he answered politely.

'I am not doubting your word, but perhaps the lady was not in such desperate straits as you imagined. Distance can distort things sometimes, you know.'

There was an air of finality about the way he turned back to his note book which precluded any further discussion. Meekly Alison told her story again, carefully remembering all the details, and after a few more formalities, the policeman left.

For the rest of the day Alison was haunted both by

the incident and the woman herself. There had been a curious familiarity about her as if she had seen her somewhere before, perhaps briefly and in some forgotten place. At times Alison closed her eyes and allowed the whole scene to parade before her inner mind whilst she sought to remember every detail of those distorted features.

She wandered restlessly from room to room, unable to concentrate on her work. The flat had suddenly become lonely and desolate and she longed for the moment when her husband would come home.

At first Ted had shown a mild interest, but as soon as he heard of the police theory his interest almost visibly died away.

'Well, that's it then, isn't it? I should forget about it if I were you, it's not your pigeon anyway.'

He turned on the television. His wife knew from past experience that it would be useless to attempt further conversation, and for the rest of the evening she managed to push the incident out of her thoughts.

It was not until the next morning as she was washing up and the sound of the 8.03 first struck her ear, that she thought again of the woman in the green dress. She paused in her work to lean forward as the engine passed the window. Then she saw it – a flash of green and there it was again, the same woman in the same dress leaning from the same carriage window.

In a daze of frightening unreality she watched yesterday's scene re-enacted in precisely the same detail. The vivid green dress shimmered in the misty morning air, the head strained backwards and the arms pawed frantically in a desperate effort to escape the unseen terror inside the carriage. In exactly the same place the door swung open and the woman was pulled back out of sight. Alison watched the unfolding of the drama until the arm reached out to shut the door and then, in a surge of panic, she ran to the telephone.

Gone today were the careful precise sentences with which she had told her story the day before. Now she rambled and shouted into the telephone, desperately compelling her listener to action and somehow she made herself understood. Afterwards she sat very still, trying to think, trying to calm herself. Nothing made any sense. Only one thing was certain – she had seen it, and what she had seen was real and terrifying.

The police did not call this time; they telephoned. It was a conversation which left her trembling with bewilderment, fear and humiliation. Miserably she had heard the cold, curt voice of authority informing her that once again the train had been needlessly delayed and searched, and nothing unusual had been found. There had been a steely edge to the police officer's voice as he had gone on to suggest that the whole incident was probably a foolish hoax.

'It might be as well if you kept away from the window when that train passes. Unless . . .' His voice trailed off on the word.

'Unless what?' Alison had asked sharply.

'Well . . . never mind. Speak to your husband about it and please, try not to see any more women in green dresses.'

Ted was even less kind. 'For heaven's sake Alison, wrap it up. You heard what the police said, it's just a joke some kids are playing on you and it serves you right, you're always peering into the carriages; people don't like being spied on. Tomorrow you just keep away from the window.'

Ted was not the most patient of men and she could not tell him that the woman was not young, at least not young enough to play practical jokes. The tears smarted in her eyes as she turned to the evening washing up. The tightly drawn curtains were only a flimsy barrier between herself and the suddenly sinister railway.

The next morning she tried very hard not to watch the 8.03 from Sutton Street. She sat rigidly at the kitchen table, afraid of her own window. The first tiny singing rattle heralded the approach of the train. It came closer, the roaring power of the engine throbbed into the room, it was bursting inside her head. The bright green dress seemed to jump and dance before her eyes.

It was unbearable. She flung herself to the window and looked straight down into the tormented eyes of the woman in green. Peering intently, Alison tried to conquer distance so that she could see every detail of the woman's face. There was still something hauntingly familiar about it, but she didn't know what.

Every detail of the macabre charade was played out exactly as it had happened before and exactly as she was to see it again a dozen times or more in the following days.

Alison became accustomed to her fantasy. She no longer tried to avoid the window when the 8.03 went by. Morning after morning, with a curious detached interest, she watched the tormented struggles of the woman in green, paying such close attention that almost daily she saw tiny new details which she had not noticed before.

But she never spoke to anyone of the woman in the green dress again; not to Ted and certainly not to the police. Instead she thought about her for hours at a time and one strange, confused thought ran through her mind over and over again. For one brief moment every morning her life became inextricably entwined with the strange woman on the train; but if that moment was not now . . . when was it?

Then the idea came to her quite suddenly. She would take a bus to Sutton Street and board the 8.03 and if the woman existed then Alison would find her on the train.

It had not been easy to find an excuse for leaving the flat so early and Ted had looked surprised. But she had managed it, and now she was at Sutton Street, waiting with mounting excitement for the train. She hastily looked over the other passengers on the platform; the woman was certainly not amongst them. The train rolled slowly into the station; a few people ran through the barrier at the last moment, but all these were men.

Alison was unable to resist her urge to start at the very front of the train and look in at every carriage window. Her heart beat faster as she approached the second to last carriage; with a slight shock of disappointment she saw that it contained only one passenger – a man. The very last carriage was occupied by noisy Cubs and Scouts off on an outing.

The whistle blew as the train was about to pull out. There was no time for hesitation. Impulsively she opened the door of the second to last carriage and jumped in.

The man, not old but not young either, sat hunched in his corner. He neither stirred nor looked up as Alison sat down opposite him. Suddenly she wished that she had not chosen this carriage. There was something frighteningly disconcerting in his total disregard of her and in his utter stillness. She even leant a little towards him to stare into his face, and still he did not move. She tore her eyes away

from him and the next moment flung a hand over her
mouth to stifle a little involuntary scream.

There had been no sound of the door opening and
the train was already moving quite fast, yet now,
suddenly and inexplicably, there was someone else
in the carriage. On the opposite seat, in the far corner
was a woman – a woman in a bright green dress, its
glowing, exotic colour seeming iridescent against
the dingy red seats. The woman was wearing a hat
now, a black hat with a large soft brim curving
gracefully down over her face. Everything she wore
seemed bright and new, from the black hat, the shiny
shoes and the vivid dress to the black leather
handbag on her arm. At least, everything was new
except her gloves. They were old and so worn that
several of the finger tips showed pinkly through the
holes.

The woman seemed very conscious of these gloves

for she was staring down at them with fixed attention, her body as rigid and unmoving as the man in the corner seat.

The bright dress seemed curiously static; it was not even rising and falling as she breathed. Then Alison realized that they were not breathing: the man and the woman both sat absolutely still, like photographs projected onto the thick dusty black-cloth of the carriage.

Since her first startled gesture Alison herself had not moved and she now felt as if she had been rendered as motionless as her two companions. She tried to speak but it was an immense effort and the words oozed slowly from her lips.

'Who . . . are . . . you?'

Neither of them gave any sign that they had seen or heard her. She turned her head. Through the window Alison saw the wood yard which was only a mile or so from her home. In a few minutes they would be passing the flat. It was then that they moved, both together and at first with curious little jerks like puppets. The man straightened himself and the woman began plucking at her gloves, trying to fold over the fabric to hide the holes.

The man edged along the seat; he was leaning sideways onto an outstretched arm which was now only inches away from the woman's handbag. He began fumbling with the catch, but it was new and stiff. The bag jerked on her arm and the woman, now aware of what he was doing, snatched it away. The man's face changed expression, and became vicious. Abandoning pretence, he grabbed the bag with one hand and with the other hit her such a blow that her head jerked back and the black hat fell off to be trampled underfoot as they struggled for the bag; and still Alison could not see the woman's face, nor force her own heavy body to move except with exasperating slowness.

The green dress danced past her as the woman let go the bag and flung herself towards the window. She leaned far out and her arms waved frantically in the air.

The man was alarmed. He dropped the bag and leapt towards her, grabbing her hair violently so that her head jerked back. Something shone coldly bright in his hand as he punched her back, once, twice, three times. A dark red stain appeared and grew larger on the back of the dress.

Alison tried to stand up, but although her body obeyed her will, it did so slowly, so very slowly. She wanted to interfere but she knew that she could not.

The woman had the door open and although her blood was spilling down on to the floor, she was gathering her last strength to leap out. They were opposite the flat and Alison looked out over the woman's head to see her own kitchen window with all its sweet familiarity, the old faded curtains and even the jam jar soaking on the sill. But someone was standing at her sink. At first the figure was blurred and indistinct, then it leaned forward and Alison saw her own face pressed against the glass.

The sight brought her an overwhelming surge of relief. This nightmare in the carriage was nothing to do with her. It was their present and not hers. In her own present moment she was where she should be – washing up at her kitchen sink. She sighed and closed her eyes, exhausted.

When she opened them again another face was peering down into hers, a face framed by a stiff white cap.

'Are you feeling better, dear?'

'I don't know,' Alison answered. 'Where am I?'

'You were found unconscious in one of the carriages. You're in the waiting room at Caitham Junction.'

They took her home in a car, but she would not let them send for Ted or a Doctor. She wanted to be alone, alone to think. What had she been doing on the train? Where had she been going and why?

She thought about it for a long time. She remembered going to bed the night before but then ... nothing. She couldn't even remember why she had got on to the train. Perhaps Ted would know. No; she knew that she must not say anything at all about it to her husband.

The dirty breakfast dishes were still stacked in the sink and automatically she began to wash up. A fast express train roared into view and Alison dropped the cup she was holding, pressed her hands over her ears and screamed. Her screams grew louder, matching the roaring crescendo of the train ...

The days grew into weeks and then months. The soft warm spring turned to a blazing summer which burned itself out into autumn. Alison no longer watched the trains go by. A heavy Venetian blind hung at the window and its slats were always turned down, making it so dark in the kitchen that she had to use electric light even in the middle of the day. Sometimes, especially in the early morning, the sound of a train made her sweat and tremble with an incomprehensible terror. Although occasionally she forgot her fear of the trains it was never for long. She would sit for hours brooding, groping in her mind for a memory, a memory that she did not want to recall but knew she must if she were ever to dispel the hazy frightening confusion into which she had sunk.

Although she did not realize it, Alison had grown

thin and gaunt. Her pinched white face with its hollow cheeks and dark-rimmed eyes were almost unrecognizable. Ted often looked at her with anxious, puzzled sympathy, for she told him nothing and he had no idea why his wife seemed so disturbed and ill, but a plan had begun to form in his mind.

He was a simple man and he thought he had found a simple solution to Alison's unspoken troubles. He came home one evening with his arms full of packages and his face glowing with the excitement of a schoolboy.

'Come here, little lady. Have I got a surprise for you!'

She came at once, smiling at his enthusiasm.

'We are going on a holiday,' he announced, 'a proper holiday. Everything's booked and we're off tomorrow for a whole week in Majorca.'

He paused dramatically: neither of them had ever been abroad before and Alison caught some of his excitement.

'I've been planning this for weeks and I thought of everything,' he said, 'I have even bought you a complete new outfit to go away in – just like another honeymoon.'

He began to open his parcels and laid out his purchases one by one on the kitchen table. A pair of shiny black shoes, an expensive, real leather handbag, a black hat with a large soft brim and, last of all, a bright green dress.

Alison recoiled; the vague memory exploded into a terrifying flash of clarity.

'Oh, damn, I forgot the gloves,' Ted was saying. 'Still, I expect you've got an old pair of black gloves somewhere.'

She stared at him desperately, but he did not

notice and as she looked into his plain simple face she knew he would not understand. He was happily explaining away some small difficulty.

'So you see, love, I'll have to meet you later at the airport terminal. Take a taxi to Sutton Street and catch the 8.03.'

Alison stood very still on the station platform. The silky material of the green dress caressed her skin and the black hat framed and softened her face, making her look quite young and pretty again.

Last night she had decided not to wear the dress or to be on this train. Even this morning her conscious mind had urged her to burn the dress and lock herself in the bedroom. But even as she thought of it Alison had known that she would wear the dress and that she would be on the 8.03 from Sutton Street. Whatever was to happen to her in the dress had already happened sometime in her future and she could not change it any more than she could go back and change her past. Every last detail had been right, even to her old black gloves with the holes in the fingers, which contrasted sharply with the smart newness of her other clothes.

The train came into the platform. The last carriage stopped in front of her but it was full of Cubs and Scouts on an outing, just as she had known it would be.

There was one man in the next carriage and he did not look up as she got in. Alison looked down at her hands, and the old worn gloves irritated her.

The train moved off and she became very occupied with her gloves as she tried to fold over the fabric to hide the holes. They were passing the wood-yard and she knew the man would begin to edge his hand close to her bag.

With daunting certainty she knew his every move.

She felt the stinging blow to her head and then they were struggling and fighting in the swaying carriage.

'I am not here, this is not me.' She heard herself shouting the words aloud. The train was passing the flats, soon she would be able to see her kitchen window.

'I know I shall be there, standing at the window, washing up.' She screamed the words and tore herself free from the grasping hands to fling herself at the window.

The heavy blow struck her back once and then again and again, and she felt the hot sticky blood trickle down her legs. Excruciating pains tore into her body and through red swirling mists she looked up at her window with a desperate hope.

The Venetian blind was drawn up and there was no one there. The window gazed back at her, starkly empty. Hopelessly she leaned far out and the door of the train swung open. She felt him jerk her back and as oblivion rushed in upon her, past present and future gathered together to make one final moment of her life for the woman in the green dress.

SUCH A SWEET LITTLE GIRL

Lance Salway

t was at breakfast on a bright Saturday morning that Julie first made her announcement. She put down her spoon, swallowed a last mouthful of cornflakes, and said, 'There's a ghost in my bedroom.'

No one took any notice. Her mother was writing a shopping list and her father was deep in his newspaper. Neither of them heard what she said. Her brother Edward heard but he ignored her, which is what he usually did. Edward liked to pretend that Julie didn't exist. It wasn't easy but he did his best.

Julie tried again. She raised her voice and said, 'There's a ghost in my bedroom.'

Mrs Bennett looked up from her list. 'Is there, dear? Oh, good. Do you think we need more marmalade? And I suppose I'd better buy a cake or something if your friends are coming to tea.'

Edward said sharply, 'Friends? What friends?'

'Sally and Rachel are coming to tea with Julie this afternoon,' his mother said.

Edward gave a loud theatrical groan. 'Oh, no. Why

does she have to fill the house with her rotten friends?'

'You could fill the house with *your* friends, too,' Julie said sweetly. 'If you had any.'

Edward looked at her with loathing. 'Oh, I've got friends all right,' he said. 'I just don't inflict them on other people.'

'You haven't got any friends,' Julie said quietly. 'You haven't got any friends because no one likes you.'

'That's enough,' Mr Bennett said, looking up from his paper, and there was silence then, broken only by the gentle rumble-slush, rumble-slush of the washing machine in the corner.

Edward chewed a piece of toast and thought how much he hated Julie. He hated a lot of people. Most people, in fact. But there was some he hated more than others. Mr Jenkins, who taught maths. And that woman in the paper shop who'd accused him of stealing chewing gum, when everyone knew he never touched the stuff. And Julie. He hated Julie most of all. He hated her pretty pale face and her pretty fair curls and her pretty little lisping voice. He hated the grown-ups who constantly fluttered round her, saying how enchanting she was, and so clever for her age, and wasn't Mrs Bennett lucky to have such a sweet little girl. What they didn't say, but he knew they were thinking it behind their wide bright smiles, was poor Mrs Bennett, with that lumpy, sullen boy. So different from his sister. So different from lovely little Julie.

Lovely little Julie flung her spoon on the table. 'I *said* there's a ghost in my bedroom.'

Mrs Bennett put down her shopping list and ballpoint in order to give Julie her full attention. 'Oh dear,' she said. 'I hope it didn't frighten you, darling.'

Julie smiled and preened. 'No,' she said smugly. '*I* wasn't frightened.'

Edward tried to shut his ears. He knew this dialogue by heart. The Bennett family spent a great deal of time adjusting their habits to suit Julie's fantasies. Once, for a whole month, they had all been forced to jump the bottom tread of the staircase because Julie insisted that two invisible rabbits were sleeping there. For a time she had been convinced, or so she said, that a pink dragon lived in the airing cupboard. And there had been a terrible few weeks the year before when all communication with her had to be conducted through an invisible fairy called Priscilla who lived on her left shoulder.

And now there was a ghost in her bedroom.

Try as he might, Edward couldn't shut out his sister's voice. On and on it whined: '. . . I was really very brave and didn't run away even though it was so frightening, and I said . . .'

Edward looked at his parents with contempt. His father had put down the newspaper and was gazing at Julie with a soppy smile on his face. His mother was wearing the mock-serious expression that adults often adopt in order to humour their young. Edward hated them for it. If he'd told them a story about a ghost when *he* was seven, they'd have told him to stop being so silly, there's no such thing as ghosts, why don't you grow up, be a man.

'What sort of ghost is it?' he asked suddenly.

Julie looked at him in surprise. Then her eyes narrowed. 'It's a frightening ghost,' she said. 'With great big eyes and teeth and horrible, nasty claws. Big claws. And it smells.'

'Ghosts aren't like that,' Edward said scornfully. 'Ghosts have clanking chains and skeletons, and they carry their heads under their arms.'

'This ghost doesn't,' Julie snapped.

'Funny sort of ghost, then.'

'You don't know anything about it.'

Julie's voice was beginning to tremble. Edward sighed. There'd be tears soon and he'd get the blame. As usual.

'Come now, Edward,' his father said heartily. 'It's only pretend. Isn't it, lovey?'

Lovey shot him a vicious glance. 'It's *not* pretend. It's a real ghost. And it's in my bedroom.'

'Of course, darling.' Mrs Bennett picked up her shopping list again. 'How are we off for chutney, I wonder?'

But Edward wasn't going to let the matter drop. Not this time. 'Anyway,' he said, 'ghosts don't have claws.'

'This one does,' Julie said.

'Then you're lying.'

'I'm not. There *is* a ghost. I saw it.'

'Liar.'

'I'm not!' She was screaming now. 'I'll show you I'm not. I'll tell it to *get* you. With its claws. It'll come and get you with its claws.'

'Don't make me laugh.'

'*Edward!* That's *enough!*' His mother stood up and started to clear the table. 'Don't argue.'

'But there isn't a ghost,' Edward protested. 'There can't be!'

Mrs Bennett glanced uneasily at Julie. 'Of course there is,' she said primly. 'If Julie says so.'

'She's a liar, a nasty little liar.'

Julie kicked him hard, then, under the table. Edward yelped, and kicked back. Julie let out a screech, and then her face crumpled and she began to wail.

'*Now* look what you've done,' Mrs Bennett snapped.

'Oh *really*, Edward. You're twice her age. Why can't you leave her alone?'

'Because she's a liar, that's why.' Edward stood up and pushed his chair aside. 'Because there isn't a ghost in her bedroom. And even if there is, it won't have claws.' And he turned, and stormed out of the kitchen.

He came to a stop in the sitting room, and crossed over to the window to see what sort of day it was going to be. Sunny, by the look of it. A small tightly-cropped lawn lay in front of the house, a lawn that was identical in size and appearance to those in front of the other identical square brick houses which lined the road. Edward laughed out loud. Any ghost worthy of the name would wither away from boredom in such surroundings. No, there weren't any ghosts in Briarfield Gardens. With or without heads under their arms. With or without claws.

He turned away from the window. The day had started badly, thanks to Julie. And it would continue badly, thanks to Julie and her rotten friends who were coming to tea. And there was nothing he could do about it. Or was there? On the coffee table by the television set there lay a half-finished jigsaw puzzle. Julie had been working on it for ages, her fair curls bent earnestly over the table day after day. According to the picture on the box, the finished puzzle would reveal a thatched cottage surrounded by a flower-filled garden. When it was finished. If.

Edward walked across to the table and smashed the puzzle with one quick, practised movement of his hand. Pieces fell and flew and scattered on the carpet in a storm of coloured cardboard. And then he turned, and ran upstairs to his room.

He hadn't long to wait. After a few minutes he heard the sounds that he was expecting. The kitchen

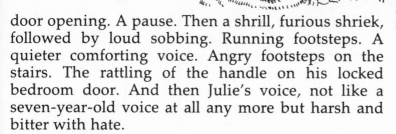

door opening. A pause. Then a shrill, furious shriek, followed by loud sobbing. Running footsteps. A quieter comforting voice. Angry footsteps on the stairs. The rattling of the handle on his locked bedroom door. And then Julie's voice, not like a seven-year-old voice at all any more but harsh and bitter with hate.

'The ghost'll get you, Edward. I'm going to tell it to get you. With its claws. With its sharp horrible claws.'

And then, quite suddenly, Edward felt afraid.

The fear didn't last long. It had certainly gone by lunchtime, when Edward was given a ticking-off by his father for upsetting dear little Julie. And by the time Julie's friends arrived at four, he was quite his old self again.

'The ugly sisters are here!' he announced loudly as he opened the front door, having beaten Julie to it by a short head.

She glared at him, and quickly hustled Sally and Rachel up the stairs to her room.

Edward felt a bit guilty. Sally and Rachel weren't at all ugly. In fact, he quite liked them both. He ambled into the kitchen, where his mother was busy preparing tea.

She looked up when he came in. 'I do hope you're going to behave yourself this evening,' she said. 'We don't want a repetition of this morning's little episode, do we?'

'Well, she asked for it,' Edward said sullenly, and sneaked a biscuit from a pile on a plate.

'Hands off!' his mother said automatically. 'Julie did *not* ask for it. She was only pretending. You know what she's like. There was no need for you to be so nasty. And there was certainly no excuse for you to break up her jigsaw puzzle like that.'

Edward shuffled uneasily and stared at the floor.

'She *is* only seven, after all,' Mrs Bennett went on, slapping chocolate icing on a sponge cake as she did so. 'You must make allowances. The rest of us do.'

'She gets away with murder,' Edward mumbled. 'Just because she's such a sweet little girl.'

'Nonsense!' his mother said firmly. 'And keep your mucky paws off those ginger snaps. If anyone gets away with murder in this house, it's you.'

'But she can't really expect us to believe there's a ghost in her bedroom,' Edward said. 'Do *you* believe there's a ghost in her bedroom,' Edward said. 'Do *you* believe her? Come on, mum, do you?'

'I –' his mother began, and then she was interrupted by a familiar lisping voice.

'You *do* believe me, Mummy, don't you?'

Julie was standing at the kitchen door. Edward wondered how long she'd been there. And how much she'd heard.

'Of course I do, darling,' Mrs Bennett said quickly. 'Now run along, both of you. Or I'll never have tea ready in time.'

Julie stared at Edward for a moment with her cold blue eyes, and then she went out of the kitchen as quietly as she'd entered it.

Tea passed off smoothly enough. Julie seemed to be on her best behaviour but that was probably because her friends were there and she wanted to create a good impression. Edward followed her example. Julie didn't look at him or speak to him but there was nothing unusual about that. She and the others chattered brightly about nothing in particular, and Edward said nothing at all.

It was dusk by the time they'd finished tea and it was then that Julie suggested that they all play ghosts. She looked straight at Edward when she said this, and the proposal seemed like a challenge.

'Can anyone play?' he asked. 'Or is it just a game for horrible little girls?'

'Edward!' warned his mother.

'Of course you can play, Edward,' said Julie. 'You *must* play.'

'But not in the kitchen or in the dining room,' said Mrs Bennett. 'And keep out of our bedroom. I'll go and draw all the curtains and make sure the lights are switched off.'

'All right,' said Julie, and the other little girls clapped their hands with excitement.

'How do we play this stupid game?' said Edward.

'Oh, it's easy,' said Julie. 'One of us is the ghost, and she has to frighten the others. If the ghost catches you and scares you, you have to scream and drop down on the floor. As if you were dead.'

'Like "Murder in the Dark"?' asked Sally.

'Yes,' said Julie. 'Only we don't have a detective or anything like that.'

'It sounds a crummy game to me,' said Edward. 'I don't think I'll play.'

'Oh, *do!*' chorused Sally and Rachel. 'Please!'

And Julie came up to him and whispered, 'You must play, Edward. And don't forget what I said this morning. About my ghost. And how it's going to get you with its claws.'

'You must be joking!' Edward jeered. 'And, anyway, I told you. Ghosts don't have claws.' He looked her straight in the eyes. 'Of course I'll play.'

Julie smiled, and then turned to the others and said, 'I'll be the ghost to start with. The rest of you run and hide. I'll count up to fifty and then I'll come and haunt you.'

Sally and Rachel galloped upstairs, squealing with excitement. Edward wandered into the hall and

stood for a moment, wondering where to hide. It wasn't going to be easy. Their small brick box of a house didn't offer many possibilities. After a while he decided on the sitting room. It was the most obvious place and Julie would never think of looking there. He opened the door quietly, ducked down behind an armchair, and waited.

Silence settled over the house. Apart from washing-up sounds from the kitchen, all was quiet. Edward made himself comfortable on the carpet and waited for the distant screams that would tell him that Sally had been discovered, or Rachel. But no sounds came. As he waited, ears straining against the silence, the room grew darker. The day was fading and it would soon be night.

And then, suddenly, Edward heard a slight noise near the door. His heart leaped and, for some reason, his mouth went dry. And then the fear returned, the unaccountable fear he had felt that morning when Julie hissed her threat through his bedroom door.

The air seemed much colder now, but that could only be his imagination, surely. But he knew that he wasn't imagining the wild thumping of his heart or the sickening lurching of his stomach. He remem-

bered Julie's words and swallowed hard.

'The ghost'll get you, Edward. With its claws. With its sharp, horrible claws.'

He heard sounds again, closer this time. A scuffle. Whispering. Or was it whispering? Someone was there. Something. He tried to speak, but gave only a curious croak. And then, 'Julie?' he said. 'I know you're there. I know it's you.'

Silence. A dark terrible silence. And then the light snapped on and the room was filled with laughter and shouts of 'Got you! Caught you! The ghost has caught you!', and he saw Julie's face alive with triumph and delight, and, behind her, Sally and Rachel grinning, and the fear was replaced by an anger far darker and more intense than the terror he'd felt before.

'Edward's scared of the ghost!' Julie jeered. 'Edward's a scaredycat! He's frightened of the gho-ost!'

And Rachel and Sally echoed her. 'He's frightened! He's frightened of the gho-ost!'

'I'm not!' Edward shouted. 'I'm not scared! There isn't a ghost!' And he pushed past Julie and ran out of the room and up the stairs. He'd show her. He'd prove she didn't have a ghost. There was no such things as ghosts. She didn't have a ghost in her room. She didn't.

Julie's bedroom was empty. Apart from the furniture and the pictures and the toys and dolls and knick-knacks. He opened the wardrobe and pulled shoes and games out on to the floor. He burrowed in drawers, scattering books and stuffed animals and clothes around him. At last he stopped, gasping for breath. And turned.

His mother was standing in the doorway, staring at him in amazement. Clustered behind her were the puzzled, anxious faces of Sally and Rachel. And behind them, Julie. Looking at him with her ice-blue eyes.

'What on earth are you doing?' his mother asked.

'See?' he panted. 'There isn't a ghost here. She hasn't got a ghost in her bedroom. There's nothing here. Nothing.'

'Isn't there?' said Julie. 'Are you sure you've looked properly?'

Sally – or was it Rachel? – gave a nervous giggle.

'That's enough,' said Mrs Bennett. 'Now I suggest you tidy up the mess you've made in here, Edward, and then go to your room. I don't know why you're behaving so strangely. But it's got to stop. It's got to.'

She turned and went downstairs. Sally and Rachel followed her. Julie lingered by the door, and stared mockingly at Edward. He stared back.

'It's still here, you know,' she said at last. 'The ghost is still here. And it'll get you.'

'You're a dirty little liar!' he shouted. 'A nasty, filthy little liar!'

Julie gaped at him for a moment, taken aback by the force of his rage. Then, 'It'll get you!' she screamed. 'With its claws. Its horrible claws. It'll get you tonight. When you're asleep. Because I hate you.

I hate you. Yes, it'll *really* get you. Tonight.'

It was dark when Edward awoke. At first he didn't know where he was. And then he remembered. He was in bed. In his bedroom. It was the middle of the night. And he remembered, too, Julie's twisted face and the things she said. The face and the words had kept him awake, and had haunted his dreams when at last he slept.

It was ridiculous, really. All this fuss about an imaginary ghost. Why did he get in such a state over Julie? She was only a little kid, after all. His baby sister. You were supposed to love your sister, not – not fear her. But no, he wasn't *really* afraid of her. How could he be? Such a sweet little girl with blue eyes and fair bouncing curls who was half his age. A little girl who played games and imagined things. Who imagined ghosts. A ghost in her bedroom.

But he *was* frightened. He knew that now. And as his fear mounted again, the room seemed to get colder. He shut his eyes and snuggled down under the blankets, shutting out the room and the cold. But not the fear.

And then he heard it. A sound. A faint scraping sound, as though something heavy was being dragged along the landing. A sound that came closer and grew louder. A wet, slithering sound. And with it came a smell, a sickening smell of, oh, drains and dead leaves and decay. And the sound grew louder and he could hear breathing, harsh breathing, long choking breaths coming closer.

'Julie?' Edward said, and then he repeated it, louder. 'Julie!'

But there was no answer. All he heard was the scraping, dragging sound coming closer, closer. Near his door now. Closer.

'I know it's you!' Edward shouted, and heard the

fear in his voice. 'You're playing ghosts again, aren't you? Aren't you?'

And then there was silence. No sound at all. Edward sat up in bed and listened. The awful slithering noise had stopped. It had gone. The ghost had gone.

He hugged himself with relief. It had been a dream, that's all. He'd imagined it. Just as Julie imagined things. Imagined ghosts.

Then he heard the breathing again. The shuddering, choking breaths. And he knew that the thing hadn't gone. That it was still there. Outside his door. Waiting. Waiting.

And Edward screamed, 'Julie! Stop it! Stop it! Please stop it! I believe you! I believe in the ghost!'

The door opened. The shuddering breaths seemed to fill the room, and the smell, and the slithering wet sound of a shape, something, coming towards him, something huge and dark and –

And he screamed as the claws, yes, the claws tore at his hands, his chest, his face. And he screamed again as the darkness folded over him.

When Julie woke up and came downstairs, the ambulance had gone. Her mother was sitting alone in the kitchen, looking pale and frightened. She smiled weakly when she saw Julie, and then frowned.

'Darling,' she said. 'I did so hope you wouldn't wake up. I didn't want you to be frightened –'

'What's the matter, Mummy?' said Julie. 'Why are you crying?'

Her mother smiled again, and drew Julie to her, folding her arms around her so that she was warm and safe. 'You must be very brave, darling,' she said. 'Poor Edward has been hurt. We don't know what happened but he's been very badly hurt.'

'Hurt? What do you mean, Mummy?'

Her mother brushed a stray curl from the little girl's face. 'We don't know what happened, exactly. Something attacked him. His face –' Her voice broke then, and she looked away quickly. 'He has been very badly scratched. They're not sure if his eyes –' She stopped and fumbled in her dressing-gown pocket for a tissue.

'I expect my ghost did it,' Julie said smugly.

'What did you say, dear?'

Julie looked up at her mother. 'My ghost did it. I told it to. I told it to hurt Edward because I hate him. The ghost hurt him. The ghost in my bedroom.'

Mrs Bennett stared at Julie. 'This is no time for games,' she said. 'We're very upset. Your father's gone to the hospital with Edward. We don't know if –' Her eyes filled with tears. 'I'm in no mood for your silly stories about ghosts, Julie. Not now. I'm too upset.'

'But it's true!' Julie said. 'My ghost *did* do it. Because I told it to.'

Mrs Bennett pushed her away and stood up. 'All right, Julie, that's enough. Back to bed now. You can play your game tomorrow.'

'But it's not a game,' Julie persisted. 'It's true! My ghost –'

And then she saw the angry expression on her mother's face, and she stopped. Instead, she snuggled up to her and whispered, 'I'm sorry, Mummy. You're right. I *was* pretending. I was only pretending about the ghost. There isn't a ghost in my room. I was making it all up. And I'm so sorry about poor Edward.'

Mrs Bennett relaxed and smiled and drew Julie to her once more. 'That's my baby,' she said softly. 'That's my sweet little girl. Of course you were only pretending. Of course there wasn't a ghost. Would I let a nasty ghost come and frighten my little girl? Would I? Would I?'

'No, Mummy,' said Julie. 'Of course you wouldn't.'

'Off you go to bed now.'

'Good night, Mummy,' said Julie.

'Sleep well, my pet,' said her mother.

And Julie walked out of the kitchen and into the hall and up the stairs to her bedroom. She went inside and closed the door behind her.

And the ghost came out to meet her.

'She doesn't believe me, either,' Julie said. 'She doesn't believe me. We'll have to show her, won't we? Just as we showed Edward.'

And the ghost smiled and nodded, and they sat down together, Julie and the ghost, and decided what they would do.

A Pair of Hands

Sir Arthur Quiller-Couch

es,' said Miss Le Petyt, gazing into the deep fireplace and letting her hands and her knitting lie for the moment idle in her lap. 'Oh, yes, I have seen a ghost. In fact I have lived in a house with one for quite a long time.'

'How you *could* – !' began one of my host's daughters; and 'You, Aunt Emily?' cried the other at the same moment.

Miss Le Petyt, gentle soul, withdrew her eyes from the fireplace and protested with a gay little smile. 'Well, my dears, I am not quite the coward you take me for. And, as it happens, mine was the most harmless ghost in the world. In fact' – and here she looked at the fire again – 'I was quite sorry to lose her.'

'It was a woman, then? Now *I* think,' said Miss Blanche, 'that female ghosts are the horridest of all. They wear little shoes with high red heels, and go about *tap, tap,* wringing their hands.'

'This one wrung her hands, certainly. But I don't know about the high red heels, for I never saw her feet. Perhaps she was like the Queen of Spain, and hadn't any. And as for the hands, it all depends *how* you wring them. There's an elderly shopwalker at Knightsbridge, for instance –'

'Don't be prosy, you know that we're just dying to hear the story.'

Miss Le Petyt turned to me with a small deprecating laugh. 'It's such a little one.'

'The story, or the ghost?'

'Both.'

And this was Miss Le Petyt's story:

'It happened when I lived down in Cornwall, at Tresillack on the south coast. Tresillack was the name of the house, which stood quite alone at the head of a coombe, within sound of the sea but without sight of it; for though the coombe led down to a wide open beach, it wound and twisted half a dozen times on its way, and its overlapping sides closed the view from the house, which was advertised as "secluded". I was very poor in those days. Your father and all of us were poor then, as I trust, my dears, you will never be; but I was young enough to be romantic and wise enough to like independence, and this word "secluded" took my fancy.

'The misfortune was that it had taken the fancy, or just suited the requirements, of several previous tenants. You know, I dare say, the kind of person who rents a secluded house in the country? Well, yes, there are several kinds; but they seem to agree in being odious. No one knows where they come from, though they soon remove all doubt about where they're "going to", as the children say. "Shady" is the word, is it not? Well, the previous tenants of Tresillack (from first to last a bewildering series) had been shady with a vengeance.

'I knew nothing of this when I first made application to the landlord, a solid yeoman inhabiting a farm at the foot of the coombe, on a cliff overlooking the beach. To him I presented myself fearlessly as a spinster of decent famly and small but assured income, intending a rural life of combined seemliness and economy. He met my advances politely enough, but with an air of suspicion which offended me. I began by disliking him for it: afterwards I set it down as an unpleasant feature in the local character. I was doubly mistaken. Farmer Hosking was slow-witted, but as honest a man as ever stood up against hard times; and a more open and hospitable race than the people on that coast I never wish to meet. It was the caution of a child who had burnt his fingers, not once but many times. Had I known what I afterwards learned of Farmer Hosking's tribulations as landlord of a "secluded country residence", I should have approached him with the bashfulness proper to my suit and faltered as I undertook to prove the bright exception in a long line of painful experiences. He had bought the Tresillack estate twenty years before – on mortgage, I fancy – because the land adjoined his own and would pay him for tillage. But the house was a nuisance, an incubus; and had been so from the beginning.

' "Well, miss," he said, "you're welcome to look over it; a pretty enough place inside and out. There's no trouble about keys, because I've put in a house-keeper, a widow-woman, and she'll show you round. With your leave I'll step up the coombe so far with you, and put you on your way." As I thanked him he paused and rubbed his chin. "There's one thing I must tell you, though. Whoever takes the house must take Mrs Carkeek along with it."

' "Mrs Carkeek?" I echoed dolefully. "Is that the housekeeper?"

' "Yes: she was wife to my late hind. I'm sorry, miss," he added, my face telling him no doubt what sort of woman I expected Mrs Carkeek to be; "but I

had to make it a rule after – after some things that happened. And I dare say you won't find her so bad. Mary Carkeek's a sensible comfortable woman, and knows the place. She was in service there to Squire Kendall when he sold up and went: her first place it was."

' "I may as well see the house, anyhow," said I dejectedly. So we started to walk up the coombe. The path, which ran beside a little chattering stream, was narrow for the most part, and Farmer Hosking, with an apology, strode on ahead to beat aside the brambles. But whenever its width allowed us to walk side by side I caught him from time to time stealing a shy inquisitive glance under his rough eyebrows. Courteously though he bore himself, it was clear that he could sum me up to his satisfaction or bring me square with his notion of a tenant for his "secluded country residence".

'I don't know what foolish fancy prompted it, but about halfway up the coombe I stopped short and asked:

' "There are no ghosts, I suppose?"

'It struck me, a moment after I had uttered it, as a supremely silly question; but he took it quite seriously. "No; I never heard tell of any *ghosts*." He laid a queer sort of stress on the word. "There's always been trouble with servants, and maids' tongues will be runnin'. But Mary Carkeek lives up there alone, and she seems comfortable enough."

'We walked on. By-and-by he pointed with his stick. "It don't look like a place for ghosts, now, do it?"

'Certainly it did not. Above an untrimmed orchard rose a terrace of turf scattered with thorn-bushes, and above this a terrace of stone, upon which stood the prettiest cottage I had ever seen. It was long and low and thatched; a deep verandah ran from end to end. Clematis, Banksia roses and honeysuckle climbed the posts of this verandah, and big blooms of the Maréchal Niel were clustered along its roof, beneath the lattices of the bedroom windows. The house was small enough to be called a cottage, and rare enough in features and in situation to confer distinction on any tenant. It suggested what in those days we should have called "elegant" living. And I could have clapped my hands for joy.

'My spirits mounted still higher when Mrs Carkeek opened the door to us. I had looked for a Mrs Gummidge, and I found a healthy middle-aged woman with a thoughtful but contented face, and a smile which, without a trace of obsequiousness, quite bore out the farmer's description of her. She was a comfortable woman; and while we walked through the rooms together (for Mr Hosking waited outside) I "took to" Mrs Carkeek. Her speech was direct and practical; the rooms, in spite of their faded furniture, were bright and exquisitely clean; and somehow the very atmosphere of the house gave me a sense of well-being, of feeling at home and cared for; yes, *of being loved*. Don't laugh, my dears; for when I've done you may not think this fancy altogether foolish.

'I stepped out into the verandah, and Farmer Hosking pocketed the pruning-knife which he had been using on a bush of jasmine.

' "This is better than anything I had dreamed of," said I.

' "Well, miss, that's not a wise way of beginning a bargain, if you'll excuse me."

'He took no advantage, however, of my admission; and we struck the bargain as we returned down the coombe to his farm, where the hind chaise waited to convey me back to the market town. I had meant to engage a maid of my own, but now it occurred to me that I might do very well with Mrs Carkeek. This, too, was settled in the course of the next day or two, and within the week I had moved into my new home.

'I can hardly describe to you the happiness of my first month at Tresillack; because (as I now believe) if I take the reasons which I had for being happy, one by one, there remains over something which I cannot account for. I was moderately young, entirely healthy; I felt myself independent and adventurous; the season was high summer, the weather glorious, the garden in all the pomp of June, yet sufficiently unkempt to keep me busy, give me a sharp appetite for meals, and send me to bed in that drowsy stupor which comes of the odours of earth. I spent most of my time out of doors, winding up the day's work as a rule with a walk down the cool valley along the beach and back.

'I soon found that all the housework could be safely left to Mrs Carkeek. She did not talk much; indeed her only fault (a rare one in housekeepers) was that she talked too little, and even when I addressed her seemed at times unable to give me her attention. It was as though her mind strayed off to some small job she had forgotten, and her eyes wore a listening look, as though she waited for the neglected task to speak and remind her. But as a matter of fact she forgot nothing. Indeed, my dears, I was never so well attended to in my life.

'Well, that is what I'm coming to. That, so to say, is just *it*. The woman not only had the rooms swept and dusted, and my meals prepared to the moment. In a hundred odd little ways this orderliness, these preparations, seemed to read my desires. Did I wish the roses renewed in a bowl upon the dining-table, sure enough at the next meal they would be replaced by fresh ones. Mrs Carkeek (I told myself) must have surprised and interpreted a glance of mine. And yet I could not remember having glanced at the bowl in her presence. And how on earth had she guessed the very roses, the very shapes and colours I had lightly wished for? This is only an instance, you understand. Every day, and from morning to night, I happened on others, each slight enough, but all together bearing witness to a ministering intelligence as subtle as it was untiring.

'I am a light sleeper, as you know, with an uncomfortable knack of waking with the sun and roaming early. No matter how early I rose at Tresillack, Mrs Carkeek seemed to have preceded me. Finally I had to conclude that she arose and dusted and tidied as soon as she judged me safely a-bed. For once, finding the drawing-room (where I had been sitting late) "redded-up" at four in the morning, and no trace of a plate of raspberries which I had carried thither after dinner and left overnight, I determined to test her, and walked through to the kitchen, calling her by name. I found the kitchen as clean as a pin, and the fire laid, but no trace of Mrs Carkeek. I walked upstairs and knocked at her door. At the second knock a sleepy voice cried out, and presently the good woman stood before me in her nightgown, looking (I thought) very badly scared.

' "No," I said, "it's not a burglar. But I've found out what I wanted, that you do your morning's work over night. But you mustn't wait for me when I choose to sit up. And now go back to your bed like a good soul, whilst I take a run down to the beach.'

'She stood blinking in the dawn. Her face was still white.

' "Oh, miss,' she gasped, "I made sure you must

have seen something!"

' "And so I have," I answered, "but it was neither burglars nor ghosts."

' "Thank God!" I heard her say as she turned her back to me in her grey bedroom – which faced the north. And I took this for a carelessly pious expresion and ran downstairs, thinking no more of it.

'A few days later I began to understand.

'The plan of Trellisack house (I must explain) was simplicity itself. To the left of the hall as you entered was the dining-room; to the right the drawing-room, with a boudoir beyond. The foot of the stairs faced the front door and beside it, passing a glazed inner door, you found two others right and left, the left opening on the kitchen, the right on a passage which ran by a store-cupboard under the bend of the stairs to a neat pantry with the usual shelves and linen-press, and under the window (which faced north) a porcelain basin and brass tap. On the first morning of my tenancy I had visited this pantry and turned the tap; but no water ran. I supposed this to be accidental. Mrs Carkeek had to wash up glassware and crockery, and no doubt Mrs Carkeek would complain of any failure in the water supply.

'But the day after my surprise visit (as I called it) I had picked a basketful of roses, and carried them into the pantry as a handy place to arrange them in. I chose a china bowl and went to fill it at the tap. Again the water would not run.

'I called Mrs Carkeek. "What is wrong with this tap?" I asked. "The rest of the house is well enough supplied."

"I don't know, miss. I never use it."

' "But there must be a reason; and you must find it a great nuisance washing up the plates and glasses in the kitchen. Come around to the back with me, and we'll have a look at the cisterns."

' "The cisterns'll be all right, miss. I assure you I don't find it a trouble."

'But I was not to be put off. The back of the house stood ten foot from a wall which was really but a stone face built against the cliff cut away by the architect. Above the cliff rose the kitchen garden, and from its lower path we looked over the wall's parapet upon the cisterns. There were two – a very large one, supplying the kitchen and the bathroom above the kitchen; and a small one, obviously fed by the other, and as obviously leading, by a pipe which I could trace, to the pantry. Now the big cistern stood almost full, and yet the small one, though on a lower level, was empty.

' "It's as plain as daylight," said I. "The pipe between the two is choked." And I clambered onto the parapet.

' "I wouldn't, miss. The pantry tap is only cold water, and no use to me. From the kitchen boiler I gets it hot, you see."

' "But I want the pantry water for my flowers." I bent over and groped. "I thought as much!" said I, as I wrenched out a thick plug of cork and immediately the water began to flow. I turned triumphantly on Mrs Carkeek, who had grown suddenly red in the face. Her eyes were fixed on the cork in my hand. To keep it more firmly wedged in its place somebody had wrapped it round with a rag of calico print; and, discoloured though the rag was, I seemed to recall the pattern (a lilac sprig). Then, as our eyes met, it occurred to me that only two mornings before Mrs Carkeek had worn a print gown of that same sprigged pattern.

'I had the presence of mind to hide this very small discovery, sliding over it with some quite trivial remark; and presently Mrs Carkeek regained her composure. But I own I felt disappointed in her. It seemed such a paltry thing to be disingenuous over. She had deliberately acted a fib before me; and why? Merely because she preferred the kitchen to the pantry tap. It was childish. "But servants are all the same," I told myself. "I must take Mrs Carkeek as she is; and, after all, she is a treasure."

'On the second night after this, and between eleven and twelve o'clock, I was lying in bed and reading myself sleepy over a novel of Lord Lytton's, when a small sound disturbed me. I listened. The sound was clearly that of water trickling; and I set it down to rain. A shower (I told myself) had filled the water pipes which drained the roof. Somehow I could not fix the sound. There was a water-pipe against the wall just outside my window. I rose and drew up the blind.

'To my astonishment no rain was falling; no rain had fallen. I felt the slate window-sill; some dew had gathered there – no more. There was no wind, no cloud: only a still moon high over the eastern slope of the coombe, the distant splash of waves, and the fragrance of many roses. I went back to bed and listened again. Yes, the trickling sound continued, quite distinct in the silence of the house, not to be confused for a moment with the dull murmur of the beach. After a while it began to grate on my nerves. I caught up my candle, flung my dressing-gown about me, and stole softly downstairs.

'Then it was simple. I traced the sound to the pantry. "Mrs Carkeek has left the tap running," said I: and sure enough, I found it so – a thin trickle steadily running to waste in the porcelain basin. I turned off the tap, went contentedly back to bed, and slept.

'– for some hours. I opened my eyes in darkness, and at once knew what had awakened me. The tap was running again. Now it had shut easily in my hand, but not so easily that I could believe it had slipped open again of its own accord. "This is Mrs Carkeek's doing," said I; and am afraid I added "Bother Mrs Carkeek!"

'Well, there was no help for it: so I struck a light, looked at my watch, saw the hour was just three o'clock, and descended the stairs again. At the pantry door I paused. I was not afraid – not one little bit. In fact the notion that anything might be wrong had never crossed my mind. But I remember thinking, with my hand on the door, that if Mrs Carkeek were in the pantry I might happen to give her a severe fright.

'I pushed the door open briskly. Mrs Carkeek was not there. But something *was* there, by the porcelain basin – something which might have sent me scurrying upstairs two steps at a time, but which as a matter of fact held me to the spot. My heart seemed to stand still – so still! And in the stillness I remember setting down the brass candlestick on a tall nest of drawers beside me.

'Over the porcelain basin and beneath the water trickling from the tap I saw two hands.

'That was all – two small hands, a child's hands. I cannot tell you how they ended.

'No: they were not cut off. I saw them quite distinctly: just a pair of small hands and the wrists, and after that – nothing. They were moving briskly – washing themselves clean. I saw the water trickle and splash over them – not *through* them – but just as it would on real hands. They were the hands of a little girl, too. Oh, yes, I was sure of that at once. Boys and girls wash their hands differently. I can't just tell you what the difference is, but it's unmistakable.

'I saw all this before my candle slipped and fell with a crash. I had set it down without looking – for my eyes were fixed on the basin – and had balanced it on the edge of the nest of drawers. After the crash, in the darkness there, with the water running, I suffered some bad moments. Oddly .enough, the thought uppermost with me was that I *must* shut off that tap before escaping. I *had* to. And after a while I picked up all my courage, so to say, between my teeth, and with a little sob thrust out my hand and did it. Then I fled.

'The dawn was close upon me: and as soon as the sky reddened I took my bath, dressed and went downstairs. And there at the pantry door I found Mrs Carkeek, also dressed, with my candlestick in her hand.

' "Ah!" said I, "you picked it up."

'Our eyes met. Clearly Mrs Carkeek wished me to begin, and I determined at once to have it out with her.

' "And you knew all about it. That's what accounts for your plugging up the cistern."

' "You saw . . .?" she began.

' "Yes, yes. And you must tell me all about it – never mind how bad. Is – is it – murder?"

' "Law bless you, miss, whatever put such horrors in your head?"

' "She was washing her hands."

' "Ah, so she does, poor dear! But – murder! And dear little Miss Margaret, that wouldn't go to hurt a fly!"

' "Miss Margaret?"

' "Eh, she died at seven year. Squire Kendall's only daughter; and that's over twenty year ago. I was her nurse, miss, and I know – diphtheria it was; she took

it down in the village."

' "But how do you know it is Margaret?"

' "Those hands – why, how could I mistake, that used to be her nurse?"

' "But why does she wash them?"

' "Well, miss, being always a dainty child – and the housework, you see –"

'I took a long breath. "Do you mean to tell me that all this tidying and dusting –" I broke off. "Is it *she* who has been taking this care of me?"

'Mrs Carkeek met my look steadily.

' "Who else, miss?' "

' "Poor little soul!"

' "Well now" – Mrs Carkeek rubbed my candle-stick with the edge of her apron – "I'm so glad you take it like this. For there isn't really nothing to be afraid of – is there?" She eyed me wistfully. "It's my belief she loves you, miss. But only to think what a time she must have had with the others!"

' "The others?" I echoed.

' "The other tenants, miss: the ones afore you."

' "Were they bad?"

' "They was awful. Didn't Farmer Hosking tell you? They carried on fearful – one after another, and each one worse than the last."

"What was the matter with them? Drink?"

' "Drink, miss, with some of 'em. There was the Major – he used to go mad with it, and run about the coombe in his nightshirt. Oh, scandalous! And his wife drank too – that is, if she ever *was* his wife. Just think of that tender child washing up after their nasty doings!"

'I shivered.

' "But that wasn't the worst by a long way. There was a pair here – from the colonies, or so they gave out – with two children, a boy and gel, the eldest scarce six. Poor mites!"

' "Why, what happened?"

' "They beat those children, miss – your blood would boil! – *and* starved, *and* tortured 'em, it's my belief. You could hear their screams, I've been told, away back in the high-road, and that's the best part of half a mile. Sometimes they was locked up without food for days together. But it's my belief that little Miss Margaret managed to feed them somehow. Oh, I can see her, creeping to the door and comforting!"

' "But perhaps she never showed herself when these awful people were here, but took to flight until they left."

' "You didn't never know her, miss. The brave she was! She'd have stood up to lions. She've been here all the while: and only to think what her innocent eyes and ears must have took in! There was another couple –" Mrs Carkeek sunk her voice.

' "Oh, hush!" said I, "if I'm to have any peace of mind in this house!"

' "But you won't go, miss? She loves you, I know she do. And think what you might be leaving her to – what sort of tenant might come next. For she can't go. She've been here ever since her father sold the place. He died soon after. You mustn't go!"

'Now I had resolved to go, but all of a sudden I felt how mean this resolution was.

' "After all," said I, "there's nothing to be afraid of."

' "That's it, miss; nothing at all. I don't even believe it's so very uncommon. Why, I've heard my mother tell of farmhouses where the rooms were swept every night as regular as clockwork, and the floors sanded, and the pots and pans scoured, and all while the maids slept. They put it down to the piskies; but we know better, miss, and now we've got the secret between us we can lie easy in our beds, and if we hear anything, say 'God bless the child!' and go to sleep.''

' ''Mrs Carkeek,'' said I, ''there's only one condition I have to make.''

' ''What's that?''

' ''Why, that you let me kiss you.''

' ''Oh, you dear!'' said Mrs Carkeek as we embraced: and this was as close to familiarity as she allowed herself to go in the whole course of my acquaintance with her.

'I spent three years at Tresillack, and all that while Mrs Carkeek lived with me and shared the secret. Few women, I dare say, were ever so completely wrapped around with love as we were during those three years. It ran through my waking life like a song: it smoothed my pillow, touched and made my table comely, in summer lifted the heads of the flowers as I passed, and in winter watched the fire with me and kept it bright.

' ''Why did I ever leave Tresillack?'' Because one day, at the end of five years, Farmer Hosking brought me word that he had sold the house – or was about to sell it; I forget which. There was no avoiding it, at any rate; the purchaser being a Colonel Kendall, a brother of the old Squire.'

' ''A married man?'' I asked.

' ''Yes, miss; with a family of eight. As pretty children as ever you see, and the mother a good lady. It's the old home to Colonel Kendall.''

' ''I see. And that is why you feel bound to sell.''

' ''It's a good price, too, that he offers. You mustn't think but I'm sorry enough –''

' ''To turn me out? I thank you, Mr Hosking; but you are doing the right thing.''

''Since Mrs Carkeek was to stay, the arrangement

lacked nothing of absolute perfection – except, that it found no room for me.

' "*She* – Margaret – will be happy," I said; "with her cousins, you know."

' "Oh yes, miss, she will be happy, sure enough," Mrs Carkeek agreed.

'So when the time came I packed up my boxes, and tried to be cheerful. But on the last morning, when they stood corded in the hall, I sent Mrs Carkeek upstairs upon poor excuse, and stepped alone into the pantry.

' "Margaret!" I whispered.

'There was no answer at all. I had scarcely dared to hope for one. Yet I tried again, and, shutting my eyes this time, stretched out both hands and whispered:

' "Margaret!"

'And I will swear to my dying day that two little hands stole and rested – for a moment only – in mine.'

THE LAMP

Agatha Christie

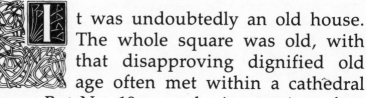t was undoubtedly an old house. The whole square was old, with that disapproving dignified old age often met within a cathedral town. But No. 19 gave the impression of an elder among elders; it had a veritable patriarchal solemnity; it towered greyest of the grey, haughtiest of the haughty, chillest of the chill. Austere, forbidding, and stamped with that particular desolation attaching to all houses that have been long untenanted, it reigned above the other dwellings.

In any other town it would have been freely labelled 'haunted', but Weyminster was averse from ghosts and considered them hardly respectable except as the appanage of a 'county family'. So No. 19 was never alluded to as a haunted house; but nevertheless it remained, year after year, 'To be Let or Sold'.

Mrs Lancaster looked at the house with approval as she drove up with the talkative house agent, who was in an unusually hilarious mood at the idea of getting No. 19 off his books. He inserted the key in the door without ceasing his appreciative comments.

'How long has the house been empty?' inquired Mrs Lancaster, cutting short his flow of language rather brusquely.

Mr Raddish (of Raddish and Foplow) became slightly confused.

'Er – er – some time,' he remarked blandly.

'So I should think,' said Mrs Lancaster drily.

The dimly lighted hall was chill with a sinister chill. A more imaginative woman might have shivered, but this woman happened to be eminently practical. She was tall with much dark brown hair just tinged with gray and rather cold blue eyes.

She went over the house from attic to cellar, asking a pertinent question from time to time. The inspection over, she came back into one of the front rooms looking out on the square and faced the agent with a resolute mien.

'What is the matter with the house?'

Mr Raddish was taken by surprise.

'Of course, an unfurnished house is always a little gloomy,' he parried feebly.

'Nonsense,' said Mrs Lancaster. 'The rent is ridiculously low for such a house – purely nominal. There must be some reason for it. I suppose the house is haunted?'

Mr Raddish gave a nervous little start but said nothing.

Mrs Lancaster eyed him keenly. After a few moments she spoke again.

'Of course that is all nonsense, I don't believe in ghosts or anything of that sort, and personally it is no deterrent to my taking the house; but servants, unfortunately, are very credulous and easily frightened. It would be kind of you to tell me exactly what – what thing *is* supposed to haunt this place.'

'I – er – really don't know,' stammered the house agent.

'I am sure you must,' said the lady quietly. 'I cannot take the house without knowing. What was it? A murder?'

'Oh! no,' cried Mr Raddish, shocked by the idea of anything so alien to the respectability of the square. 'It's – it's – only a child.'

'A child?'

'Yes.

'I don't know the story exactly,' he continued reluctantly. 'Of course, there are all kinds of different versions, but I believe that about thirty years ago a man going by the name of Williams took No. 19. Nothing was known of him; he kept no servants; he had no friends; he seldom went out in the daytime. He had one child, a little boy. After he had been there about two months, he went up to London, and had barely set foot in the metropolis before he was recognized as being a man 'wanted' by the police on some charge – exactly what, I do not know. But it must have been a grave one, because, sooner than give himself up, he shot himself. Meanwhile, the child lived on here, alone in the house. He had food for a little time, and he waited day after day for his father's return. Unfortunately, it had been impressed upon him that he was never under any circumstances to go out of the house or to speak to anyone. He was a weak, ailing, little creature, and did not dream of disobeying this command. In the night, the neighbours, not knowing that his father had gone away, often heard him sobbing in the awful loneliness and desolation of the empty house.'

Mr Raddish paused.

'And – er – the child starved to death,' he concluded, in the same tones as he might have announced that it had just begun to rain.

'And it is the child's ghost that is supposed to haunt the place?' asked Mrs Lancaster.

'It is nothing of consequence really,' Mr Raddish hastened to assure her. 'There's nothing *seen*, not *seen*, only people say, ridiculous, of course, but they do say they hear – the child – crying, you know.'

Mrs Lancaster moved towards the front door.

'I like the house very much,' she said. 'I shall get nothing as good for the price. I will think it over and let you know.'

'It really looks very cheerful, doesn't it Papa?'

Mrs Lancaster surveyed her new domain with approval. Gay rugs, well-polished furniture, and many knickknacks, had quite transformed the gloomy aspect of No. 19.

She spoke to a thin, bent old man with stooping shoulders and a delicate mystical face. Mr Winburn did not resemble his daughter; indeed no greater contrast could be imagined than that presented by her resolute practicalness and his dreamy abstraction.

'Yes,' he answered with a smile, 'no one would dream the house was haunted.'

'Papa, don't talk nonsense! On our first day too.'

Mr Winburn smiled.

'Very well, my dear, we will agree that there are no such things as ghosts.'

'And please,' continued Mrs Lancaster, 'don't say a word before Geoff. He's so imaginative.'

Geoff was Mrs Lancaster's little boy. The family consisted of Mr Winburn, his widowed daughter, and Geoffrey.

Rain had begun to beat against the window – pitter-patter, pitter-patter.

'Listen,' said Mr Winburn. 'Is it not like little footsteps?'

'It's more like rain,' said Mrs Lancaster, with a smile.

'But *that, that* is a footstep,' cried her father, bending forward to listen.

Mrs Lancaster laughed outright.

'That's Geoff coming downstairs.'

Mr Winburn was obliged to laugh too. They were having tea in the hall, and he had been sitting with his back to the staircase. He now turned his chair round to face it.

Little Geoffrey was coming down, rather slowly and sedately, with a child's awe of a strange place. The stairs were of polished oak, uncarpeted. He came across and stood by his mother. Mr Winburn gave a slight start. As the child was crossing the floor, he distinctly heard another pair of footsteps on the stairs, as of someone following Geoffrey. Dragging footsteps, curiously painful they were. Then he shrugged his shoulders incredulously. 'The rain, no doubt,' he thought.

'I'm looking at the spongecakes,' remarked Geoff with the admirably detached air of one who points out an interesting fact.

His mother hastened to comply with the hint.

'Well, Sonny, how do you like your new home?' she asked.

'Lots,' replied Geoffrey with his mouth generously filled. 'Pounds and pounds and pounds.' After this last assertion, which was evidently expressive of the deepest contentment, he relapsed into silence, only anxious to remove the spongecake from the sight of man in the least time possible.

Having bolted the last mouthful, he burst forth into speech.

'Oh! Mummy, there's attics here, Jane says; and can I go at once and *eggz*plore them? And there might be a secret door. Jane says there isn't, but I think there must be, and, anyhow, I know there'll be *pipes*, *water pipes* (with a face full of ecstasy) and can I play with them, and, oh! can I go and see the boi-i-ler?' He spun out the last word with such evident rapture that his grandfather felt ashamed to reflect that his peerless delight of childhood only conjured up to his imagination the picture of hot water that wasn't hot, and heavy and numerous plumber's bills.

'We'll see about the attics tomorrow, darling,' said Mrs Lancaster. 'Suppose you fetch your bricks and build a nice house, or an engine.'

'Don't want to build an 'ouse.'

'House.'

'House, or h'engine h'either.'

'Build a boiler,' suggested his grandfather.

Geoffrey brightened.

'With pipes?'

'Yes, lots of pipes.'

Geoffrey ran away happily to fetch his bricks.

The rain was still falling. Mr Winburn listened. Yes, it must have been the rain he had heard; but it did sound like footsteps.

He had a queer dream that night.

He dreamt that he was walking through a town, a great city it seemed to him. But it was a children's city; there were no grown-up people there, nothing but children, crowds of them. In his dream they all rushed to the stranger crying: 'Have you brought him?' It seemed that he understood what they meant and shook his head sadly. When they saw this, the children turned away and began to cry, sobbing bitterly.

The city and the children faded away and he awoke to find himself in bed, but the sobbing was still in his ears. Though wide awake, he heard it

distinctly; and he remembered that Geoffrey slept on the floor below, while this sound of a child's sorrow descended from above. He sat up and struck a match. Instantly the sobbing ceased.

Mr Winburn did not tell his daughter of the dream or its sequel. That it was no trick of his imagination, he was convinced; indeed soon afterwards he heard it again in the daytime. The wind was howling in the chimney, but *this* was a separate sound – distinct, unmistakable: pitiful little heartbroken sobs.

He found out too that he was not the only one to hear them. He overheard the housemaid saying to the parlormaid that she 'didn't think as that there nurse was kind to Master Geoffrey. She'd 'eard 'im crying 'is little 'eart out only that very morning.' Geoffrey had come down to breakfast and lunch beaming with health and happiness; and Mr Winburn knew that it was not Geoff who had been crying, but that other child whose dragging footsteps had startled him more than once.

Mrs Lancaster alone never heard anything. Her ears were not perhaps attuned to catch sounds from another world.

Yet one day she also received a shock.

'Mummy,' said Geoffrey plaintively. 'I wish you'd let me play with that little boy.'

Mrs Lancaster looked up from her writing table with a smile.

'What little boy, dear?'

'I don't know his name. He was in an attic, sitting on the floor crying, but he ran away when he saw me. I suppose he was *shy* (with slight contempt), not like a *big* boy, and then, when I was in the nursery building, I saw him standing in the door watching me build, and he looked so awful lonely and as though he wanted to play wiv me. I said: "Come and build a h'engine," but he didn't say nothing, just looked as – as though he saw a lot of chocolates, and his mummy had told him not to touch them.' Geoff sighed, sad personal reminiscences evidently recurring to him. 'But when I asked Jane who he was and told her I wanted to play wiv him, she said there wasn't no little boy in the 'ouse and not to tell naughty stories. I don't love Jane at all.'

Mrs Lancaster got up.

'Jane was right. There was no little boy.'

'But I saw him. Oh! Mummy, do let me play wiv him, he did look so awful lonely and unhappy. I *do* want to do something to "make him better".'

Mrs Lancaster was about to speak again, but her father shook his head.

'Geoff,' he said very gently, 'that poor little boy *is* lonely, and perhaps you may do something to comfort him; but you must find out how by yourself – like a puzzle – do you see?'

'Is it because I am getting *big* I must do it all my lone?'

'Yes, because you are getting big.'

As the boy left the room, Mrs Lancaster turned to her father impatiently.

'Papa, this is absurd. To encourage the boy to believe the servants' idle tales!'

'No servant has told the child anything,' said the old man gently. 'He's seen – what I *hear*, what I could see perhaps if I were his age.'

'But it's such nonsense! Why don't I see it or hear it?'

Mr Winburn smiled, a curiously tired smile, but did not reply.

'Why?' repeated his daughter. 'And why did you tell him he could help the – the – thing? It's – it's all so impossible.'

The old man looked at her with his thoughtful glance.

'Why not?' he said. 'Do you remember these words:

> *What Lamp has Destiny to guide*
> *Her little Children stumbling in the Dark?*
> *'A Blind Understanding,' Heaven replied.*

'Geoffrey has that – a blind understanding. All children possess it. It is only as we grow older that we lose it, that we cast it away from us. Sometimes, when we are quite old, a faint gleam comes back to us, but the Lamp burns brightest in childhood. That is why I think Geoffrey may help.'

'I don't understand,' murmured Mrs Lancaster feebly.

'No more do I. That – that child is in trouble and wants – to be set free. But how? I do not know, but – it's awful to think of it – sobbing its heart out – *a child*.'

A month after this conversation Geoffrey fell very ill. The east wind had been severe, and he was not a strong child. The doctor shook his head and said that it was a grave case. To Mr Winburn he divulged more and confessed that the case was quite hopeless. 'The child would never have lived to grow up, under any circumstances,' he added. 'There has been serious lung trouble for a long time.'

It was when nursing Geoff that Mrs Lancaster became aware of that – other child. At first the sobs were an indistinguishable part of the wind, but gradually they became more distinct, more unmistakable. Finally she heard them in moments of dead calm: a child's sobs – dull, hopeless, heartbroken.

Geoff grew steadily worse and in his delirium he spoke of the 'little boy' again and again. 'I do want to help him get away, I do!' he cried.

Succeeding the delirium there came a state of lethargy. Geoffrey lay very still, hardly breathing, sunk in oblivion. There was nothing to do but wait and watch. Then there came a still night, clear and calm, without one breath of wind.

Suddenly the child stirred. His eyes opened. He looked past his mother towards the open door. He tried to speak and she bent down to catch the half-breathed words.

'All right, I'm comin',' he whispered; then he sank back.

The mother felt suddenly terrified; she crossed the room to her father. Somewhere near them the other child was laughing. Joyful, contented, triumphant, the silver laughter echoed through the room.

'I'm frightened; I'm frightened,' she moaned.

He put his arm round her protectingly. A sudden gust of wind made them both start, but it passed swiftly and left the air quiet as before.

The laughter had ceased and there crept to them a faint sound, so faint as hardly to be heard, but growing louder till they could distinguish it. Footsteps – light footsteps, swiftly departing.

Pitter-patter, pitter-patter, they ran – those well-known halting little feet. Yet – surely – now *other* footsteps suddenly mingled with them, moving with a quicker and a lighter tread.

With one accord they hastened to the door.

Down, down, down, past the door, close to them, pitter-patter, pitter-patter, went the unseen feet of the little chidren *together*.

Mrs Lancaster looked up wildly.

'There are *two* of them – *two!*'

Gray with sudden fear, she turned towards the cot in the corner, but her father restrained her gently, and pointed away.

'There,' he said simply.

Pitter-patter, pitter-patter – fainter and fainter.

And then – silence.

ACKNOWLEDGEMENTS

The publishers would like to extend their grateful thanks to the following authors, publishers and others for kindly granting permission to reproduce the extracts and stories included in this anthology:

JIMMY TAKES VANISHING LESSONS by Walter R. Brooks. Published in the United States of America by Alfred A. Knopf, 1965. Reprinted by permission of the author and Brandt & Brandt. Copyright © 1950 by Walter R. Brooks. Copyright © renewed 1978 by Dorothy Brooks.

THE SHADOW-CAGE from *The Shadow-Cage and Other Tales of the Supernatural* by Philippa Pearce (Puffin Books, 1978). Published in the United States of America by Thomas Y. Crowell. Reprinted by permission of Penguin Books Ltd and Harper & Row, Publishers, Inc. Copyright © Philippa Pearce, 1977.

THE HAUNTED TRAILER by Robert Arthur. Reprinted by permission of the Regents of the University of Michigan, Ann Arbor, Michigan. Copyright © 1953 by *Weird Tales*, Renown Publications Inc., renewed 1968 by Robert Arthur.

LET'S PLAY GHOSTS! by Pamela Vincent. Previously published by Armada Books. Reprinted by permission of the author. Copyright © Pamela Vincent, 1972.

NOW YOU SEE IT by David Campton. Reprinted by permission of the author and ACTAC (Theatrical and Cinematic) Ltd. Copyright © David Campton, 1980.

THROUGH THE DOOR from *The Phantom Roundabout and Other Ghostly Stories* (1977) by Ruth Ainsworth. Reprinted by permission of André Deutsch Ltd and Modern Curriculum Press. Copyright © 1977 by Ruth Ainsworth.

THE EMPTY SCHOOLROOM by Pamela Hansford Johnson. Reprinted by permission of Curtis Brown Ltd.